whitney.hayes@paranormalbooktivity.co.uk or
customer.service@milestonepress.co.uk

This is a work of fiction. Names, characters, places, and incidents either are the product of the author's imagination or are used fictionally. Any resemblance to actual persons, living or dead, business establishments, events, or locales is entirely coincidental.

First Edition, 2020

eBook ISBN 978-1-9162558-0-7
Paperback ISBN 978-1-9162558-1-4

Published by Milestone Press Ltd.
Printed in Great Britain.
www.MilestonePress.co.uk

Written by Whitney Lynn Hayes
Cover Design by Whitney Lynn Hayes
www.instagram.com/whitneylynnhayes

Illustrations by Michalis Karageorgis
www.instagram.com/artymoik

Follow the Paranormal Booktivity franchise on:
www.ParanormalBooktivity.co.uk

Paranormal Booktivity

The Mystery of the Stolen Spell Book

Book One in the Paranormal Booktivity Series

By Whitney Lynn Hayes

MILESTONE PRESS Ltd

Dedication

For my familiar, Micio.

Contents

ROBIN

Friday 23rd October

17:39 PM, Central Park, New York

Robin shifted her weight on a wooden bench soaked in last night's downpour. With her hands clasped together between her thighs, she wondered whether there would be a dark patch on the bottom of her jeans when she eventually stood up. They felt damp. Perhaps it was just the cold.

Thankfully, there was no one in sight to see either way.

Sat near the edge of the park on alert for the sound of a distinct rhythm of honking, Robin's ears pricked up to every shuffle. But she could not hear the car she waited for. Indeed, not much could be heard.

No running or skating or laughing—just distant murmurs from passersby, occasional barking, and a slight whistling of the wind through the many Scarlet Oaks and American Elms around her.

A sudden gust whooshed past and blew her hair forward and onto her face. It made lone leaves and debris dance at her feet and the chill of it sent tingles down her spine.

As she unlocked her fingers and brushed back red locks behind both ears, her phone slipped out from where it was tucked in her sleeve. After peeking at the time, again, and checking, again, for nonexistent notifications; she reached down to unzip her suitcase and let her phone slide to the bottom of its deep front pocket.

Then, digging, her fingertips passed the spine of a book, the side of a water bottle and crinkling packets of snacks before reaching the thick, soft fleece of her gray cardigan—which she tugged on, pulled out and put on immediately.

Yes, it was well and truly fall.

With her head tilted upwards, Robin gazed as she waited. She watched the sun as it hung in a tinted sky through squinting eyes. Then, she closed them as her thoughts trailed back, amidst lingering shivers, to a warmer time with a warmer sun. When it seared sidewalks and stalled bumble-bees, when it scorched and blinded, when it simmered and then simmered down, lulling spirits all the while.

Just as the memory reached its vivid peak, the unmistakable sound of footsteps disrupted Robin's trance. Her eyes opened to the crunching of stone pebbles in the rectangular pit behind her and, turning around, she saw a stranger stop a few feet away from the bench. It was a short, heavy-set man, wearing a black leather jacket over a navy-blue hoodie which came up and over a baseball cap he wore so low she could barely see his face.

'Excuse me, Miss. I heard about a shortcut through the park to the *Shake Shack*. You know where that is?' he asked, in a distinctive New York accent.

'No, sorry. I'm not from here,' Robin replied.

'Yeah, you don't look it. That's a nice suitcase,' he continued, 'You a tourist or you got friends here?'

The hairs on the back of Robin's neck raised. But it wasn't the cold. Something about this encounter did not feel reminiscent of the typically quaint conversations she was accustomed to.

Instinct seized hold, her gut turned and, without switching her gaze, she made a mental note of the quickest path to the main streets.

'A couple of friends, yeah,' she answered, slowly shifting towards the edge of the bench.

'A couple of friends,' he repeated, nodding. The man raised his cap slightly, looked around the surrounding area, and then back to Robin. 'But they aren't here now, are they?'

Robin said nothing.

Her eyes fixated on the man's left hand; fidgeting in the large front pocket of his hoodie where there seemed to be an unusual bulge. Beads of sweat mingled in between her palms as he took a step forward.

Sprint to safety, every part of her body told itself. But her legs were limp noodles.

Then, more footsteps. This time, though, they did not belong to the strange man. The scuffling against the concrete made Robin's head jerk in the opposite direction. Could it be an accomplice?

'Hey! Hey there,' a woman called out, winded, as she half skipped and half power-walked towards the bench. 'There you are,' she said.

'Hello,' Robin hesitated, keeping the potential burglar in her periphery.

Middle-aged, pale, with thick glasses and a full head of auburn frizz; the woman sat down next to Robin and began to dig into a bright-red satchel she placed on her lap. 'Can we help you?' she said after a pause, addressing the man whilst still nose-deep in her bag.

He did not reply. Instead, he simultaneously adjusted his cap, took a step back, and took another look around their immediate surroundings, seemingly unsure how to proceed. But before he could decide, the woman pulled out what she had presumably been looking for, a flip phone. As she dialed, the man hurried and vanished behind the nearby grove.

'Well,' the woman started after a brief pause, 'it appears I arrived just in time.'

However sure Robin was that the almost-offender would not resurface, she continued to peer through the trees. When she felt comfortable enough, she settled her back up against the bench.

'I suppose. Yes, you did,' she said to the woman. 'I'm sorry, do we know each other?'

'No, you don't know me. My name is Amber. Amber Grebe. I could see from behind those trees over there,' she explained, gesturing, 'that you might need some assistance. You can never be too careful in New York. I take it you're not from here?'

'Is it that obvious?'

Amber smiled in response. After an exaggerated shudder and a loud exhale, she put on a pair of woolen burgundy gloves she retrieved from her coat pocket. 'Chilly,' she said with an inflection in an evident attempt to make conversation.

'Yes. I was just thinking that before… I was just thinking that.'

'I miss the West coast during these months. I grew up there, all around really. I go back to visit my sister and her children during their summer break, usually. Didn't get a chance to this year, though. Did you do anything nice over the summer?'

Robin tried to think of something interesting to mention. But all she could visualize was a mundane montage of the endless days spent sitting at her desk in her Boston studio apartment, surrounded by books and stained mugs, in front of the living room window.

'No,' she replied, 'not really.'

Amber pursed her lips and nodded with a slight frown, before going back to dig in her satchel.

Robin sighed as she repeated her answer inside her head. She had spent yet another summer caged indoors, studying, even with the college year being over. She remembered the lighthearted tone she used with her fathers over the phone during those months; saying she was grateful to feel some level of heat, at least, to enjoy even a few rays penetrate the glass. But, despite Robin's propensity to look on the brighter side of things, she could not help feeling a familiar longing all summer long. A tug in her chest which she could feel more powerfully now. A pulling sensation that reminded her of where she ought to be. Because, of course, she would have preferred to have spent that time elsewhere, doing other things. And where and what could be better for Robin Wilson, than summer in Melvin, Massachusetts?

Her fathers had reassured her that she wasn't missing anything; joking that although the sun had come out of hiding to pay a brief visit to their little town, it had rolled into hibernation soon after.

Robin was happy to hear anything about Melvin. She was certain that, however brief and in however small a town, it had been another perfect summer. Complete with fireworks and apple pies, gatherings on checkered blankets with charred meat and iced drinks, and balmy nights ever accommodating to those first magical stirrings for young couples and more irreplaceable memories for groups of old friends. Everything entirely characteristic of picturesque towns like Melvin.

Robin checked the watch on her wrist. The time read 18:04 PM. Then, she stared up at the sky, at the sun whose rays only recently penetrated her living-room window but had now waned into a distant cousin of itself, streaming streaks of timid light through thick clouds onto this north-eastern corner of the world. She continued to watch as she waited. It always comforted her to do so. To close her eyes and feel the warmth on her face, rapt in quiet pensive moments. She knew that no matter where she was—even now, over two-hundred miles away from home—it would always be the same sun. A concept, a constancy, that made her feel safe and never alone.

As it began to set over a sea of tall trees, Robin's eyes fixated on the glowing orb slowly descend in its blurry splendor. She knew it was the same sun her parents could see back home, and she felt closer to them. Mesmerized, she gazed; still lost in thoughts of summers in Melvin. A season, and a place, she had missed for the third year in a row.

The sky began to darken as Robin's knees shook in anticipation; rhythmically, left to right, as the soles of her shoes tapped on the concrete.

Amber placed a comforting hand on Robin's shoulder. 'He's not likely to return,' she said, 'I wouldn't worry.'

'Oh, no. I mean, yes, I don't think so either. But I'm not nervous,' Robin explained, 'Thank you, though. I'm just… anxious, I suppose,' she elaborated.

'Oh?'

'I'm waiting for friends to pick me up.'

'How nice,' Amber said, clasping her hands together, 'What will you do, I wonder? Where will you go?'

Another gust swept more debris, dust, and small pebbles through the park and past the path in front of them. More crunchy leaves twirled at Robin's feet and crept under her tapping soles. She looked down and as she observed their coloring—pumpkin orange and candy apple red—her gloaming trance resumed instantly.

Yes, summer was well and truly over. But there was no point in dwelling, Robin reaffirmed to herself with another deep sigh. Because although it was her favorite season, fall was a close second—and despite having spent the beginning of fall away from Melvin, she was grateful, in any case, to have spent it in New England.

Fall in New England; four words that paint orange and chocolate-brown dreams in the imaginations of every person in the world. Where leaves morph into vivid colors as they fall from deciduous trees and float on the first brisk airs which surround you on long walks through parks. Few sights compare to this magical period of death and rebirth when harvests end and school years begin. And fewer places play host to the season in such glorious fashion.

Indeed, every year millions flock to these six north-eastern states to bear witness. But even during this busy period, in the small town of Melvin, Massachusetts, tourist activity is scarce. Every year, plastic bats and turkey hands turn into golden tinsel and strings of red and green lights. Wrapping paper is recycled and footprints on the white-blanketed ground melt into slush and are replaced with budding flowers.

Trees become greener and fragrant spring airs become warm and occasionally humid. All the while, the comings-and-goings of Melvin's citizens keep on at a steady pace. For although the seasons change, not much else does.

For many, Melvin remains an utterly mediocre place uninspiring and unimpressive to the outside world. For some people, though, this was the definitive description of paradise. For people like Robin Wilson, no town could be more alluring. She could not imagine living anywhere else. Even after spending three years at *Harvard Medical School* in Boston—a city she could not objectively fault—she desperately missed the silent uncomplicated beauty that was Melvin.

As the sun disappeared completely into the evening, Robin blinked the last glimmers of sunlight from her sight, dismissing any nostalgic longings from her mind, from her heart. Soon, its hidden presence would allow its sister moon to reflect and protect. Soon, she would be where she belonged.

'Home,' she replied, 'We're going to go home.'

18:15 PM, West 75th Street, New York

'Come on, Curtis, we're late!' Ashley called from the bedroom.

'Yeah, *we*,' Curtis mumbled.

'I heard that,' Ashley yelled. 'Now come on!'

Curtis smirked as he heard Ashley grunt and grumble in Spanish, clearly struggling with bags he could hear bump and crash into each other as she shuffled through the hallway. He would offer to help but knowing Ashley she would flick his hands away and grumble some more.

'I'm ready, hon. I've kind of been ready for a while,' he responded in a high-pitched tone so as not to aggravate her any further.

Ashley made her way into their living room. She let go of the handle on her suitcase, propped a bag on top of it, dropped the rest, and stopped in front of him. Then, she pursed her lips and blew strands of hair from her mouth and face. 'Mhm. That's why you're sat comfortably in front of your laptop,' she said, pointing to it, 'which is on and not packed away. That's why your shoes are off,' she said, gesturing towards his feet.

'What? My socks are on.'

Curtis' grin disappeared when Ashley shot him a familiar expression. He knew she meant business. So, he checked the laptop screen one last time; ensuring every scanned map, photo, and document he had been working on were successfully copied to both his phone's internal and external memory, sent to his e-mail, and cautiously saved to every storage space he could think of. Then, Curtis pressed the off button, held it down, and lowered the screen.

'See?' he said as he stood up and wheeled his chair back before going to hug Ashley.

'Oh, no. No, no, no. I know that look. There's no time for that. We're late now.'

'What? We said we'd pick Robin up at... 18:30,' Curtis said, checking his watch, 'we have plenty of time and we're close to the park.'

'Yeah, but we still have to have dinner and then who knows what traffic will be like.'

'On the road to Melvin? Yeah. There won't be any traffic.'

'There could be an accident or something that holds us up. I had a very ominous dream last night.'

'Oh, no… not a dream!'

'I'm serious. The car wouldn't start. Seriously. I got in and it just wouldn't start.'

'Holy unrealistic hunch, Batman!' Curtis joked.

Ashley went to shove Curtis, who took her hand, spun her around, and held her tight.

'Seriously,' she said, trying not to laugh, 'it just wouldn't start. And I don't trust your Dad's car. And—'

Curtis' diverting pecks and smooches distracted Ashley for a few seconds. But she was right; they would have to be on the road, and soon—but he'd do anything to calm her down, to make sure she was relaxed enough to enjoy a reunion with her best friend. He knew Ashley's nerves were just a temporary outlet of anticipation rather than anything else, anything too serious anyway. She couldn't wait to see Robin, she couldn't wait to go back home to Melvin—and Curtis fully understood, because neither could he.

The couple embraced one last time and then split apart. Simultaneously coordinated, they rushed in unison until they were ready. Ashley wrapped a scarf around her neck and tucked it into her coat. Curtis pulled on his beanie and slipped his sneakers on. They looked at each other, smiled, and sighed. They were going home.

But as Curtis unlocked the door and reached for his set of keys, his phone began to ring.

'Robin?' she asked with discernable panic in her voice.

Curtis shook his head as he looked down at his phone before proceeding to answer it. 'It's just Aaron,' he said simply.

18:20 PM, Melvin, Massachusetts

Those of us who are lucky enough to have one close friend, to have had them in our lives for a priceless amount of time, feel like the richest people alive. Even when those friends are far away, even when you have not been in the same room together for years. You could try—if there were ever a reason—but you could probably not remember what life was like without them.

On occasion, you might find yourself reminiscing about how you became friends in the first place. Not how or when you first met, but that precise moment that magically and unexpectedly shifted everything. The moment that made your friendship something you would die for, something to live for.

Aaron Jackson and Nathaniel Berger were doing just that. They talked and laughed for hours on the plane journey, and once safely on the road to Melvin, they talked and laughed all the way from the airport.

They remembered simpler times, playing games in Curtis' treehouse, dozens of slumber parties at Aaron's house, and those few slightly awkward but delicious Shabbat dinners at the Berger household. They laughed at the memory of Ashley's infamous fall into the drinks table at her quinceañera, and how livid Robin's fathers were the day they found a shoebox of opossum babies she had stashed in their closet.

After an extra-early start with *CBS This Morning*, a mountain of maple syrup covered flapjacks complete with crispy bacon and freshly squeezed orange juice, after one last sweep of their dorm room and after another inspection of their inventory checklists; Aaron and Nathaniel zipped, weighed and secured their bags, cases, and suitcases, and arrived at *Gainesville Regional Airport* with plenty of time. Flying up from Florida; they landed in Boston, on time of course, where Andrew, Aaron's brother, was already waiting in their father's car.

Close since elementary school, Aaron and Nathaniel graduated from *Susan B. Anthony High* together, where chance or perhaps destiny led both their paths to the *University of Florida*; where Aaron studied engineering, and Nathaniel majored in theology. It was exhausting work, and they were both relieved to have only one more year ahead of them.

Like everyone else, they were always ecstatic whenever a much needed and well-deserved break came around. For three years, Aaron and Nathaniel spent sweltering summer breaks and world-famous spring breaks in the Sunshine State; studying and relaxing rather than partying. Thanksgivings were tricky, considering their timetables, but they always managed to fly up to Massachusetts in December for Christmas, at least, although not for New Year's Eve.

Curtis and Ashley made the trip down from New York for that first Christmas break. It was wonderful. And it almost felt normal, like nothing had changed. Except—and of course—everyone missed Robin.

This year, though, everyone would finally be together again. These five best friends made every effort to tear themselves away from their daily routines and plan what they hoped would be the most memorable Halloween ever. Because Halloween was not just a favorite holiday. For Aaron, Nathaniel, Curtis, Ashley, and Robin; it was a day that marked the foundation of their friendship.

The group had spent their youth sneaking VHS tapes of slasher films past their parents at sleepovers. They had grown up exchanging the scariest reads they could find. After-school clubs ended with risky sprints in and out of quiet, poorly lit bathrooms with dingy mirrors, perfect for playing *Bloody Mary*.

When they were old enough, they intermittently braved trips to increasingly spookier locations in Melvin, delving deep into the exhilarating realm of paranormal investigations.

This week, they planned to take a trip down memory lane by reenacting childhood games, bigger and better than ever, with a series of explorations all leading up to the spectacular climax of Halloween night. And everyone was excited, to say the least.

As Andrew turned off the engine, and as Nathaniel bolted out of the back seat to grab his bags,

Aaron's first thought went to Robin, to Ashley, and Curtis. He took out his phone from his back pocket and started to dial to check on their progress.

'Are you calling the guys?' Nathaniel shouted from behind the car, pulling his suitcase out of the trunk. 'Tell them I'm staying at yours tonight. So, my phone will be off.'

'Yeah,' Aaron replied, 'No problem.'

23:15 PM, Route 1, Massachusetts

Watching water droplets slide and merge in patterns on the car window, attempting to peer through the misty glass as only night and fog stared back, Robin's heart drummed inside her chest. Though she could not see a road sign, or anything really, she knew they were gradually getting closer to Melvin.

She could hear Ashley's unsurprisingly energetic voice buzzing in her right ear and Curtis' occasional input from the driver's seat in front of her. She tried to focus on the conversation but found herself tuning in and out. She felt groggy; stuffed from dinner and low in energy after hours of excitement and adrenaline. With her forehead pressed against the cold glass, she tried not to close her eyes, as she would surely fall asleep as her thoughts trailed in a state of dream-like limbo from memory to fantasy.

Robin thought back to the day she was accepted into *Harvard Medical School,* back in 2012. She remembered how excited she was. Besides obvious reasons, its location meant she would be able to come home whenever she wanted, she had thought. But since her transition from high-school-graduate to college-student, Robin had only seen Melvin in photographs. She had not been able to come back for summer breaks, which she spent studying and volunteering in various wards. She had not even been able to come back for one Thanksgiving. Not even for Halloween, her favorite holiday. Robin's studies kept her incredibly busy, even over Christmas breaks—which she spent nose-deep in medical books instead of presents.

It didn't matter now, though. Nothing did. In the grand scheme of things, three years was a small price to pay for an education which would allow her to fulfill her dream. Robin had not told anyone yet, but she had already begun communications with friends over at Adam's hospital in Melvin—and she knew that in less than a year, come graduation, she would be able to move back home for good.

The thought made her smile and her heart sing. She wondered what her friends would think, and what their plans were.

Curtis and Ashley seemed happy in New York, and it would be easier to land contracts in a big city. Nathaniel probably hadn't thought that far ahead, knowing him. And with Aaron, she couldn't guess, but in any case, she knew he had a good head on his shoulders and would be fine either way. Still, she couldn't help but wonder whether he would stay in Florida or move somewhere else.

She wondered what he was doing at that very moment. She couldn't wait to hug him. She wondered how Nathaniel was. It was late. By now, both Aaron and Nathaniel were probably sleeping comfortably. She imagined them, mouths agape, curled up in sleeping bags, in front of the TV, on Aaron's bedroom floor. The thought lulled her immensely. As Curtis drove and as Ashley talked, she felt a familiar calm begin to sweep over her. And in the presence of two of her four closest friends, on their way home in Curtis' father's unpredictable Toyota Corolla, things were finally beginning to feel normal again.

A loud screech jolted both Robin and Ashley from their positions. It was Curtis toying with the radio controls which were being affected by the lack of a strong signal. They were getting close.

Robin had known Curtis since they were children. Though he was never considered the brightest one in any group, she thought the world of him. Ever since her father called her to their front door, where a boy from across the street stood on the balls of his sneakers; waiting, hoping she could come out to play, holding a pail of mud and worms which he would then give to her. *How nice*, albeit *gross*, she remembered thinking.

In his youth, Curtis Jones seemed to everyone the typical American boy; with slightly-below-average grades, slightly-above-average looks, and an evident penchant for mischief and dirt. The Widow Brenton learned to stay sat in her rocking chair if she heard the doorbell ring several times at once, as it was probably Curtis playing *Knock-Knock Ginger* before running back home next door. On the other side, Mr. Holbrook would chuckle upon noticing muddy tracks left across his paved front lawn; because Curtis often ran across and through the shortcut—a small entrance between the two houses—to get to his treehouse which perched in between both garden plots.

In high school, he sprouted like a mushroom and towered over nearly everyone. You could not miss him. And everyone knew him. Kind, generous, and popular; he somehow managed to participate in nearly every sports club.

Now though—despite still enjoying the occasional huddle and very much looking like a stereotypical quarterback—no one would think of Curtis as an athlete anymore, primarily at least. In the end, Curtis left Melvin in the pursuit of his true passion, music.

Susan B. Anthony High's semi-annual newsletter gave a big shock to local readers and alumni when it confirmed that, studying a mixture of composition and orchestral conducting at the *Juilliard School* in New York and upkeeping a popular YouTube channel with hundreds of thousands of followers, Curtis was well on track to achieving his musical dreams. Dreams which included, and would mean nothing without, his long-term girlfriend, Ashley.

Ashley Cruz was well on her way, too. She was currently harnessing her love of ballet and gymnastics into a Bachelor of Fine Art, studying dance at *Juilliard* alongside Curtis.

An eternal cliché. The pair were the ultimate high school sweethearts. Having met through Robin after the two girls quickly became best friends all those years ago, the couple had been together since anyone could remember. Naturally, everyone expected them to go the distance—a normal occurrence for those native to small towns.

Even with the couple moving to a big city—and which city is bigger than the Big Apple—Ashley and Curtis' dynamic endured.

Unchanged by the temptations which come with such a fast-paced environment, or the stresses caused by a grueling education at one of the finest schools in the country, the couple appeared to maintain a storybook love. Quippy comebacks, sarcastic digs, and even heated arguments provoked by Curtis' scoffs and continued by Ashley's Latin fire, were all part of their charm. For the quiet moments in which no one was looking, where both felt they were the only two in the entire world, were the moments that counted. The cornerstone of their enchanted union.

Robin could not hold back a big contented grin at the thought of them, at the sound of them together.

Ashley leaned forward to lovingly rub Curtis' head from the back seat when she noticed he was still distracted. 'Keep your eyes on the road,' she said, sitting back down.

'Keep your eyes on the road *what*?' he challenged.

The inflection in his voice, as well as the combined tension in Curtis' eyes in the rearview mirror, along with Ashley's raised eyebrow, pushed Robin to reply instead.

'Please,' said Robin, 'please keep your eyes on the road, Curtis.'

'Thank you, Robin. I will do,' he said with one hand on the wheel, whilst the other fiddled with the radio, 'just give me five seconds.'

'I think what Robin meant to say was, "*Please try to avoid killing us all, thanks.*"'

'Yeah, well, at least she said it politely.'

'What are you even trying to do with that thing?'

'Calm down, there aren't any other cars on the road.'

'My God. And you know where everyone is driving to or from tonight?'

'Have you seen any other cars?'

'I don't know. I'm not the one who has to keep their eyes on the road!'

'Guys,' Robin intervened, 'come on. Now, Ashley's right. Curtis, what are you trying to do?' she asked, sitting up, 'Tell me and I'll do it for you, so you can focus on driving.'

'I'm trying to find a station that works. Preferably classical.'

Robin unbuckled her seatbelt and knelt over as she carefully positioned herself between the two front seats. 'Hold me,' she asked Ashley as she adjusted the dials.

'Why do you need music?' Ashley grunted as she tugged on the back of Robin's belt to keep her in place.

'Because as much as the sound of incessant chattering and you ladies occasionally cackling in the back provides a certain type of ambiance, I think I'd prefer it right now. Besides, you know music wakes me up.'

'Wait. Are you tired? Do you want me to take over?' Robin offered.

Before Curtis could reply, he felt a faint flick on the back of his head.

'Incessant? Who's cackling?' Ashley demanded.

Curtis sighed and turned around. Ashley barked and provoked. And Robin bent down, attempting to slide back into her seat, attempting to get out of the war zone.

'Guys…' Robin started, trying to calm the pair when a bright flash sparked through the fog and surrounded the car.

Lightning zigged and zagged across the night sky and thunder began to crash and roar as the car swerved off the tarmac's slippery surface onto the grassy side of the road.

Curtis tried, desperately, to regain control of the car. Ashley tightened her grip on Robin, who tried and failed to dislodge her hips which were stuck in the thin gap between the two front seats.

'Ashley, help me,' Robin pleaded.

'I'm trying,' Ashley cried back.

As the struggle, which seemed to last forever but which lasted only seconds, ensued; they hoped that there truly were no other cars on the road. Neither of the three could see anything, through the swirling blur and thick fog, though each of them tried to keep their eyes open, just in case.

Curtis finally managed to level the car back onto the road. Trying to focus through rain and mist, he heard a sudden cry he was sure did not come from the girls.

'Curtis!' Robin yelled, still stuck, seeing a flash of a figure, of something or someone sprint in front of the car, 'Watch out!'

In seconds, Curtis' foot on the breaks made the tires screech, the car jolt, and Ashley scream. Then, they came to a halt.

'Are—Are you okay?' he mumbled to the girls; his voice trembling, his eyes fixed forwards.

Ashley immediately unbuckled her seatbelt. 'Robin? Robin?!' she cried, pulling Robin's body into the back of the car. Taking her unconscious head in her hands, on her lap, she wiped the strands of forlorn hair away from Robin's face. But when she looked down at Robin's head, at her fingertips, she saw blood. 'My God. Oh my God, Curtis—'

'Shh,' Curtis whispered forcefully, staring through the glass as the window wipers danced rhythmically, backward, and forwards in the rain, staring at something through the fog. The *someone,* standing a dozen feet in front of the car, staring back at him.

23:00 PM, 8 Almond Avenue

'Okay, guys, I'm done. What are we watching?'

'Hold on, Aaron. Let me polish off Drew and we can check out your Dad's *My Cloud,*' Nathaniel mumbled, licking the bottom-left corner of his lip as he struggled with Andrew's gaming controller.

Sounds of the aggressive tapping of buttons and occasional laughter filled the lower level of the Jackson household. Andrew, Aaron's elder brother, sat calmly on Nathaniel's right in the living room; cross-legged on the floor, with his back propped up against an overstuffed armchair with a faded floral pattern. 'Yeah, I'd like to see that,' he said, sniggering.

Aaron resisted the urge to laugh, looking down at them from the couch.

Nathaniel planned to stay at the Jackson's for this first weekend, seeing as his family would not be home. His younger brother, Daniel, attended boarding school and his parents were away on business and would not return until Monday.

Nathaniel and Andrew were competing, although it was not close, in yet another match of *VAN-GO*: an old driving game in which players could race through increasingly difficult tracks, unlocking graphics based on famous paintings in the process. They had started what they said would be a *quick game* while Aaron checked and organized his equipment.

Varied types of digital recorders in different sizes, EVP and EMF devices, flashlights, along with their respective batteries and cases, were tested and logged. Everything, technology-wise, the group would need to conduct a successful paranormal investigation later in the week. However, Aaron was thorough and made sure to take as much time as he needed. Indeed, an hour later; Nathaniel and Andrew were still playing.

'Let's just flick through YouTube,' he suggested, putting everything away, meticulously, in his big metallic case.

'I have literally watched everything on YouTube,' Nathaniel replied.

Andrew scoffed. 'How have you seen *everything* on YouTube?'

'He hasn't,' said Aaron.

'Everything good, anyway. I've watched like every documentary out there. The accurate ones. None of that conspiracy junk.'

Aaron cleared his throat. 'Berger… you do know you're the first one to believe in *any* conspiracy theory? I mean, I wouldn't be surprised if you were the one posting those videos.'

'Ha!' Andrew laughed, 'You go to click subscribe, look at the bio and there's Berger in a hat and a fake mustache, talking about reptiles in the White House.'

'You guys think I'd rock a mustache?'

The Jackson brothers looked at each other and said nothing.

'Well?' Nathaniel insisted.

'I think you rock the look you have now,' Aaron said diplomatically after a long pause.

'And what's that then?'

Aaron thought for a moment and Andrew took the opportunity to intervene.

'Pasty white boy,' he said, amused.

Nathaniel squinted, nodded, and started to clap sarcastically when the *bloop-bloop* noise indicating the game was over made his face turn.

'Ha-ha. Look at that! Guess you lost again, Berger,' Andrew said, slapping Nathaniel's shoulder.

As Nathaniel gawked, back and forth from the controller to the television set in disbelief, Aaron and Andrew jeered and laughed uncontrollably.

'Stop it now,' said Mrs. Jackson, slapping the side of Andrew's head as she crossed the room.

'Ow! Mom?'

'Stop it, you hear? Nathaniel is a guest in this house,' she said, shuffling through the living room, placing a cream ceramic bowl covered in cling foil on the coffee table in between the boys. 'I have never seen a young man go through puberty with clearer skin. Unlike you two,' she scolded her sons before turning to face Nathaniel. 'You have a *very* nice complexion, Nathaniel,' she said.

'Thank you. See guys? I told you I was a ladies' man.'

'But Mom,' Aaron chimed in, chuckling, 'Drew's right. I mean, how does anyone manage to stay that pale in Florida?'

Aaron and Andrew both howled and slapped at their knees, before stopping abruptly as Mrs. Jackson leaned over to issue a synchronized whack.

'Stop that you two. I mean it. I'll never understand boys. Always feelin' like they got to rip on each other to have fun. Curse that old gypsy woman who told me I'd have girls. Two times.'

'Ah, that's okay Momma, they're just jealous of my charms. And I'm okay with that.' Nathaniel grinned.

Mrs. Jackson uncovered the bowl and scrunched the foil into a ball. Then, she stroked Nathaniel on the cheek before reaching behind him to kiss Aaron and, crouching down, gave Andrew's head a loving pat on her way out.

'You boys eat and go to bed, you hear? It's late. And put what's left of that in the fridge when you're finished. And remember to close the fridge, Drew. Nobody wants to deal with me in the mornin' after having to throw a whole carton of milk out.'

The three boys looked at each other and smirked. 'Goodnight, Momma,' they said in unison.

'Two times she said I'd have girls, God bless her,' Mrs. Jackson murmured. She grunted as she switched off the kitchen light. 'Good God, though, I love having you kids in the house,' she mumbled, making her way upstairs.

It was almost midnight.

The heavy rain on the windows made the entire house feel warmer from the inside. A deep, low rumbling traveled downstairs, meaning Mr. Jackson was well and truly asleep. Soon, Mrs. Jackson would be too. But the boys—thrilled to be in each other's company, and without a care in the world—were wide awake.

'So, come on guys, are we watching something or what?'

'You're not tired?' asked Andrew.

Aaron sighed. 'Nope.'

'How about you Berg?'

'No,' Nathaniel answered with his mouth full.

'What? Are you guys still on Florida time or something?'

'There's no time difference between Florida and Melvin, fool.' Aaron laughed.

'Yeah,' Nathaniel mumbled, 'but technically, Florida does have two different time zones. So… you can see where he got confused.'

Andrew put his controller on the coffee table, took the remote and threw it into Aaron's lap. 'Man, whatever, I'm bored. Just pick something.'

'A movie?'

'I'm down for a movie. What genre?' Nathaniel asked, dipping into the bowl, going back for more of Mrs. Jackson's southern-fried popcorn-chicken. 'Ah,' he continued, 'I love how you guys have chicken just like… on hand, all the time.'

Aaron looked at Andrew and grinned, and Andrew looked at Nathaniel. 'That's racist,' he said, staring with a straight face.

'No way.'

'Yep,' Aaron agreed, 'Sorry dude, but that's racist.'

'I didn't mean *you guys* as in black people in general, just your family.'

'Oh, that's better.'

'Besides, Jews can't be racist.'

Aaron burst into laughter.

'How do you figure that?' Andrew asked.

'You know, because of Egypt and stuff. We're victims too. I feel you, bro.'

'Man, what? That was centuries ago.'

'So was slavery.'

'He's got you there, Drew.' Aaron smiled, wiped his eyes, and exhaled. Then, composing himself, he persisted, 'Come on guys, stop getting distracted. What're we doing?'

'You just said, bro. A movie.'

'Yeah, but which one?'

'Let's watch a scary movie,' Nathaniel suggested, '*What's your favorite scary movie*?' he mocked.

At that moment, something rumbled and crashed outside.

Thunder.

Their necks jerked. Startled, they turned towards the window—despite the thick curtains blocking out any lightning—and waited, in silence, for another booming roar.

But seconds passed, and all they could hear was the patting and dripping of rain on the glass and in the gutters on the roof.

Nathaniel wiped his greasy hands on his jeans and gripped his knees. 'Well… if that isn't a sign for us to watch a horror movie, I don't know what is.'

'Right. I think I'm officially out. You boys enjoy.'

'Ha! Come on Drew. You scared?' Aaron teased.

'Hey, now, it's not my fault you guys are all desensitized. Y'all are too used to getting the bejesus scared out of you on the regular. It's like y'all are constantly trying to reenact *Ghostbusters* or whatever. I'm the only normal one here.'

'Fair, but movies aren't real.'

'They're all based on something real though, am I right? Like that *Emily Rose* thing. Man, I didn't sleep for days after seeing that.'

'Exorcisms? Oh yeah, I get it,' Nathaniel said in agreement, 'totally real.'

'Totally *scary*.'

'Remember the beginning of *The Conjuring*? Those paragraphs—'

'Those paragraphs that explained it was based on a true story?!' Andrew exclaimed, 'See? I rest my case.'

Aaron shrugged. 'I don't buy it.'

'How about some comedy? I think pops has some old *SNL* sketches somewhere. There'll be time for you guys to get the bejesus scared out of you tomorrow, right?' Andrew suggested.

Aaron looked down at his case and thought about the morning.

He had everything that would allow him to oversee the "digital side of things" as Ashley put it when she assigned everyone tasks that spring when the vacation was organized. He even managed to get his hands on some new equipment he could not wait to show Curtis and the girls. He was ready for action, for a fright. And he knew Nathaniel was, too. Though, he could not be sure about the others.

'I don't know Drew,' said Nathaniel, 'I mean, we're meeting everyone tomorrow. But we haven't settled on a first site yet. I'm hoping we can all decide on one, though. I'm craving a good haunting.'

'Yeah, me too. I think they'll want to rest though, don't you? First day back in Melvin? They'll want to chill for a couple of days,' Aaron supposed.

'Guess we'll see tomorrow,' said Nathaniel.

'That'll be nice… to catch up with the group,' said Andrew.

Aaron nodded and handed Nathaniel the remote, who nodded back.

'It'll be nice to see Robin, huh, Aaron? A little catch-up session with Miss. Wilson?' he continued.

'Hey. Shut up.'

'Is that a euphemism?' Nathaniel asked.

'Berger, shut up.'

'What? I'm not the one who said, "*catch up*" in a seedy manner.'

'Right. Well, I don't know what seedy means,' said Andrew, 'But I do know our boy's been hung up on a certain Miss. Wilson since Clinton was in office.'

Aaron's facial expression went from irritated to bewildered and back to irritated in a manner of seconds. 'So, you don't know what *seedy* means, and you don't know what *shut up* means.'

'Whatever bro, you do you. I'm just saying—'

'I think you've said enough.'

'I am just saying…' Andrew continued, 'It's not like you've brought anyone home, you know, into the family. And you've never mentioned any girls from Florida. And I know there are some fine beach-bunnies down there.'

'You don't know what I get up to. For all you know I have a fine… Floridian "beach bunny" waiting for me right now.' Aaron gestured.

'He doesn't,' said Nathaniel.

'What? No…' Andrew said, sarcastically propping a hand up and over his mouth.

'Whatever. I'm beat. It's late. Too late for a movie now.' Aaron grunted, sat up, and took out his phone from his back pocket to check the time, as both his brother and best friend pleaded with him to stay when he noticed something. The number nine next to the phone icon. He had missed nine phone calls whilst his phone was on silent. But who would call at this hour?

Aaron quickly adjusted the volume, setting it to vibrate before checking his phone log. But before he could, another incoming call popped up on the screen.

As the phone continued to vibrate, Nathaniel lent forward and asked, 'Who is it?'

'It's Robin,' Aaron answered, 'She's probably calling to say they've arrived.'

'Great. Answer her then.'

Aaron stood up from his seat and gestured for the boys to keep quiet before answering. 'Hello? Wait… Ash? Ashley, what's wrong? Slow down… Where are you guys?'

Nathaniel shot up from the floor. 'What in the world is happening?' he asked.

'Okay just stay there, okay? We're coming to get you guys, we're coming to—'

Aaron stood still and stared at the phone in his hands. The look on his face said everything. Something had gone wrong.

'What's going on?' Andrew asked, standing up, as Nathaniel and Aaron stared at the phone.

'It cut off. I don't know. They were in an accident. Robin's hurt. She's hurt.'

Nathaniel tugged at the tight black ringlets on his head. 'Heck...'

Andrew reached into his pocket. 'Go,' he said, handing Aaron a set of keys, 'both of you. Take Pops' car. I'll hold down the fort, cover for you if Mom wakes up.'

AARON

Saturday 24th October

00:05 AM, Route 1

It had stopped raining and it was not as cold.

If you looked forward, where the fog had mostly cleared and was visibly clearing still, you might find a comforting sense of relief wash over you. If you looked down, however, at the mirror-black puddles on the ground, at the ominous droplets of Robin's blood on Ashley's white converses, you would not feel so at ease.

'What did Aaron say?!'

Ashley squinted at Robin's phone and pocketed it. 'They're coming to get us,' she told Curtis as she held Robin against her torso in the back of his father's car.

'Try calling the sheriff's office,' Curtis barked.

'Again? Curtis… no one is going to answer. It's late. Too late. We're not in New York. And with this signal… I was lucky enough to get through to Aaron.'

'Well, we have to try something,' he said, raising and waving his phone in the air, keeping an eye on the non-existent signal bars.

Ashley had never seen Curtis so agitated. Anyone who knew them would agree that he was the more laid-back half of the pair. Now, though, he wouldn't even look at her. He just stood behind the open car door, staring into the road, digging into the metal with his palm as if he would rip the door from its hinges as one would clip a nail.

00:35 AM, Route 1

What was it? Cocoa butter or shea? She must have asked a dozen times over the years, but could never remember what it was, only how it smelt. Thinking about it now, there never was a sticker or label on the bottle; on the pale-yellow bottle which lived in the same place on his nightstand and was always full and new. He loved to fidget, she remembered he couldn't help but to pick at things. Like with orange-soda bottles he would get at the drugstore on hot days after school. He would always pick at the label with his fingernails, tear it off and fiddle with it; fidget, as he spoke to her. So, she never knew what it was, what kind of cream it was he used every day. She only knew how it smelt, and how she felt when she smelt it. How she felt when her brain occasionally remembered the smell for her, triggering memories of brief moments in which they found themselves alone and away from the group.

Robin could smell the nameless and intoxicating fragrance so strongly now; it was almost as if Aaron were inches away from her nose. The more she thought about the smell, the more she could feel his presence surround her. And the more she tried to concentrate, the more she could hear, she swore, the faint yet persistent calling of her name, as if through an extra inner ear from within her imagination. Was it him? "*Am I dreaming*?" she thought to herself. 'Am I awake?' she mumbled aloud.

'Robin?' a voice beckoned, 'Can you hear me?'

Though Robin seemed to gradually drift further away from her limbo-like state, the heaviness of her eyelids, of her head, and the stiffness of her neck, endured. She put every effort into lifting her head but could not. Now though, at least, she could hear clearly.

'Robin?' the voice continued.

It was Aaron. She was sure of it—sure that she was not dreaming, sure that she was awake and in his care. That certainty drew in strength, and as she opened her eyes, as her vision cleared, she let out an exasperated sigh of relief.

'Hi,' Robin breathed.

Aaron smiled back. 'Hey.'

Robin's eyes trailed over him, taking in every detail. The faded lettering on his burgundy *University of Florida* sweatshirt, the thin stubble on his angular jawline, his perfect grinning teeth, and the look in his eyes. And the… pale, skinny unknown hand on his right shoulder?

The strange hand was Nathaniel's, of course. There he was as well; bent over, resting on Aaron. Then, he slowly but very deliberately peeked his head forward. 'Is she alive?' he asked.

Curtis smacked Nathaniel's bicep with enough force to wobble him like a feeble plate of Jell-O and almost knock over Aaron, who was kneeling on the ground, in the process. 'Of course, she's alive, moron,' Curtis started, 'What kind of foolish thing…'

'Careful,' Aaron warned—trying to find his balance whilst maintaining a firm grip on Robin's head.

Robin grunted as she shifted her position slightly. Then she looked up at her friends. At Curtis rolling his eyes, at Nathaniel as he stared back at her with his mouth agape, and at a mute Ashley standing behind the boys, anxiously chewing on the tassels of her scarf.

'Hi, guys.'

'SHE LIVES!' Nathaniel announced before bolting across the road, theatrically; running away from Curtis, who he knew would chase after him.

Curtis did, of course. And, of course, Ashley went after the howling boys like a tired mother, though not before shooting Robin a loving smile and a relieved nod.

Aaron and Robin smirked and sighed and chuckled.

'Home sweet home, huh?' Robin joked as Aaron cautiously helped her up from the ground.

'Ha. Not quite,' he said, steadily releasing her as she stood upright, hand on head. 'Come on,' he continued, 'let's get you home.'

01:00 AM, Downtown Melvin

Curtis' father's car had started, miraculously, despite all the poor vehicle had been through in the past 24-hours alone.

After hugs and back pats and reassurances, Curtis and Ashley got in. They drove to Ashley's mother's home; where Ashley planned to spend the week and where Curtis would stay for a while, for the night at least, before visiting with his father.

Curtis drove slowly and, all the while, Aaron's father's car could be seen in the rear-view mirror as Nathaniel drove just a few meters behind them with his watchful eyes fixed on the car as well as the road.

Aaron kept an eye on Robin in the back seat. They all looked after each other, just as they always had done. And now they would have an entire week to do so. Now, they were together again, and everyone felt more at ease, as if nothing untoward had happened that night. They were together, they were home, and that was all that mattered.

After an eventful and early reunion—as stars twinkled through the dissipating fog and as Mr. Jackson's engine ran on the corner of Bainbridge Drive—Aaron, Nathaniel and Robin quietly watched as Curtis and Ashley waved goodbye. They waited as Ashley unlocked the door to her childhood home with surgical precision so as not to wake her mother. Then, they watched as Curtis snuck in behind her, lowering his head, carrying their bags.

The door shut behind the couple and after a slight pause and a long, collective sigh of relief, the three remaining friends were off into the night.

The narrow, familiar streets of Melvin were empty. No nocturnal critters could be seen, and no cooing, scurrying, or screeching heard. It was too early for birds and too late for anything else. The sleepy town of Melvin was, for all intents and purposes, fast asleep. Closed signs hung in front of the post office, the pet store, and the bakery. Nothing was open. And no lights were left on in stores or houses. Only sporadic streetlamps illuminated sections of roads, guiding their way, twitching, and blinking as they drove.

Now that half of the group was home and the other half were on their way, Nathaniel, invigorated by a burst of energy, seemed typically chipper; chattering away about how cool a "mini-adventure" this had been and how it was a shame Aaron's father only had *Boyz II Men* cassettes in his car but no *Beastie Boys*. Robin could manage a faint smile whilst Aaron made sure Nathaniel stayed focused to get them back quickly and safely. With only some dried blood left on her forehead, next to a large band-aid, she was mostly fine, but felt a deep tiredness sweep over her—and she could not wait to be in her old bed.

The evening had come to an end.

Aaron insisted Nathaniel take the car back to his parents' house first so that he could let Andrew know everything was fine, provided he was still awake. He would make sure Robin got back home safe and sound.

So, he did.

When they arrived, Nathaniel parked as smoothly as he could, which he successfully managed despite not having his license for as long as everyone else. As they got out, they tried to avoid slamming the car doors shut, especially after retrieving Robin's suitcase from the trunk.

Aaron and Robin waited briefly, on edge, as Nathaniel snuck in. All three expected the all-knowing and ever-irritable Mrs. Jackson to be wide-awake and have a thing, or two, to say. But when he closed the door behind him and no lights switched on, they knew they were home free.

With the handle of Robin's suitcase in his left hand, and Robin's hand in his right, Aaron walked Robin to the only place she wanted to be—home.

01:15 AM, 13 Carmine Crescent

They took short, unhurried strides.

Aaron stopped intermittently, taking breaks from carrying Robin's heavy suitcase. He would have rolled it if the sound of it struggling on the sidewalk did anything but echo into the night and through Melvin's empty streets.

Robin tried to muffle giggles as they caught up, as Aaron tried—unnecessarily, yet with the best of intentions—to distract her from what had happened. She was fine. They both were. Oddly, the events of the past few hours had no adverse effect on either's mood.

Nor did the darkness or their exhaustion. Nothing could penetrate the bubble of glowing joy that surrounded the pair as they walked, side by side.

Though it did not seem like it in each other's company, the way to Robin's house did not take long. Even considering the scarcity of working streetlamps or the fact that Robin had not walked these streets in a long time, neither felt lost nor confused, only certain. So much so that their eyes, for the most part, remained fixed on each other rather than ahead of them.

Robin's shoes, her feet, her head, and her heart would never, could never, forget the ins and outs of the town she grew up in. And for Aaron, the route to her house from his was a route which would always remain a familiar one; forever ingrained in his memory. A few minutes and a few turns. It was a few yards away from Curtis' house and, more importantly for Aaron in his youth, Curtis' treehouse.

Both houses were detached and, though not as large as Aaron's, Nathaniel's or even Ashley's family homes, appeared quaint and well-kept from the outside; complete with flowerpots, hanging plants and, much to the insistence of the Widow Brenton, perfectly placed garbage cans on their respective curbs.

Perched in a small cul-de-sac, alongside only a few other houses, Robin's was positioned right in the middle of the curve in the road and was unmistakable due to the distinctive glossy sheen of the carmine-red front door. The shimmer from the polished silver numbers one and three could be seen twinkling from afar in the sunlight, Aaron recalled; thinking of times he would walk Robin home during their last years of high school when Curtis began to make his way to Ashley's house more and more. The memory beckoned reality in that, in seconds, something appeared to glimmer in the moonlight not far ahead. It was just how he remembered it, how they both did. They were there.

True to form, Halloween decorations were already up. Although, the meticulous detail of the autumnal arrangement could not be seen at this hour. Robin's heart fluttered at the anticipation of seeing everything in the morning.

A faint glow of artificial light leaked through the living room window's thick curtains and she knew that her fathers were awake, waiting for her. It was typical, she thought, but also understandable considering the circumstances. She was grateful that Aaron managed to get a message to them on his and Nathaniel's way to the highway earlier that night.

'I should go,' Robin whispered, as they both peeked through the window.

Aaron nodded in response. He picked up Robin's suitcase one last time, made his way up the three steps towards the front door, and placed it upright on the top step. Then, he walked down and stopped in front of Robin.

He did not say anything, but Robin knew Aaron well enough to understand why he was lingering. He would want to watch her close the door behind her, to know that she was safe, before leaving.

In turn, Aaron knew Robin well enough to guess that she would want a few moments to herself; a few moments alone to breathe in her house, to breathe out this incredibly long day, before going inside.

Robin took three deliberate steps and sighed. She looked back and smiled at Aaron, mouthing *"Thank you"* as he smiled back. Then, he waved before disappearing into the darkness.

Robin turned back and faced the door; the door she had longed to see, to open, to shut, to knock on, to salute from, for three years. The carmine entrance to her core.

Tugging on her keys from within her tight denim back pocket, attempting to find the right one on the jingling set of what seemed like a hundred keys and various keyrings must have alerted her parents to her presence because, almost immediately, Robin heard frantic stomps, flicking and clicking, presumably of light switches, and the distinctive sound of a latch unlocking.

The door swung open to reveal the fatigued and careworn, emotive, and relieved faces of Finn and Christopher Wilson. Finally, after one collective sigh, Robin was home.

10:00 AM, 13 Carmine Crescent

Robin woke up in the comfort of her old bed.

Surprisingly, in the fleeting moments between asleep and awake, she did not feel confused as to where she was, as one might expect. She did not think she was in Boston but rather drifted into reality with a firm sense of certainty.

Then, Robin raised her hand to her head and softly caressed the area her band-aid covered. She would have to take it off and change it. After breakfast, of course. "*How unsightly*," she thought. There would be a scratch or some mark. "*Definitely*." There was no pain, though, so at least there was that.

Robin stretched, yawned, and arched her back as she sprawled across her, pleasantly large in comparison, queen-sized bed and, as she blinked Friday away, as her eyes adjusted to the morning sun streaming through her bedroom window, she fully took in her surroundings.

She looked across the plum walls of her fairly small—but still bigger than at Harvard—bedroom. At the human anatomy poster that Nathaniel had gotten her for Christmas one year. At the *Final Destination* poster featuring Devon Sawa, her first celebrity crush, which she would kiss before bed for years in secret as a teenager. At the cut-out newspaper articles about her father, Finn, and his students at his dance school, *Stardust*, winning various competitions over the years. At a photo of her, at however many years old, Finn and Christopher in a pink elephant ride at a funfair one July 4th, long ago. At a photo of her and Christopher, one Thanksgiving, dressed as pilgrims at the history museum where he worked. At the fluffy violet frame Ashley had bought her for her sixteenth birthday; containing a photo of them as children in full ballet gear at Finn's studio where they first met.

What a room, filled with such memories, with love, she thought.

Then, she wondered, noticing the extreme amount of purple one room could contain, how it was that she had forgotten she, at one point, had a favorite color. Perhaps she had been too busy, as of late, to have one, if that was possible. As her eyes trailed across her room and as her thoughts trailed into the past, the sight of one singular item made Robin instantly sit up.

Pinned into the top left-hand corner of the full-length mirror behind her bedroom door was one unforgettable photograph. It was of her, of Curtis and Ashley, Aaron, and Nathaniel, dressed as Catwoman, Superman, Wonder Woman, Batman, and Robin on their last Halloween together before college. Though she had woken up with a clear mind as to where she was, she had momentarily overlooked the reason for her being there in the first place and then, upon seeing the photograph, remembered she was supposed to meet with the gang today to begin their Halloween-themed antics.

Frantically, she looked around for her phone, realizing that she had neglected to set an alarm. Although she did not know what time it was, she, correctly, assumed she was late.

Rushing through a blur of yesterday's events in her mind, as she threw on a gown and a pair of fresh socks, Robin remembered that she had slipped her phone into the front pocket of her suitcase yesterday afternoon in the park. Then, she remembered Ashley giving it back to her after having borrowed it on the highway in the early hours of the morning. She thought long and hard, trying to remember where she had placed it, only to remember that she had, once again, slipped it into the front pocket of her suitcase!

Not seeing the suitcase in her bedroom, Robin opened the door and hurried downstairs.

She flew down the stairs and, holding onto the banister, used her momentum to swing left and turn towards the hallway. There was no suitcase to be seen. She did see her parents sat at the dining table, however, in the far-right corner of their living room. They were both fully dressed and there were no breakfast plates or mugs in sight. This was a bad sign, Robin deduced. It was probably already late in the afternoon and her friends, undoubtedly worried about her from last night and wanting to leave her to rest, were in all likelihood already having fun without her.

'Where did you guys put my suitcase last night?' she asked, looking around the living room.

'It's in the kitchen, Bubba,' said Finn, gesturing. 'I took out some of your clothes this morning to do a load of laundry. I wasn't sure if you had the time to get everything washed before you packed and didn't want to wake you to ask.'

'Thanks,' she said, sprinting towards the kitchen.

'Um, Robin…' Christopher started, 'Robin, honey, come back here for a moment, won't you?'

'Sorry, Dad,' she said, returning with her phone, 'I'm late and I have to meet the guys.' Robin continued to look down at her phone. Her fingertips went pale from pressing down on the *on-button* too hard and for too long. 'Shit! I mean, shoot! Sorry. No battery.'

'Robin,' Christopher insisted.

'Charger…' Robin mumbled to herself, going back to the kitchen to rummage through her open suitcase.

'Robin,' Christopher said in a firm voice, 'You can do that in a moment. Kindly join your father and me at the breakfast table.'

'I can't, Dad.' Robin said, rushing back into the living room to find a free socket for her charger. 'I'm late and I need to charge my phone and get ready and the guys…'

'Robin!'

Robin felt like she was a teenager again. Her father's *"Taxi Driver voice"* always rendered her speechless, however rare it was he felt he had to use it. She stopped and looked them both over.

'Wow…' she started, 'Listen, I know you guys might be feeling anxious about what happened last night… and I know you're happy I'm home and want me to be safe… but…' Robin stopped talking as her reasoning slowly vanished, as she observed her parents and began to fully comprehend the situation.

Something else was wrong.

She had been so focused on her friends and their plans that she failed to fully take in her parents' demeanor when she first came downstairs. There they were, sitting in unusual and tense silence, evidently waiting for her at the table, with no eggs or coffee but only an A4 letter-brown folder in between them. As Robin walked over to give the folder a closer look, she saw there was nothing on it. No label or logo or note to characterize it in any way.

'Wait. What is that?' she asked, 'What's going on?'

When she looked up at her parents, at Finn and Christopher, a lump instantly formed in her throat as she noticed they had been crying. Their bloodshot eyes immediately summoned thoughts of the worst in her mind.

Were they in financial trouble? Robin didn't fully understand what the word foreclosure meant but it started darting through her thoughts. Did someone get hurt or ill? Were *they* ill? God forbid, someone they knew died or was dying. God forbid one of them was dying.

'Sit down, Bubba,' said Finn, caressing Robin's upper back and shoulders as he positioned her onto a chair in the middle of them.

'What's going on?' she repeated herself.

'Now, Robin, I don't want you to worry. It's...' Christopher paused and lifted his sleeve to look at the watch on his wrist before continuing. 'It is 10:00 AM, so you have some time, and I'm sure your friends will wait for you and understand if you're a tad late.'

News that Robin was not late, yet anyway, to meet the gang went straight over her head. She could not feel relieved or happy, or anything positive, whilst the tension perched deep in her stomach.

'Your father and I must speak to you,' Christopher continued, 'We have to speak to you about something important. You see, it's important that you understand that... um, well...'

'What your father is trying to say, Bubba, is that we have something to tell you,' Finn interrupted.

'Yeah… I can see that.'

Christopher cleared his throat. He removed his round glasses, wiped each lens with the fabric from the right sleeve of his brown sweater, and wiped his brow with the back of his hand before putting them back on. 'You see, Robin… This folder contains information that affects you, or will affect you, which affects all of us, really.'

Robin's emotional state went from worried to irritated as he rambled when, thankfully, Finn stepped in.

'I think what your father is *still* trying to say,' Finn started, 'is that this folder is from the adoption agency in Melvin.'

"Oh," Robin thought.

Relieved, yet slightly frustrated; she had no idea why her parents had to be so incredibly dramatic about something as wonderful as adopting a new child. She had thought the worst and for nothing. It made complete sense, the more she thought about it. She had been away for college and, in their minds, would be away for several years yet whilst she figured out her career and her future. Of course, they would be pining to take care of something new—and with Christopher being allergic to cats and Finn being terrified of dogs, a child made sense.

Christopher and Finn were two of the kindest souls she had ever known, her absolute heroes. They were amazing parents to her, and she did not doubt they would be the same towards anyone else. She knew how much it had meant to them when they were finally able to adopt her all those years ago, and, considering the amount of time and effort it took them to adopt her from Boston the first time, she reckoned it would be easier to go through the Melvin Adoption Agency, this time.

She thought it was wonderful. Robin had always wanted a sibling, a large family. And she knew that, when the time came for her to tell her fathers she planned on moving to Melvin next year after graduation, they would be all the happier to have her there to help integrate the newest member of the Wilson family.

'I think it's fantastic that you guys want to adopt again. Or foster. Whatever you've decided. I'm fully behind you.'

Christopher and Finn looked at each other. Then, they looked down at the folder—as if they couldn't bear to look at Robin.

'What…?'

'Bubba, we're not adopting anyone. You're our only child. You're our daughter… our…' Finn's eyes teared up and, now, she was worried again.

If Finn, the calmer, more collected, rational half of the two had lost his cool; whatever they had to say must have been serious.

'This is a Reversed Details Request form, Robin.' Christopher explained. 'We received a letter informing us that one of your relatives has requested to contact you. And, seeing as it was a closed adoption, legally the agency can't give him or her any information which would identify you to them. They can, however, give your adoptive parents, us, their details, and inform us that, should you wish to initiate contact with this person, you can do.'

The acid in Robin's stomach began to churn again, turning into bile in her throat.

'Relative? What relative?'

'We don't know, sweetheart.'

Robin looked at Finn, at the tears streaming down his face, as he said nothing. She looked back at Christopher, at his pursed lips seemingly holding back a lump in his throat, too.

She had never felt this way before.

Robin sat there on edge with clenched fists, vibrating with emotion, unsure of what to say as a million thoughts raced through her mind.

'I… don't… understand,' she said, slowly and purposefully through gritted teeth, pronouncing each word, trying to pace herself. 'You said… you told me, that I was an orphan. In Boston. That you adopted me from an agency in Boston. That I had no living relatives. That's why I felt safe going to school there. Because I knew I wouldn't ever have to worry about random people trying to find me. Random people, who didn't want me, trying to find me and mess me around.'

'Sweetheart…' Christopher started.

'No.' Robin barked, standing up. 'You said I didn't have any living relatives. And, now, I have some repentant criminal uncle, fresh out of prison who's found Jesus and wants to reconnect or something, or some older sister, with a gaggle of kids, in need of a kidney? Some… *person*, who's been in Melvin the whole time, by the way, the town that I've been from this *entire* time, some creep who could have been spying on me this entire time, wants *me* to contact *them*? Now? How does that make any sense? What else have you lied about over the years?'

What more could be said after such an eruption of emotion?

The conversation did not last long, after that. That morning, Robin's fathers tried and failed to console their daughter in light of the most disturbing news which could have ever rocked their little family.

Unable, or unwilling, to confront the issue at the time; Robin angrily zipped and lugged her suitcase upstairs, ignoring the pleas and cries of her parents as she shut the door of her childhood bedroom behind her.

She didn't have time to think about this right now.

She shook her head as if she would shake away the memory and the reality of the conversation which had only just taken place and began to get ready, quickly.

Ten or so minutes later, dressed and ready to go, Robin sat on the edge of her bed and waited a few more minutes for her phone to charge just enough for her to check if her friends had sent any messages with a change in plans. She waited for it to reach 1% battery life, for it to turn on, for it to reach 2%, at least, etc. Then, she began to receive a plethora of notifications. When the vibrating stopped, she looked to see if anything warranted her immediate attention. Most were social media messages from friends at college wishing her fun during her break, and there were no updates in the group chat between her, Curtis, Ashley, Aaron, and Nathaniel. However, there was one new text message. It was from Aaron, sent quite early that morning.

She read it aloud, quietly, to herself, with an inquisitive inflection. The text read; *"Check the bottom drawer of your desk."*

'Check the bottom drawer of your desk…'

Robin placed the phone down on her bed and got up to investigate. Upon opening the third drawer in her desk, she found a card with her name written on the top, and upon picking up the card she noticed a gift box underneath the card.

She sat down on her bedroom floor next to the open drawer with her back up against her wardrobe and opened the card.

'Dear Robin…' she started, *'I'm using your stationery, I hope you don't mind…'* Robin stopped to look at the front of the card again and noticed it was indeed one from her collection—a red and gold general occasion card with a red-breasted-robin design. *'I hope you don't mind,'* she continued, *'but I forgot to get a card. I asked your fathers if I could leave this here before seeing you tonight and they said it was fine. I promise I won't look through your stuff. I just wanted to leave you this present and avoid any awkwardness in front of the group. We've all missed each other's birthdays over the past few years, so I got you something. It's nothing special and didn't cost much,*

but it made me think of you when I saw it. I know how much you love Melvin and how much you've missed it since you've been away. So, I wanted you to have a piece of home wherever you go. See you at PB. Love, Aaron.'

Robin smiled and put down the card before opening her present. It wasn't wrapped, it was just a small, simple, navy-blue velvet box. *"It must be jewelry,"* she thought. She opened the box slowly and it clicked in place to reveal a necklace. She was right. It shone like white gold, although Aaron mentioning price in the card meant it was probably silver. It was a silver pendant, on a silver chain, in the shape of a crescent moon. In the middle was a small gemstone.

Robin continued to look at the necklace Aaron had bought her. It wasn't something she would pick out for herself, and she didn't recall ever mentioning a fondness for the moon. If anything, everyone knew how much Robin loved basking in the sunlight. Still, she thought it was incredibly kind of him to get her something, anything, and equally considerate of him to look up her birthstone. Although, the more she looked at it, the more confused she became.

Robin's birthday was in July. This meant her birthstone was a ruby. And the more she inspected the necklace, the more she realized the gemstone wasn't a ruby at all. It was a darker, deeper red. It was a garnet rivet.

'How odd,' she said to herself.

She looked at the card again, skimming over Aaron's words. *"I wanted you to have a piece of home wherever you go."*

'Wait a minute,' she said aloud as an epiphany brewed.

Robin eventually realized what Aaron meant, what the present meant. The garnet stone in the middle of a curved moon was her house; her door, her carmine-red door in the middle of a crescent-shaped road, of Carmine Crescent. It was a *piece of home*.

At that moment, Robin could not help but cry.

She knew that he had meant the best for her, as he always did, and she also knew that under any other circumstances a gift like this might bring her to tears of a different nature.

Now, though, unsure of so much—of her parents, of who she was, or where home was or what that even meant—Robin could not escape the flood of immense sadness as she looked down at the pendant.

She would, of course, eventually approach her feelings. She would eventually talk to her parents about the situation and make some form of decision. She would, at some point this week, thank Aaron for his present. But, for now, she put the necklace into the box, the box and card back into her desk drawer, got up, wiped her face, and left.

10:00 AM, 8 Almond Avenue

'Drew, your laundry's in your room. Drew? Do you hear me?' Mrs. Jackson balanced the half-full laundry basket on her hip and, with her one free hand, reached down to yank Andrew's headphones off as he was, predictably, sat on the living room floor gaming.

'Ow! Ma?'

'Do you hear me, Drew?' she repeated herself. 'Your clothes are in a pile on your bed. No amount of money can make me open your chest of drawers to put them away. God only knows what foul things are in there.'

'Man, ain't nothing in there,' Drew dismissed as he put his headphones on and continued with his video game.

'Man?' Mrs. Jackson scoffed. 'You just run on up there and put that pile away, you hear? Make sure those clothes stay as neat as you found 'em. Lord knows I'm not ironing them again, Drew,' she said, yanking his headphones off again.

Andrew exhaled and paused the game. Then he got up and walked behind his mother into the kitchen as she made her way through and up the stairs.

'Yeah, yeah. I'll get to it. *After* breakfast,' he said, taking a seat at the table across from where Aaron was already sat, grinning cheekily as he ate his cereal and eavesdropped.

'As long as you get to it, I don't mind if you have an espresso with the President first,' Mrs. Jackson shouted as she made her way upstairs.'

'Yeah, yeah, whatever,' Andrew mumbled.

Aaron tutted and shook his head. 'That's messed up, bro.'

'I know right? How am I gonna meet Obama?'

'No. I mean you.'

'What?'

'You do realize you're a grown man, right?' said Aaron, putting down his spoon.

'Hell yeah. I'm as grown as they get.'

'Right,' Aaron whispered, 'So, what in the hell are you doing making Ma do your errands at her age? At your age?'

Andrew shook his head as he stood up to grab a bowl, a spoon, and the open milk carton on the counter before sitting back down. 'Man, don't sweat me right now, Aaron. Yesterday was a long day. I just need to kick back today. Finish your fruity pebbles, go play with your friends and leave me be,' he said. Then, Andrew grabbed one of the cereal boxes on the table, filled his bowl, topped it with milk, and started to, try to, enjoy his breakfast.

'Nah, bro. That's not right.'

Aaron got up from the table shaking his head. Having finished his cereal, he placed his bowl and spoon in the sink. He had already showered and was dressed, ready to meet Curtis, Ashley, Nathaniel, and Robin. He wouldn't need anything until tonight, probably, but he made sure all his equipment was ready and packed that morning, too. He should, he told himself, just leave to see his friends and start enjoying his vacation. But something was niggling at him, in the back of his mind, and Aaron was not the type to stay quiet about anything.

'I understand you staying for the weekend to see me and everything,' he started, turning towards his brother, 'but how do you have enough clothes here for Ma to be doing a load of your laundry and leaving it in your old room?'

'Not everything revolves around you, bro,' Andrew said simply.

It was a nonsensical response and the situation was even more so.

That morning in the bathroom, Aaron noticed various products—aftershave and deodorant and a third toothbrush—he knew belonged to Andrew. And the more he thought about it, the more he realized too many of Andrew's things were scattered around the house. He knew it was unlikely that anything major had happened, like Andrew losing his house or his job. He guessed, knowing his brother, that he had simply gotten lazy as of late, possibly after yet another break-up, and started staying at their parents more frequently, as he had done periodically in the past. But enough was enough. Andrew was in his thirties and their parents were not, and ought not to be, in the position to baby him anymore. He had to say something. He had to defend his parents.

'Not everything revolves around you either, Drew. Mom and Dad have stuff to deal with. Whatever trouble you've gotten yourself into, again, you can get yourself out of, alone. We're both out of the house, finally, or should be. This is the time for them to start reconnecting and saving before retirement, not spending money on extra food and stuff for you.'

'Listen. Aaron. Seriously. Just stop. Stop talking about stuff you don't know a thing about.'

'What? What don't I know? That my older brother still has the mentality of a teenager? It's pathetic. Get your life together.'

Andrew stood up and faced his brother. 'I said… you need to stop talking.'

'Or what?' Aaron challenged, inches away from his brother's face.

Just then, Mrs. Jackson barged into the kitchen, pushed the boys apart, and stood in between them. 'Woah,' she said, 'What in Christendom is going on here? What are we Italians? This ain't no episode of *The Sopranos* for there to be this much tension in my kitchen this early in the morning. What's going on here?'

Andrew pushed at the air dismissively with both hands and sat back down at the table. 'Nothing. Ain't nothing happening, Ma.'

'It doesn't look like nothing,' she snapped, jerking her head. 'Aaron, what's going on?'

Aaron wasn't sure he should involve his mother in yet another fraternal tiff, but the part of him which was genuinely worried pushed him to speak.

'I'm not sure Drew staying here is the best thing for you guys right now,' he said.

'You told him?' Mrs. Jackson asked Andrew.

Andrew shook his head and continued eating his cereal. 'You told me not to.'

'Told me what?' Aaron asked, confused.

Mrs. Jackson sighed. 'Sit down, baby,' she said.

Aaron took a seat next to Andrew, who said nothing. Then, he looked towards his mother for answers.

'Now, I don't want you to worry. You still go out and have a good time with your friends, you hear? We were gonna tell you soon. As I said, it's nothing to worry about.'

'What's going on, Ma?'

'Drew has moved back in with us. For a little while. Just for a little while.'

'Why?'

'To help out, for a little while.'

'Help with what?' Aaron pressed, becoming more and more agitated.

'Well, your Dad… your Dad is taking some time off. Well, he's come home for a while. So, your brother has kindly left his job and taken your Dad's place at the security firm… and offered to stay here, just for a while, to help. It's cheaper and Lord knows we could all use the extra money.'

Aaron still didn't understand what his mother was getting at. It was certainly no explanation. 'I don't get it. So, Drew's filling in for Dad, why? And why do you need the money? What's going on?'

Andrew let his spoon clank on the bowl and sat back in his seat and exhaled as if he was going to say something. But nothing came out.

'Baby,' Mrs. Jackson started, taking Aaron's hand, and crouching down to look him in the eye, 'Your Dad has Dementia.'

A strange noise—he was not prepared for and could not hold back—escaped Aaron's lips, and, in a powerful combination of shock and confusion, he found himself utterly speechless.

'There are so many different types, apparently,' his mother continued, 'that the doctors don't quite know what we're dealing with yet. And tests and hospital bills are expensive so, we're just all taking it one step at a time.'

Aaron cleared his throat. He didn't know what to say, even if he could. He didn't know what to think either. It didn't matter that they waited to tell him, or why they waited. What mattered was how his father was, which was unclear. He just wasn't sure how to feel.

'Now, we'll all talk about this later. I'm gonna go finish my errands and check on your father before I make his breakfast. Y'all just make sure you stay calm, okay? All that testosterone. We're a family and we'll get through this together, okay? You have fun with your friends, baby,' she said, kissing Aaron on the cheek, 'and don't you worry about a thing. Not a thing, you hear?'

Mrs. Jackson looked over her boys, gave them faint pats on their shoulders, and went back upstairs.

They watched her go and then, turned and looked at each other.

There was nothing left to say. Andrew did not want or expect an apology, and Aaron wasn't going to give one. There was nothing to say.

Aaron got up and took the open milk carton from the table. He pinched and folded the corner before putting the carton back inside the fridge. 'Mom hates it when you leave the milk out,' he said, before walking out of the kitchen, passing through the living room, and leaving the house with just his jacket in hand.

11:00 AM, *Paranormal Booktivity*, 7 Graeme Road
Every town has one. A road of considerable length that runs straight through. A road that no one in the town ever needs directions to, and if a tourist ever asked you how to get to a specific spot on that road, you'd chuckle and exhale before saying *"Right"*, before preparing to give them extremely detailed instructions on how to get there. Well, Russell Road was Melvin's, and there were no tourists, and everyone knew where it ran. Past Susan B. Anthony High, past Adam's hospital, past everything that made Melvin what it was. And if one were to look closely at a map of Melvin, if one were to look at Russell Road stretch across that map, one would see a type of cross near the center where two small no exit alleys ran directly opposite each other, off the main road. They were Graeme Road and Neil Street.

Both alleys contained low-level terraced houses that had mostly been converted into apartments, bar a few converted shops under second-floor apartments.

On Neil Street, Tony Woods lived with his daughter, Fiona, above the general occasion shop he ran, *Merry Masks,* which sold everything from cards and wrapping paper to costumes and some antique items. The Zhous lived in a few apartments on Neil Street; one above *The Black Dragon,* the go-to Chinese food place for many in Melvin, which did not deliver, and which had no space to accommodate anyone wanting to sit in but which you could collect from, and the two apartments next door. *Tara's Tibs,* which everyone just called the packie, sold a bit of everything, and there was a late-night pharmacy that closed at 21:00 PM, considerably late for Melvin, too.

It was a useful couple of alleys for those who lived there. In fact, except for the limited space and the hustle and bustle coming from town on Saturday mornings, one might say it was a perfect place to be. This was truer if you lived on Graeme Road and could look down from the windows on the other side of the top-level apartments which faced a small but beautiful communal stone courtyard, and especially if you were partial to the smell of coffee—strong and sweet. Because on Graeme Road there was a shop, the only shop on Graeme Road in fact, which just so happened to sell the best coffee in Melvin. They even sold home-made pastries as well. Unique and quaint, and irreplaceable, at the center of Melvin sat *Paranormal Booktivity*; a Halloween-themed bookshop which everyone knew was open all-year-round, with the exceptions of Halloween itself and Thanksgiving Day. The owners also owned the courtyard which housed the oldest tree in Melvin. A deciduous tree whose spindly branches seemed to reach out and draw you in like monster claws inviting you to an unforgettable night out. The tree's silhouette was carved onto the wooden sign which hung outside the front of the shop, which the Dodson sisters owned and lived atop of.

Though you wouldn't guess it by looking at them, the Dodson sisters, Willow and Tamarind, had more money than anyone could count, allegedly; where at some point in Melvin's history the Dodson family owned half the town and will have surely saved and invested however much over so many years. The two sisters were the only two left of their line. After inheriting a substantial sum from a dearly departed aunt decades ago, they donated several properties and plots of land to the city of Melvin, earning them a key to the city from Madam Mayor Miller. Apart from that, and apart from the fact that they generally kept to themselves at home and in their shop, no one in Melvin knew much about them at all. No one except for Nathaniel Berger, Aaron Jackson, Robin Wilson, Curtis Jones, and Ashley Cruz, who happened upon their shop as children and spent most of their free time there ever since.

Today, after years of school and semi-adulthood and life in general, the gang would be together at *Paranormal Booktivity* again.

'Not to chastise the future Mrs. Berger, but this is a huge blunder in etiquette,' said Nathaniel.

Curtis made a noise, seemingly in retort, like a dismissive snort under his breath.

Ashley's head jerked as she shot Curtis a puzzled look before turning back towards Nathaniel. '*"Blunder in etiquette?"* That's brutal,' she said after a brief pause, 'especially to your future wife.'

'A *faux-pas* if you will,' Nathaniel compromised.

'Yeah, that's better,' Ashley teased, nodding her head with her lips exaggeratively pursed.

Once again, Curtis unwillingly interrupted the conversation with a sudden and involuntary spasm accompanied by a loud sneeze.

'*¡Qué susto!* Curtis, are you okay? Do you want to move, baby?' Ashley asked.

'No, I'm fine.' Curtis affirmed through gritted teeth.

'Are—are you sure?'

Tamarind Dodson's cat, Jefferson, purred in a ball on Ashley's lap as they talked. Mostly content to sit on windowsills or bookshelves and observe the shop's customers in between naps, Jefferson would rarely approach people, as you would expect. He was generally happy being a cat, but he was friendly enough. If you went to pet him, he would stretch in unison with your strokes and raise his long tail in approval. If you went to pick him up, he would not put up a fight like some cats would, which Ashley and Robin always appreciated as they would take turns holding him whenever the group spent time there. A Maine Coon, he was very long and quite fat, and his fur made him look even bigger. Again, the girls especially appreciated this. They loved to run their fingers through his soft coat and when he sat on them during wintertime, they would call him a "big, fluffy hot-water-bottle".

For a phase in their teenage years, Nathaniel had tried, to no avail, to train Jefferson to do certain things like come when called or even fist-bump him with his paw. Cheese-coated chicken-filled treats Nathaniel knew Jefferson loved would be the bait. But even the sound of Nathaniel rattling a bag of *Cheesy Meow-Mix* from the packie only swayed Jefferson to blink slowly and turn his head, evidently unimpressed at Nathaniel's patronizing attempts to make him "YouTube famous".

Aaron, growing up with no pets in the Jackson household, felt weary about how and where to touch cats in general; finicky creatures he could not identify with. Though, he did think Jefferson was cute and enjoyed being around him. He was so tame he never meowed, as if it were above his majestic bearing to communicate with humans. He never even got into the typically mischievous and silly hijinks you would expect from a cat; like knocking things off surfaces or tugging at strings of fabric. You probably would not mind Jefferson even if you hated cats. In fact, the only customer that ever had a problem with Jefferson was Curtis.

Curtis learned the hard way, when his father brought home an enthusiastic Jack Russell called Jock from the rescue shelter for his seventh birthday, that he was allergic to most animals. Fortunately, Jock found another home that same week. Unfortunately for Curtis, school trips to the Weddleton farm to pet lambs and see calves being born never happened and after-school trips to Paranormal Booktivity could only happen if he had his miraculous menthol nasal spray with him; a spray he did not need in New York and therefore completely forgot to buy for their stay in Melvin.

'Dude. Weak,' said Nathaniel.

Curtis did not reply but merely squinted at Nathaniel before attempting to hold back another sneeze. He couldn't, of course, and woke Jefferson up in the process. The poor creature looked up at Curtis with big innocent eyes as Curtis' gaze, his resentful squinting, shifted from Nathaniel to Jefferson. The pair continued to stare, dramatically, at each other, as if they were in some form of Mexican stand-off in an old Western. Their audience—Ashley and Nathaniel—remained perfectly still. But in an anti-climactic move, Jefferson, clearly over the situation, merely got up, stretched, yawned, and walked over Curtis' lap before making his way upstairs.

'I think the cat won this round,' Nathaniel teased.

'Poor baby…' Ashley exclaimed.

'Thank you.' Curtis sniffled, wiped his eyes, and continued, 'I'll be okay,' he said.

'Not you,' Ashley clarified, 'Jefferson. Poor Jefferson. He knows you hate him!'

Curtis gasped, and Nathaniel laughed.

'I'm sorry,' a voice called from the background across from their booth, 'I just can't find it.'

Curtis, Ashley, and Nathaniel looked towards the glass counter displaying an array of individual pastries and beautifully decorated cakes at the front of the café. A pale hand covered in rainbow moonstones entwined around thin silver rings perched on the counter. Followed by a forearm, an elbow, another hand, and two cat green eyes; the woman propped her head up from behind the counter. It was Tamarind.

At Nathaniel's request, she had been searching through flatware in cabinets underneath the till for his childhood mug. A short, round mug that looked more like a cereal bowl if not for its two big handles on opposite sides, with several DC character silhouettes painted on a red background. Nathaniel brought it with him once as a young boy and left it there. Any time he was there, he would drink out of that mug and only out of that mug.

'*Faux-pas*, indeed. How am I supposed to have my hot cocoa now?' he grumbled.

Ashley rolled her eyes as Nathaniel sulked on the table.

'I'm sorry, dear,' Tamarind said as she resurfaced, balancing a large box of glasses and mugs and espresso cups. 'Ooft,' she grunted, 'at least you've inspired me to organize these cabinets. I found all sorts of things under here. I'd forgotten we had these!' she exclaimed, holding up a tiny salt and pepper shaker pair.

'Yeah, everything but my mug.'

Ashley tapped Nathaniel's arm. 'Don't be so ungrateful,' she said, 'at least they're looking.'

Nathaniel zipped up his sweater until the collar covered his chin and mouth, folded his arms on the table, and let his head collapse in the hole between them and his chest. 'They'll never find it,' he mumbled quietly.

'Maybe Willow will find it upstairs, hmm? No, no. In fact, she will find it. I am willing her to. We have that kind of connection, y' know? I am putting positive vibes into the universe and—'

'Do positive vibes travel *up* wooden stairs?' Nathaniel interrupted, poking his head up from the fortress of sadness he had created with his woolly sweater.

'Of course, numbskull,' Curtis rebuked, through his nose, 'They're like orbs, they float through the air, through anything. They can go anywhere.'

'What do you know, cat prey?' Nathaniel spat.

'No, no. He's right.' Tamarind affirmed, 'I'll send them upstairs and in no time, Willow will come down, mug in hand. You'll see.'

As Tamarind's silver-coin covered violet skirt jingled in sync with the clanking flatware in the box she balanced on her knee moments before placing it on the counter, Curtis, Ashley and Nathaniel turned around and looked in the direction of the stairwell, half hoping and half expecting to see Willow wander down at any moment. But she did not.

'*Right…*' Nathaniel replied after a long pause. 'I suppose I'll just have to have a slice of cake with no hot cocoa to accompany it. Tamarind, I shall have—'

'No. We'll wait for the rest of the gang,' Ashley said, rather firmly, tapping Nathaniel's hand on the table twice.

Nathaniel raised his other hand, elongating his index finger, and opened his mouth. But before he could muster a sarcastic or witty reply, Curtis sneezed, quite loudly, again.

'Dude… weak. Jefferson's not even here.'

'Okay, baby,' Ashley started, digging in her purse. 'Here,' she said, handing Curtis a ten-dollar bill, 'I want you to go to the packie and see if Tara has that nasal spray. You're going to need it this week.'

Curtis simply nodded, unable to respond lest another fit came over him. Holding his nose and mouth so tightly with one hand, as if they would fall off his face if he didn't, he took the money with the other and shot out the door.

'Poor Curtis,' said Tamarind, blowing strands of long night-black hair from her face before dragging a stool towards the kids and sitting down with them.

The echo from the bell on the door dissipated and they could hear the frantic scuffling of Curtis' footsteps on the cobblestone street outside stop and then start again after what sounded like a brief exchanging of words. Then, the bell rang again as the shop door opened and Aaron walked through it.

Ashley waved. 'Buenos días, Aaron.'

'Mornin' buddy,' said Nathaniel.

'Aaron!' Tamarind exclaimed.

'Ha-ha. Hey, T. Hi guys.'

Aaron beamed as Tamarind shot up from the stool and hugged him.

'Look at you! You're so tall and, what is that?' she asked, trailing her fingers against Aaron's stubble before pinching his cheeks together. 'You are just so handsome I could shrink you down and pop you on top of one of my chocolate cakes!'

'Little cake man? I'll buy that,' Aaron mumbled through pursed lips as Tamarind maintained a firm grip on his cheeks.

'Tamarind… I think that's enough,' Nathaniel said, staring as she continued to hug Aaron.

'Don't be jealous,' Ashley whispered.

'Yeah. T? I missed you too but you're gonna crush me,' Aaron chuckled as she held on tight. Tamarind was shorter than him and had been for years now, but she had a strong grip and it was only enhanced by her love and the time he, and everyone, had spent away from Melvin.

Just then, the shop's bronze doorbell trilled once more. But it was not Curtis back from the shop. It was Robin.

'Robin!' Ashley shouted, 'Are you okay?'

'You're still alive. You made it, girl. You're my hero. There's barely a scratch on you,' Nathaniel went on.

Aaron and Tamarind separated as they both turned around.

'Hi.' Aaron looked her over. She seemed fine, bar one seemingly fresh flesh-toned band-aid on her forehead.

With everyone's eyes on her, Robin felt uneasy. Perhaps they would instantly see that something was wrong. Maybe Aaron would notice she was not wearing his birthday present. Would she be forced to explain her demeanor?

'Hey guys,' she said, 'sorry I'm late.'

'Oh!' Tamarind shrieked. 'Don't you ever apologize for being you, you gorgeous girl!' She took Robin and Aaron in her arms and they smiled at each other, at Tamarind's shrill eccentricity they did not realize they had missed so much.

'Ugh,' Nathaniel grunted, 'here we go again.'

Ashley placed her hand over Nathaniel's mouth and continued to stare at the three with her head slanted and a loving smile, sighing with contentment.

At this point, Aaron and Robin found the morning's revelations and drama had completely vanished from their minds. They felt the tension slowly release from their bodies. Aaron soaked in Tamarind's loving embrace, her floral scent, and Robin basked in the comfort of being amongst people who she loved and who loved her back. In this place with these people, their friends, their family, surrounded by an autumnal air filled with endless childhood memories, everything began to feel good again, feel right.

As Robin slowly opened her eyes, the serene smile on her face was replaced with one of deeper contentment, signaled by the tears her eyes welled up with as she saw someone else. 'Willow,' she breathed, gliding out of the group hug and through the shop towards her.

Willow Dodson stood, smiling towards the idyllic scene in her café, on the second-to-last step of the stairs, holding a mug everyone recognized.

Robin could not rush to her quickly enough. In seconds they were hugging and rocking, laughing, and crying.

'Oh, heck, you guys,' Nathaniel whispered, 'T's magical positivity orbs worked.'

'*What*?' a baffled Aaron mouthed.

Tamarind lifted her arms and nodded as if to say, *I told you so.*

'I'm just gonna…' Nathaniel whispered again, licking the corner of his lip as he leaned over from where he sat at the edge of the booth. Then he took his DC mug from Willow's hands which were cupped behind Robin's back.

With her hands now free, Willow gently took hold of Robin's face. She wiped away the tears from her cheeks and lightly brushed a finger over Robin's band-aid. 'Are you okay?' she asked. Robin nodded as more tears rolled past Willow's fingertips. Then, they hugged some more. As they continued to embrace, they appeared two halves of one whole. Robin's bright red hair flowing over a butterscotch cardigan covering milky skin in perfect contrast to Willow's leafy, earth tones covering her caramel complexion and cropped dark hair. Willow was grateful to even see Robin, to know she was well, let alone hold her. Robin gave in to the maternal, supporting touch she missed every day in Boston.

'So,' Nathaniel started, 'who do I have to hug to get some cocoa around here?'

'Always got to break the mood, eh, Berger?' said Aaron.

Willow and Robin looked back and laughed. Then, Willow placed her hands onto Robin's shoulders, gesturing for her to join her friends, and she did.

'Nah, I reckon Nathaniel's right. I mean now that we're all together. Besides, I'm starving. Like, I already had breakfast, but I could literally eat a dozen tacos right now.' Ashley said as Robin and Aaron scooched into the booth.

'*PB* lattes and cake anyone?' Tamarind suggested.

'Wait… all together? Where's Curtis?' Willow asked, following Tamarind behind the counter.

'Oh, yeah,' said Robin, 'where *is* Curtis?'

'Jefferson attacked him. So, he went to get ammo,' said Nathaniel.

'Oh dear,' Willow exclaimed.

'What? No way Jefferson attacked anyone,' said Robin.

'He didn't,' Tamarind called out, fumbling with the coffee machine as she balanced a stack of small plates in her hand.

'He said something about the packie before I came in?' said Aaron.

'Sí. He went to find something for his allergies,' Ashley explained.

'Oh, that makes sense,' Robin said, eyeing Nathaniel as he grinned cheekily.

'Well, he won't be long,' said Tamarind, 'we can get started on breakfast at least. What do you reckon he'll have, Ash? *PB* latte and a slice of pecan pie, right?'

Ashley nodded. 'Same for me please.'

'Right. So, four lattes and one cocoa for Nathaniel. Two pecan pies—'

'Three, please,' said Nathaniel, raising his hand.

'Three pecan pies,' Tamarind continued, 'how about you guys?' she asked, looking towards Aaron and Robin.

'I've already eaten. Thanks, T,' said Aaron.

'How about you Robin?'

Robin shook her head and smiled. She couldn't think of food. She could barely stomach the revelation she was forced to sit through with her fathers earlier that morning, but she continued to smile. She could not bear the thought of anyone noticing something was wrong. She would not be the one to ruin their special week together.

'What're you doing there, Willow?' she asked, distracting herself.

As Tamarind balanced and brought plates and cakes and cups and saucers to the table, Robin noticed Willow fiddling behind the counter; carefully fingering through books, on Jefferson's favorite shelf, just behind the bowl in which her goldfish, Prankers, casually swam.

'I'm just looking for… Ah, found it!' she called, revealing a long green pamphlet which appeared to have been hiding underneath the fishbowl, 'I left it with Prankers for safekeeping. I remember now.'

'What's that for Willow?' Nathaniel asked with his mouth full.

'What do you kids know about Prankers Pond?'

'Oh, that's easy,' said Ashley.

'Yeah,' Aaron continued, 'T always talks about the time you nearly drowned there, Willow. When you were kids—'

'That's right,' said Nathaniel, before swallowing another bite of pecan pie, 'You fell in and you don't know how to swim, like me, and Tamarind saved you. But you were still scared of the water and—'

'And then she got you Prankers,' Ashley continued, pointing towards the bowl, 'that's why you named him, well, *Prankers*.'

'Wow!' Tamarind smiled and clapped her hands together, 'What a bunch of storytellers!'

'Ha-ha, they're right, though. Thanks for that, by the way,' said Willow, patting Tamarind's arm before linking it with hers. 'You guys *are* right…' she continued, looking towards the kids, 'but what *else* do you know about Prankers Pond?'

'It's haunted,' said Robin.

'Bingo.'

'What? Nuh-uh.' Nathaniel shook his head. 'If it were haunted, I'd know about it.'

'Yeah, because you know everything,' Aaron teased.

'Technically,' Willow started, opening the pamphlet in her hands to reveal a detailed map, 'it's not the lake itself that's rumored to be haunted, but the woods behind it,' she said, tapping it.

'Yeah, I remember this now—' Ashley began.

'And you never told me?' Nathaniel interrupted.

'Hmm… I don't think you were in Mrs. Steinem's history class, were you? In 6th grade?'

'Nah, we had Mr. Roper,' Aaron answered for him.

'Well, we had to do this small project on local witches, and most people went for Salem and stuff like that—'

'Pfft… Salem!' Tamarind scoffed.

'Right! But this one girl talked about someone who was drowned for being a witch, or something like that, in Prankers Pond, I think? I remember it now.'

'Yeah,' Robin continued, 'it was a little girl. And she didn't drown. She was hanged in the woods. There's a memorial there to this day.'

'Margaret Bishop,' said Willow, 'she had just turned seven years old and her mother and younger brother were found murdered.'

'What about her father?' Nathaniel asked, eyes wide with excitement and a mouth full of pie.

'All they found,' said Tamarind, waving her hands around theatrically, 'were a pair of his muddy boots next to a pile of his hair and...

'And? And?!' Nathaniel begged.

'A ripped shirt! Woo!'

'Fantastic. So... he killed his wife and son, shaved off his beard as a disguise, and moved away. Mystery solved,' Aaron asserted.

'Probably.' Willow shrugged and nodded.

'But they never found him,' said Robin, 'and they blamed witchcraft. They blamed the little girl.'

'Li'l Maggie,' Tamarind bellowed behind the fabric of her purple scarf she lifted halfway above her face for dramatic effect. 'They say... to this day... you can hear the chilling, eerie laughter of a young girl playing in the woods... confused as to her fate, forever in a state of ghost-like innocence!'

'Nope. Nah. I'm alright with that,' said Nathaniel, shaking his head frantically. 'They can say whatever they want to say, but I don't want to find out. Child ghosts are creepy as hell!'

'Hell indeed!' Tamarind grinned, 'Mwahaha!'

Everyone chuckled.

'Ah, I don't know. Sounds kind of cheesy,' said Aaron.

'I think it sounds kind of fun.' Robin shrugged.

'Right. So, when are we going?' asked Aaron.

'Ha-ha,' Ashley laughed, 'I'm so hyped for this one, you guys! And it's so close, we could go tonight.'

'We can fill you in and get you guys ready for tonight if you want,' Willow offered.

'Awesome,' Nathaniel said with an obvious lack of enthusiasm.

The shop doorbell rang once more as Curtis burst inside, lifting his arm into the air, shaking a small blue tub he held between his thumb and index finger.

'Ah-ha!' he exclaimed, 'the packie had no sprays but the pharmacy equipped me with this magical menthol rub. Now I will use this to defeat… Wait, where is Jefferson? Wait, what have I just interrupted? Oh, hey guys,' he said, waving towards Aaron and Robin, 'What did I miss?

Don't fear the reaper
CURTIS

Sunday 25th October

00:00 AM, Palmers Woods, Massachusetts

It was officially Nathaniel's twenty-first birthday. But the gang was not celebrating, yet. They were fast asleep in three tents under a starry New England sky: Ashley with Curtis in the first, Aaron heads-and-tails with Nathaniel in the second, and Robin in the third.

Though their original journey home did not go as fluidly as they might have hoped, being together during their first full day in Melvin could not have exceeded expectations more so. Eating and planning, walking, and talking, splitting up and finding each other, reuniting, and checking in with the Dodson sisters at *PB*. All the while warm, nostalgic stirrings ignited sparks of excitement for what awaited them.

No one commented on it, but everyone had thought about how extraordinary it was that, in the relatively short time they had all been apart, they had all forgotten what "normal" felt like.

It is in the little things that you find some part of yourself clicking into an older version of your life, like muscle memory when riding a bicycle or a new battery that gives life to an antique watch.

Yes, finally, they were together again. Together in Melvin during the week coming up to Halloween. All of which could mean only one thing; it was time for the first in a series of paranormal investigations.

It did not take long for them to get ready after deciding to go with Willow's suggestion to seek out the fabled ghost of Lil' Maggie in Palmers Woods.

Months earlier, in the time spent organizing and finalizing details for their trip, Ashley assigned each friend specific tasks and areas to cover to ensure their adventures would go as smoothly as possible.

Unsurprisingly, it all set off like clockwork.

After breakfast at *PB*, Nathaniel sprinted off to his uncle's house, his mother's brother Mortimer's house, in desperate hopes of finding his uncle's wife meaning he could avoid a long trip to her office—and he did. Mary Miller was the Mayor of Melvin. The gang knew that if the area they planned to ghost hunt in required any camping or filming permits or licenses, they would have to pick another spot as it would be too late to apply for and have access to them in less than 24-hours.

They were hopeful, but still, they knew that if that were the case, Mayor Miller would know. And she did.

Nathaniel got back to the group in enough time to tell them the good news, and everyone split up again.

Curtis had made a prior study of several detailed maps of Massachusetts before the trip. After uploading digital close-ups to everyone's phones, after Willow and Tamarind pointed out the specific areas they'd be investigating, he planned to print off paper copies for everyone at the library, just in case.

In addition, Curtis planned to mark out useful destinations they could find en route, from the closest hospital and late-night pharmacy to diners and gas stations.

Robin accompanied him to the library, where she would attempt to find as much information about the area's history as possible.

Guided by friendly and helpful staff, she looked through the microfiche and relevant literature she was directed towards to gather facts. Then, she took what she could to inspire an extensive list of questions she would jot down in various categories; questions the group would then ask the spirits out loud in the hopes of triggering emotional reactions or even verbal answers for Aaron to record.

Being the "digital master" he was, according to Ashley anyway, Aaron was naturally put in charge of the equipment and its placement.

Of course, the standard array of flashlights and backup batteries were stocked up and handed out.

The EMF meters, which Aaron was careful to keep well away from all other electrical devices, would be able to detect disturbances in electromagnetic fields and indicate potential spiritual activity if readings spiked above their average number.

He made sure highly sensitive and expensive microphones, EVP recorders, and cleverly placed video cameras, including high definition 1080p full spectrum camcorders, were always on; constantly recording the group and their surroundings.

His pièce de résistance was a pack of five brand new infrared thermometer guns he bought before the trip. These would allow the gang to measure extreme drops in temperature, further adding to their mere coincidence versus spooky activity debate.

Ever the matriarch of the group, Ashley oversaw everything else.

Everything and anything they might need that might slip from everyone else's minds during the week. Packs of tissues, baby wipes, mini bottles of hand gel, towels, changes of clothes, first-aid kits, painkillers, water bottles and snacks, and even a foldable plastic chair and table set from Walmart and a deck of cards. Two large duffle bags with hot pink and black detailing, which may as well have been one big Mary Poppins style carpet bag, fit perfectly in the trunk of Curtis' father's car along with everything else.

Finally, not that anyone asked, and despite Curtis being the closest thing to an expert, Nathaniel was invariably in charge of music—equipped with a large black wallet of CDs of compilations he mixed himself, including songs by groups like the *Beastie Boys, Red Hot Chili Peppers,* and *Nickelback,* to name a few.

They were ready.

Unfortunately though, no level of readiness to capture evidence could ever guarantee the emergence of any such material, which in itself would always be vulnerable to scrutiny, nor could its emergence guarantee it being recorded in satisfactory quality or at the right angle, or recorded at all for that matter. Too many extraneous variables can and probably will arise on a spook filled night such as Saturday's; a night which would intrinsically provide chilling thrills due to its mere purpose and the paranoid company of those around you.

Any paranormal investigator, amateur or not, would know this. And the group knew this. So, it was no surprise when, perhaps disappointingly but probably for the best, nothing spooky happened all evening. From the time they left *Danny's Diner* off Route 1 to when they arrived at their location, from when they set up camp and readied their equipment to when they were ready for bed.

Still, it was good fun either way.

They were sure they would find more than enough to talk about the next morning. And there would certainly be plenty of footage and recordings to examine. Also, they were determined to find spookier areas to explore in the coming week.

Suffice to say everyone fell asleep quickly, confident that nothing but their alarms or sunlight streaming through small gaps in the zippers of their tents would wake them up.

03:00 AM, Palmers Woods

The concept of tough love is difficult for many of us to accept. We certainly don't welcome it. In the first instance, how do we go about understanding it? If it is indeed a type of love at all, can that atone for the pain it causes? And if it isn't, can any form of love exist without pain?

If you struggle to deal with those who appear harsh, possessive, critical, and even terrifying in their professed love of you, and, accordingly, make every effort possible to cut them out of your lives, you will, unfortunately, find that you are still not able to escape this paradoxical type of relationship. This is because it exists, inherently, in you, battling always, in your subconscious. It is a person in and of itself. A nameless being who lingers in the unseen crevices of your brain, feeding off the shadows of your day, waiting for you that opportune moment to take hold—waiting for you to fall asleep.

As you lay your head to rest you unknowingly give into its power. As you close your eyes and try desperately to think of pleasant fantasies, relaxing scenes, and then nothing at all—you try to slip past it, unnoticed, but can only slip deeper into its claws. And when it has hold of you, of your mind, all you can do is watch those fantasies become undone, powerless as disturbing scenes unfold in front of you as you lie back and wish for anything else, for nothingness.

Indeed, it exists in all of us. It appears in our slumber, in the limbo-world beforehand, and it hides the next day in the same purgatory you experience between asleep and awake. It cannot be killed or changed. The only thing that can change is your perception of it.

If you could look beyond the awkward, uneasy, itchy, violating feelings it implants, you might see how this entity, this creature, truly loves you—how it aims to protect you by using your fears.

When it reminds you of the most embarrassing moments in your past; it's telling you they don't matter anymore, that you're older, wiser, and stronger now. It desensitizes you to the memory so that each time it affects you less and less. When it reminds you of the biggest mistakes you've made; it's warning you to never make them again. When it shows you things to be anxious or afraid of; it's preparing you for those eventualities, even if they never come to pass. It draws back curtains to reveal things that may never happen, to reveal your hopes and dreams, and the obstacles you must face to achieve them. It enlightens you to the gravity of what you fail to admit is going wrong in your day-to-day life, what you repress, and what you ought to work on. It morphs into symbols and abstract colors and situations and people you once knew. That is how it speaks to you.

If you could only speak its language, communicate with it, ask it questions. If you could only remember its teachings, the next morning, and try to interpret them, try to learn from each message.

One by one, they all gave in to their monsters, to their worries and heavy cares in the nanoseconds before sleep.

Everyone has problems. And this was especially the case for Aaron Jackson, who found himself in the toughest situation he had ever been in.

In recent years he saw average teenage drama and unrequited love become replaced with missing home and typical student problems; like looming deadlines, ever-increasing debt, and having to tolerate Nathaniel's quirky habits 24/7. But even in the most frustrating moments, he could recognize that he was incredibly fortunate. You had to give it to him; wise beyond his years, Aaron almost always felt blessed.

Now though, at twenty-one-years-old, he was forced to face a thought which most of us must face in our lifetimes, but which no one ought to face at that age—the thought of losing a parent.

Aaron never prepared himself for the eventuality. Like most of us, he never thought he had to. Being young is often synonymous with assuming you have all the time in the world to learn how to cope with whatever might come your way and, following that, the inability to deal with such things.

Aaron closed his eyes and tried to forget about it all. He imagined silhouettes of palm trees and picturesque beaches under the hot Florida sun he had become accustomed to. As he did, he began to relax to the thought of what freedom after college might look and feel like. But the more he drifted off, the more he began to see these images morph into flashes of his family. The fear in his mother's eyes, the fear she tried to undermine as she comforted him and said that everything would be okay even though they all knew it could never be. The bitter resentment in his brother's clenched jaw when he made it clear he had sacrificed enough, that it would be Aaron's turn to step up and soon.

Clear, clean, open spaces turned into darker prisons. Rooms like tombs with no windows or doors but with muddied, pest-infested walls closing in all around him until they were only inches away from his body.

Helpless, there was no escape.

Sat, curled, bunched in a ball on this cold imagined floor, he was somehow able to see the unnatural inward movement of each inch of the walls through tightly shut eyelids.

Rocking, backward and forwards, he could not speak but he could hear his internal voice screaming, *"This is not real! Wake up!"* Still, however loud his inner screams, they could not cover the sickening sound which surrounded him; the scraping chittering of a million creepy crawlies penetrating his ears. He could not wake himself up. But when enough was enough, he felt the entire weight of his body lift from the floor and he stood, tall and upright. Up and out of that nightmare, somewhere else. In a different room entirely. Was he still dreaming? Was it still a nightmare?

A blinding white light gradually dulled to reveal pale wallpaper and uncomfortably cheap furniture. He had not seen this place before. He looked around and took in the strong, unmistakably clinical smell of bleach and something else, something odd, like off food and something foul. Aaron looked around some more. As he looked down, he found the source; a tray with plates and bowls, abandoned, filled with moldy food and squirming maggots.

Cringing and flinching and turning away, all Aaron could see wherever he looked was the pure neglect and decay of every inch of that horrible room. Dust and cobwebs and bedpans, full to the brim, forlorn on the floor. The sight of it all made his gut churn as the repulsive scent filled his throat. He felt the impulse to vomit, but something stopped him.

A hand. Fast and strong, gripping his forearm, forcing him to turn around.

As he did, he saw what it was, who it was, in the bed next to the table. A heartbreaking, skeletal version of what he knew, deep down, was once his father.

'*Dad*?' the word came out like a frog leaping out only to be drowned in his tears. He kept repeating himself. But Aaron spoke to no avail. Because the man, this final stage of a man, did not answer, could not answer. All he did was stare. Stare into Aaron's very soul as if to ask, to beg, for something; something Aaron could not understand. '*Dad*?! *What do I do, Dad*? *What do I do*?'

Aaron Jackson awoke in a sweaty, panting state of confusion in a tent in the woods underneath that starry

New England sky, next to his best friend who snorted and snored in a blissful state of obliviousness.

He did not dry himself off or get up for a drink of water. He did not wake Nathaniel or distract himself by scrolling through apps on his phone.

Instead, Aaron crouched back down into his sleeping bag and lifted the soaking wet blanket over his head, desperate to escape the traumatic images whirling in his mind's eye, desperate to fall back asleep, hopeful to fall into a different dream, this time.

'Curtis…' Ashley whispered, '*Curtis*?!' she whispered again, forcefully, pushing his shoulder as he lay beside her.

'Hmm? Huh? What?' Curtis mumbled.

'Did you hear that?'

'Hmm? Hear what?'

'*That*!'

'What? Go back to sleep babe.'

'No, no. That scream. And that… rustling!'

'Scream?' said Curtis, turning around to face Ashley. Sitting up slightly, he balanced the weight of his torso on his elbow and forearm. Then, he stopped, with his eyelids half shut, to listen intently. But he could hear nothing.

'No,' he said, 'it was probably an animal call, hon. Tonight's got us all spooked.' And with that, he collapsed on his side and instantaneously fell asleep again, with his hand on Ashley's—a feeble, albeit loving, attempt to comfort her.

'It sounded human. I know what I heard. Do you hear me? *Curtis*?' It was no use, though. Curtis was well and truly asleep. Ashley raised her eyebrow and exhaled. 'Great,' she said to herself, turning onto her back with her hands crossed over her stomach which she noticed felt unusually bloated. '*Great*.'

It had been Aaron, waking up. But Ashley did not know. And now she felt nervous.

"Mind over matter," she thought to herself. Ashley did not need Curtis or anyone to relax her. She knew that she *had* heard *something*, but she also knew that whatever it was had a perfectly rational explanation behind it. She would put herself back to sleep.

On her back, Ashley closed her eyes and began an exercise she often used after a show or long day of classes. Something slow and perfect for just before bed, after proper cool-down exercises or a nice hot bath. She would start by tensing muscles, specific parts of her body, and holding the tension as she counted before releasing it. Then she would move up. Starting with her toes, she would aim to end with her head but would often fall asleep well before she reached it.

She lowered her hands, aligning her arms along the sides of her body and started as she always did. Flexing her toes up and down. Up and then down. She could feel her shins stretch with them. Then she moved on to her calf muscles. Tensing them and relaxing as she felt the tension release and slip away. And then the same with her strong, dancer's thighs.

She paid attention to her breathing. In and out. In and then out again. Counting all the while. Soon, it was as if she were in her bed in New York, with Curtis snoring comfortably beside her.

She arched her back slightly and felt a pleasant crack. But as she continued to stretch, the familiar feeling left her body and became pressure instead; pressure she felt build on her torso until it flattened the arch in her back. Until she could somehow feel the cold, gritty floor through the sleeping bag, through the tent.

Hot, uncomfortable pressure became hands on her stomach weighing her down, pushing her down. They were not hers. They felt alien and foreign and inhuman; long and spindly and strong. Pushing and reaching down, reaching in, pulling now, and tugging at her insides. She could feel them move inside her and it hurt more than any average cramp, more than anything most people have ever felt, a specific type of pain Ashley knew all too well.

In agony, tears began to stream down Ashley's face. Her eyes were open now. She knew she was not asleep. And she knew she was not alone. But she could see no one, nothing, in the tent with her. Not even Curtis. She could not move an inch, not even to turn her head, but she could see in her periphery, even in the darkness, that he was not next to her anymore.

She tried to scream but something was stopping her, like an extra hand over her mouth. All the while the sinking pressure on the bottom half of her body did not let up. Struggling to breathe, Ashley was petrified and alone. She did not feel like herself anymore. What was this, that could make her feel so vulnerable?

She could only remember one other time in her life in which she had felt anything close to this horror, and the memory made her burst into tears.

All in an instant, the pain, the physical pain at least, stopped as she shot up.

Sobbing violently, calling for Curtis, howling, stuck in the memories of her suffering. *'CURTIS!'* she howled, *'WHERE ARE YOU?!'*

But there was no reply.

She did not know where he was, but she would not leave the tent alone to retrieve him.

Why could no one hear her? Where were Aaron and Nathaniel if not in the tent next to theirs? Where they off, somewhere, together? Three boys awake and having fun. Could Robin be with them?

'ROBIN!' Ashley screamed.

"Robin," Robin heard in her sleep, in her dreams. *"Robin,"* someone whispered.

In the pitch black, Robin tried to ascertain whether it was a man's voice. One of her fathers'? Or was it a woman's?

Her ears pricked up to the sound and she waited to hear it again. She waited and listened, but nothing happened.

Robin could feel her eyes begin to adjust to the darkness. She started to see outlines and shapes. She tried to make them out, reaching out with her hand to touch what was maybe only a foot in front of her. It felt like leaves. Small, waxy, wet leaves against her fingertips. She smiled to herself as she realized what she could not put her finger on before—the distinct smell of rain-drenched flora. Then, she felt a nice, cool breeze caress her skin as she caressed the leafy structure.

Robin felt oddly at ease, even in the darkness—the darkness which surrounded her, but which gradually dissipated.

As it cleared, she realized she was now enveloped by a white mist. Fog, thick and tall around her and a series of perfectly trimmed shrubbery; a maze.

"Robin," a voice called again. This time it was not a whisper, but guttural and low. Robin did not feel so at ease anymore. This time, she did not want to know who it was coming from. But a shadowy figure rushing beyond her line of sight, the figure of whoever it was calling her, intrigued her too much.

She would follow them.

She could not tell, just by seeing glimpses of the person's back, who it was or, again, whether they were male or female. The figure kept disappearing behind corners as she chased it, but Robin felt a strong, strange impulse to determine *who* it was and continued. Walking at first and then running. Picking up her pace to find the curious and seemingly cloaked figure when she turned around a final corner and stopped.

There they were. There he or she was. Standing, with their back towards Robin. Still, not moving, not saying a word.

Robin walked up to them, slowly. With her arm elongated and her hand fully stretched, ready to reach out and touch them, to turn them around, ready to find out who it was.

But as she grabbed the figure's shoulder, the fabric from the cloak was all that remained in her hand, drooping before falling onto the ground as if the person's body turned from flesh into a pile of dust which was then swept away with the wind.

Robin woke up with a start, sweating in her tent.

'ROBIN!'

Now, she knew *that* voice, at least. It was Ashley's.

'Ashley?' Robin said, wiping her eyes as she tripped crawling out of her sleeping bag. Grunting, she quickly pulled on her boots, leaving the laces untied, and pulled on a sweater before feeling around for a flashlight. 'Ashley?' she said again, unzipping her tent, kneeling as she poked her head out, looking around as she turned on and shone the flashlight in every direction. 'Are you okay? Where are you?' she whispered forcefully.

Robin got out and stood up, ready to walk over to Curtis and Ashley's tent when she saw something in the distance.

It was Curtis. She was sure of it. And he was alone.

Walking, slowly, he passed trees going further into the woods.

What could he be doing?

Robin shone her flashlight on him and saw space, a gap, between his side and his right arm where it stretched out by his body. She thought she could see his hand, his fist, clenched as if he were holding something, but she could not see what. 'Curtis,' she called, 'Curtis!' she called again, but he did not answer.

07:30 AM, 8 Almond Avenue

'Thanks, Momma,' said Nathaniel, mumbling and eating his words as he sat and ate through the pop tarts, cookies, and snacks from the wooden tray Mrs. Jackson set down on Aaron's desk.

'Thank you, Mrs. Jackson,' said Curtis, fiddling with the SCART cables behind Aaron's surprisingly old television set.

Aaron smiled and nodded as his mother kissed him on his forehead. Then, she gave the boys their share of affection, too, before shifting out of the room.

He took sheets and spare pillows and proceeded to set up the inflatable mattress on the floor in the space between his bed, desk, wardrobe, and chest of drawers where Curtis stood, having finally figured out how to hook up the DVD player to the T.V.

'Why don't you get up and do something helpful?' said Curtis in Nathaniel's direction.

'What for? It's all done.'

'*What for*? Good Lord, I swear you're always eating.'

'Oh gosh, *what*? *"You're always eating?"* You sound just like my mother,' Nathaniel mocked.

'When are your parents coming back by the way?' Aaron asked.

'Tomorrow. Why?'

Despite having previously said it would be fine for Nathaniel to stay at his house for as long as he wanted to, Aaron thought it best for Nathaniel to go back home as soon as possible. He didn't think it was a good idea for either of them to be there now, considering the tension in the house. *He* didn't even want to be there.

Nathaniel would probably go back home Monday morning anyway, Aaron deduced. Saying anything now would solve nothing, so he simply shrugged.

Nathaniel shrugged too and went back for more cookies.

Curtis shrieked. 'Good God, how are you so darn skinny?'

'Hmm? What now?'

'You're literally always eating.'

'So? What's it to you?'

Curtis exhaled, brushed the air in front of him with both hands, and sat on the inflatable mattress, trying to get comfortable. But his heavy build seemed to deflate the corner he sat on as it raised the opposite corner a few inches from the ground. 'Remind me why we're not downstairs on the couches? With the Xbox?'

Aaron would explain. But his mission to avoid another confrontation with his brother was not his friends' concern. So, he merely shrugged again.

'Hey,' Nathaniel continued, 'I won't always be twenty. No, wait, twenty-one. I won't always be twenty-one. And with this metabolism. I've got to take advantage of my situation. Live it up now before I get old and have to worry about getting a beer gut.'

Curtis nodded with his thumbs up. 'Beer gut. Yeah, that's a problem.'

'Ha,' Aaron chuckled. 'You looked just like Ashley then.'

'Ugh, please don't bring Ashley up,' said Curtis, sighing and running his fingers through his buzz cut before dragging his hands down his face and sighing again.

'Dude. I think that was a compliment. Say thank you,' Nathaniel teased.

'What's wrong?' Aaron asked.

'I don't know. Probably nothing. I just feel like… I don't know, man.'

'Feel?' said Nathaniel, scrunching his face. 'Ooh… Can we say that?'

'Shut up, dude. Seriously, Curtis. What's up?' Aaron pressed.

'Yeah, Curtis. You've been tense all morning. And taking it out on me. So, spit it out,' Nathaniel added.

'I don't know, she just seemed a bit distant on the ride back,' Curtis explained, 'and when we dropped the girls off. She didn't even invite me in.'

'Yeah,' Nathaniel started, 'because we're doing split sleepovers.'

In their late teenage years, when curfews were pushed back, and incrementing steps of freedom were steadily earned, a typical morning after a paranormal investigation would involve a split sleepover; where the boys would sleep at one of their houses and the girls would do the same.

This was because, understandably, the night before would involve practically no sleep.

The set-up had worked well for those years. They would nap the night's terrors off and meet up later in the day to eat together, to watch and listen to any footage they had collected.

But last night's adventure was different than any other trip, for many reasons. Namely, because they had all seemingly slept through what they would consider peak spooky hours. Perhaps it was because they were older, now, or perhaps it was due to something else. In any case, the group still split up in line with tradition, intending to meet that night, instead, to celebrate Nathaniel's birthday.

'Hmm.' Curtis wavered for a moment. Nathaniel was probably right, he thought, but something still felt off.

'Nah, I noticed it, too,' said Aaron.

'Really?'

'Yeah but like, with Robin too. And you. We're all tense. It was a weird night.'

'Was it?' Nathaniel shrugged, 'I didn't notice.'

Aaron and Curtis both sneered in Nathaniel's direction, then they all burst out into a sort of exasperated laughter and sighed in unison.

'Okay, yeah. I guess you're right,' said Curtis, wiping his face again before letting his hands fall on his knees.

'Yeah,' said Aaron, 'So, let's pick a DVD and chill.'

Nathaniel crawled onto and over the inflatable mattress, fumbling and falling exaggeratively as he did, reaching for the box of disks in wallets Aaron kept on the other side of the room.

'It's just…' Curtis hesitated.

Nathaniel exhaled forcefully, lying down flat on the mattress with his fingers through his curls as the mattress jiggled. 'What now?'

'I'm just… I'm still really nervous you guys.'

'Nervous about what?' Aaron asked.

'Pass me my backpack.'

Aaron sat up from the edge of his bed, took Curtis' bag, and threw it towards him.

Catching it, Curtis unzipped the smaller front pocket and retrieved a small black velvet box. He opened it to reveal a ring, which he placed on the palm of his hand to show his friends. It had a peach-toned stone in a rose-gold setting with three small slanted diamonds on the top, resembling a pumpkin.

It was an engagement ring.

An engagement ring Curtis explained he had custom made for Ashley months before and intended on giving her at the end of the week, surrounded by everyone they loved.

'Nervous about giving her this,' he continued, 'I don't think I can wait until Halloween night.'

08:00 AM, 6 Bainbridge Drive

'Does Curtis know?' Robin asked.

'Of course. He was there,' Ashley replied.

'No. Of course. But I mean, does he realize the effect it's still having on you?'

'Hmm. I don't know that it *is* still affecting me, though.'

'Ashley, something like that doesn't just disappear.'

Ashley thought for a moment. She drank the last gulp of water from the glass Robin handed her minutes before and placed it back on her bedside table.

Robin could see Ashley's hand tremble as she held the glass and her facial expression shift as if the pause did not indicate she was unsure of what to say but rather how to say it.

'With all due respect, Robin,' Ashley started, 'you don't know what something like *that* does.'

Robin moved closer to Ashley on her bed. She took Ashley's hands in hers and rubbed the back of them with her thumbs. As she looked in her eyes, she felt hers well up at the thought of what Ashley had revealed, at what had happened to her. Then, an immense feeling overcame her. A heaviness, a searing hot flash on the nape of her neck—guilt. Robin could only feel guilty for neglecting her best friend when she most needed her support. She had missed Melvin, her parents, her friends. But now Robin started to realize what that meant, the full extent of what it meant to be so far from what she considered home, the price of it all.

'No. No, Ashley, I don't know what it must have been like for you. And,' said Robin, pausing to clear her throat before continuing, 'I'm so sorry I wasn't there for you, that I wasn't there to help. I'm sorry you felt like you couldn't tell me about this. But last night—'

'Last night…' Ashley interrupted, 'last night something happened. Something real happened last night. This isn't about me dealing or not dealing with anything, Robin. You saw how strange Curtis was acting. And your dream sounded so strange. Something weird happened, to all of us I bet. I bet the boys are sat talking about it right now.'

Robin stared into space as she thought back to that morning in the woods. To the sound of Ashley's screams, the sincerity, and the fear in them. To the oddness she could not explain in Curtis' behavior, to the look on his face as he turned around, facing the rays of her flashlight, before disappearing into the woods. To her disturbing dream.

'You don't believe me,' Ashley pressed.

'It's not that.'

'Look. I'm sorry I didn't tell you before…'

'No,' said Robin, 'don't apologize. I understand. Honestly. We've been best friends all our lives. I love you. I just… I'm worried, that's all. I want to know you're okay.' Perhaps for the first time in Robin's life, she understood why someone would keep a secret, a big secret, from those they loved. She would be a hypocrite to expect anything different from anyone else, even Ashley.

'I was okay. As okay as I could be. I'll be okay,' said Ashley, 'but I know what I felt last night. This morning. And God knows what got to Curtis, too.'

'Has he been okay recently? Do you guys talk about it at all anymore?'

'No,' Ashley said simply.

'Maybe it's affecting him too, y' know.'

Ashley scoffed. Then, she remembered the night they drove down to Melvin, all three of them. She remembered how strange Curtis had acted that night, too, with Robin passed out in the back of the car. 'Something's wrong,' she concluded, 'I just don't know what it is.'

Both girls sat in thought.

'I know one thing,' said Ashley, breaking the silence, 'I won't go through that again.'

'No. No, you're right. Let's tell the guys tonight.'

'Tell them what?' Ashley panicked.

'That we're done. For the entire week. No more adrenaline hunting, no more scary childish junk. We're together, finally, and we should just enjoy that,' Robin explained, 'We can find other things to do this week.'

Ashley nodded and sighed and slid further into her bed, pulling up the covers over her shoulders and turning on her side.

Then, Robin stood up to turn Ashley's bedroom light off before slipping into bed next to her.

'Let's get some rest. We'll tell them tonight,' Robin reassured her.

21:15 PM, *El Salero*

'Hola and welcome to *El Salero*. Would you guys like some chips and guacamole while you decide?' the aloof waitress said in a boorish manner to the group, sat in a corner booth at the back as she poured water from a pitcher into their glasses.

Predictably, Fiona Woods still worked at *El Salero*, the only Mexican restaurant in town. She still had badly dyed hair, an unnecessary number of piercings, and wore clothes that anyone in Melvin might consider edgy or rebellious but which anyone from a big city would consider cute at best. She was friendly enough, if not a bit standoffish, and was relatively well regarded by mostly everyone in town. Though this was certainly due to her kind father's reputation and that of his store, rather than Melvin's citizens' general opinion of her or her delinquent boyfriend Mike Henderson, who had irritated practically everyone with his arrogant demeanor since he hit puberty, but especially since he acquired an incredibly loud and audibly faulty motorcycle which he insisted on obnoxiously driving everywhere.

Mike Henderson had lived through an average childhood, from what anyone could tell, and had loving parents, whom he still lived with. He even worked as a mechanic with his father at *Mick's Auto Garage* on the outskirts of town. But he had struggled at school for the longest time and never finished. No, Mike Henderson was not considered clever. Grunting and scoffing and spitting were the extent of his vocabulary it seemed, and if he did speak it was in petty insults or vague threats. The overcompensating, unmistakably short, thug beat his way through disputes over the years.

The gang knew this well, especially Nathaniel, who got the brunt of his wrath as a pre-teen when Mike Henderson heard rumors of Nathaniel's unrequited love towards Fiona. It was how Aaron and Nathaniel met, after all—when, following a brief aggressive exchange it was Aaron's lucky intervention which stopped Nathaniel from winding up in hospital one Valentine's Day weekend long ago.

The rumors were true, of course. However, in Nathaniel's defense, as he quite often ranted, everyone had a crush on Fiona, and he swore it was not him but Christian Thomas who left an anonymous love letter at her house. In any case, Nathaniel had not been afraid of Mike Henderson for years. Especially now, being twenty-one and having over a foot on him height-wise, where Mike preferred picking on younger and smaller victims.

So, there they were, at the Saltshaker, as many called it, where the food and the accents were not authentic, as Ashley always pointed out, but where Fiona Woods, who was still dating Mike Henderson, still worked, for Nathaniel's twenty-first birthday celebration.

'Yes. I'd love some,' Nathaniel replied. 'Gracias,' he called as she left.

The group sat in unusual silence.

Tense and awkward, the five friends smiled and fidgeted while thoughts and efforts to converse were increasingly eclipsed by the loud and cheesy music.

'Why are we here again?' Ashley huffed.

'Because it's my birthday,' Nathaniel affirmed, quite proudly, 'my twenty-first at that!'

'I meant, why are we *here*?' said Ashley, waving circles in the air around her, 'Again!'

'Because Nathaniel chose to come here.' Robin took Ashley's hand and held it under the table. She squeezed it gently as if to send a telepathic message to her best friend that everything would be alright and then smiled towards Nathaniel.

'That's right.' Nathaniel nodded. 'Thanks, Robster. I like the food.'

'You like Fiona,' Curtis grumbled.

Nathaniel gasped. 'I do not… anymore.'

Aaron slumped into his hands. 'Dude. Seriously. We're not stupid.'

'What? What?!' Nathaniel's bewildered face could have won him an Academy Award.

'Pfft, *what, what*?' Curtis mocked.

'Yeah, dude. Seriously. You didn't learn your lesson eons ago? With—' Aaron stopped to look around, to see if anyone was in earshot, and continued, '—with Mike 'The Fist' Henderson?' he whispered.

Nathaniel, still seemingly in shock, looked over the group with his mouth wide open. Then, Curtis, who made a fist and smirked in jest, and Aaron, who found the gesture funnier than it was, laughed for perhaps the first time all day, before quickly having to simmer down as Fiona Woods returned to their booth with the chips and guacamole promised moments earlier.

'Don't worry Nathaniel,' said Robin as soon as Fiona was out of earshot, in the typically soothing and genuine voice characteristic of her entire persona. 'No one expects you to forget your first love. Even if it was eons ago,' she continued, looking at Aaron. 'Besides, these two certainly didn't,' she said, gesturing towards Ashley and Curtis.

The couple said nothing, but now it was Curtis who had a hold of Ashley's hand underneath the table. They both felt more at ease a squeeze or two later.

Fiona came and left, again, and so did their food. Wooden boards underneath sizzling pots with colorful peppers covering chunks of chargrilled meat soaked in spicy sauce atop incredibly filling rice, each steaming with mouthwatering aromas.

Now, the table was clean and empty. They were all full and content. Sometimes food is all it takes. Good food and good, albeit quiet, company. Still, amidst polite conversation, something serious had been left unsaid and Robin felt inclined to initiate what she hoped would be a brief, uncomplicated conversation.

'So,' she started, 'are we going to say what we're all thinking?'

No one replied. Everyone was deep in thought.

'Ooft.' Nathaniel grunted, leaning back into the booth as he patted his belly a couple of times. 'I know what I'm not thinking. I don't think I could eat another bite. I hope you guys aren't going to surprise me with a birthday cake.'

'And I think that's the first time I've ever heard you say that,' said Curtis.

'Same,' Aaron agreed.

'Cake!' Ashley exclaimed. 'I forgot the cake! How could I do such a thing.' Unsurprisingly, Ashley rambled and ranted and exaggerated, apologizing as if she had just driven over a beloved pet. *'¡Estúpida, idiota, tonta!'* she continued.

'Oh no…' Aaron sat up and budged near the end of the booth, confused and awkward, looking for more napkins.

'It's okay Ashley! I didn't want a cake. I'm serious,' Nathaniel reassured.

'I don't think it's about the cake,' said Robin, rubbing Ashley's back as Ashley wept into her sleeves pulled up around her hands.

'Really? She's usually so organized…' Nathaniel whispered.

'Oh, for God's sake, Berger!' Aaron shot a look at Nathaniel which said *"Shut up"* for him.

'It's okay, baby.' Curtis put his left arm around Ashley and kissed her forehead. With his right hand, he took one of the napkins Aaron had managed to get from a nearby table and gave it to her to wipe her face with.

'No, no…' Ashley whimpered, 'It's not okay.'

'But… I mean, he's eaten so much today already. Like, really. A whole lot.'

'It's not about the frigging cake!' Robin insisted.

'Ash? What's wrong?' Aaron asked, 'You can talk to us.'

Ashley blew her nose and wiped remnants of tears from her thick eyelashes before looking towards Robin for an encouraging nod of approval.

'I'm just... very tired. Last night was stupid and horrible,' she said simply.

It wasn't much of an explanation, but it was enough.

Ashley rested her head on Curtis' shoulder as Robin continued for her.

'We talked this morning after you guys dropped us off and, honestly, we're both feeling a little weird after last night,' Robin explained.

'I knew it,' said Curtis.

'What do you mean?' Aaron asked.

'Well, I mean, I can't speak for Ashley but, I know I had a bizarre dream...'

'You too?' Aaron inadvertently asked.

'Mhm.' Robin nodded.

'Well I didn't,' said Nathaniel, 'I slept like a baby. Like a log. Like a smooth, baby log.'

'I know,' said Aaron, evidently frustrated.

'I don't remember dreaming about anything,' Curtis said, trying to remember.

'See, well, that's another thing, Curtis,' said Robin, going for her bag underneath the table. 'Ashley and I saw something last night and we think you should all see it too...' Robin pulled out one of Aaron's cameras from her bag and placed it on the table.

'I knew I was missing one,' Aaron exclaimed, 'How did you—'

'I am sorry, Aaron. I am. But I just had to see if we managed to record it…'

'What was it? Oh no,' Nathaniel started, 'It was a ghost, wasn't it? If it was a ghost, I don't want to see it. Actually, no, show it to me. Actually—'

'Robin,' Aaron interrupted, 'what did we record?'

Robin paused and looked at her friends. 'Ashley?' she said, handing over the figurative torch.

Ashley sat up and sighed. Her face was dry but, perhaps out of habit, she wiped her eyes with both sleeves once more before answering Aaron's question. 'Curtis' odd behavior,' she said.

'What do you mean by, "odd"?' Curtis demanded.

'Yeah, what do you girls mean?' Aaron asked as well, taking the camera in his hands to turn it on.

'Well,' Robin started, 'you can see for yourselves. It's paused at the right moment, just before it all starts.'

'This is one of the cameras I set up near the woods,' said Aaron, instantly recognizing the still of the footage.

'Look at the time-stamp!' said Nathaniel.

'03:03 AM,' said Curtis, with a sad and bewildered look on his face.

Ashley linked her right arm around Curtis' left and caressed his hand as they all smooshed together in the booth to watch the footage. It showed nothing, at first. Just trees swaying in the wind on Aaron's night-vision camera. Then, perhaps twenty-odd seconds in, a figure very briefly blocked the feed. It was Curtis. Trudging slowly towards the line of trees and then stopping in front of them before disappearing into Palmers Woods.

'What am I doing?' said Curtis aloud in shock.

'It looks like you're… talking,' Ashley said warily.

'To whom?!' Curtis shouted.

'There's no one there,' said Nathaniel.

Ashley and Robin shrugged.

'If you go back a few seconds, Aaron,' said Robin, 'it looks like Curtis is holding something. There,' she said, pointing as Aaron rewinded the video, 'with his right hand. Can you zoom in at all? To see what it is?'

Everyone scooched closer to see what it could be. But there was nothing there.

Curtis sat back in his seat. 'What could I possibly be saying…'

'Didn't you guys watch this with the audio on?' Aaron asked the girls.

'There's audio?' said Ashley.

'I didn't realize,' said Robin.

'Yeah, you just… see, here?' said Aaron, signaling towards a specific button on the camera's side, 'You just tap this, here.'

The group got closer again.

Aaron made sure to turn the volume up just enough so that they could hear. The restaurant was far from full, and any staff members were far from sight, but he did not want to risk it either way.

The audio was muffled but they could make out some words. It sounded like Curtis was simply saying a single phrase, repeatedly, before he stopped and all one could hear were his footsteps as he made his way into the woods.

The phrase sounded like, "*Life is short*." It was unmistakable, the group didn't even have to say it out loud. They merely looked at each other, bewildered.

'Wait,' said Nathaniel, 'Aaron? Can you go back to the beginning? Not of the tape, but to the beginning of all this meshugas.'

Aaron nodded and rewinded the tape to where Robin had originally paused it and let it play with the audio running.

The group had already seen the footage several times by now, and so all leaned in with their ears pricked up to try to hear everything new. And they did.

Something on the tape made them all jerk backward and stare at each other in horror.

'Play that back,' said Curtis after a brief pause.

'No, Curtis, no…' Ashley pleaded, panicked.

'Play it again.' Curtis affirmed, looking at Aaron. It was as if he could not believe what he was seeing, what he was hearing.

Aaron braced himself and repositioned the camera in his hands as it had almost fallen onto the table during the previous jolt.

Then, he played the video from the beginning with the audio on, again. And they all heard it, again. They all heard what anyone would agree was the distinct sound of a small child, a little girl, laughing.

Baby take my hand
ASHLEY

Monday 26th October

00:05 AM, Downtown Melvin

It was settled. The group would go to the *Melvin Monster Mash* that Friday evening at the community center opposite the town hall. Fiona had told them about it as they left *El Salero*, offering them all bright orange flyers advertising the event—one of which Nathaniel eagerly took, of course.

It looked like their week would not go as they had originally planned after all. But life rarely does.

Ever a skeptic, Aaron was eager to weed through the rest of the footage caught on his other cameras that night. But he did not push it. He would wait to look through them himself, or with Nathaniel once things had died down. Perhaps even when they returned to Florida.

After seeing the disturbing tape at the restaurant, it seemed the majority vote steered towards any other activity.

The girls had certainly made it clear they would not be involved in anymore "ghost nonsense" as Ashley put it. And the boys responded by promptly nodding in agreement.

No one used any binding words, like *ever* or *never*. It was simply clear that no one wanted this week to be tainted in any way. It was too important. They could all agree on that in any case.

During the ride back, each pitched ideas on what they *could* do for the rest of their vacation.

But it was late, tensions were high, and Nathaniel was unsurprisingly hungry again.

So, as they had done nights before, they each retired to their separate homes—excluding Nathaniel who would stay with Aaron for one more night—having agreed to meet at *PB* in the morning, bright and early, to refer to their guides; the Dodson sisters.

Willow and Tamarind would undoubtedly have several fun suggestions for activities that were uplifting and merely "spook-adjacent" as Nathaniel put it and which, most importantly, would also avoid upsetting Ashley or Robin any further.

08:45 AM, 8 Almond Avenue

'I'm so sweet like a nice bonbon, Mom said rock it till the break of dawn!' Nathaniel rapped, or sang, or tried to, with his mouth full of lemon bonbons as the group walked into town.

They had all met outside of Aaron's house in what appeared to be good spirits. Everyone seemed well-rested. Naturally, Nathaniel's mood was highest on the energy spectrum. He was excited to go home today—after spending some time with his friends at *PB* of course. Today, his parents would be back from one of the property investment conferences in Connecticut they recently began to attend.

'I can't wait to see what presents they got me, you guys,' he said, as his backpack jingled and jangled, as his thin sticky fingers continued to explore the near-empty contents of the crinkling packet of candy he took from one of the Jackson's kitchen cabinets earlier that morning. 'I gave them a list before we came down. A big list. I bet they get me everything I wanted. And why not? I'm like a man now. A whole man,' he went on as he advanced ahead of the group, with Aaron and Robin walking side by side behind him, and Curtis and Ashley walking arm-in-arm behind them.

'Hey, Berger,' Curtis called from a few feet behind him, 'How many dolls did you ask for this year?'

'You mean action figures?'

'I think he said dolls,' Aaron chimed in.

'Yeah, how many do you *"figure"*, Aaron?' Curtis joked, 'Like ten?'

'Oh, yeah. At least,' Aaron teased.

'You guys joke. But my action figures taught me how to fight. You could say, they gave me action… Karate-chop action, watch out!' In one swift yet ungainly motion, Nathaniel crumpled up the packet and threw it in the air. It managed to hit Curtis on the shoulder—though, it may not have done had Aaron's reflexes been slower, had he not dodged the candy packet's determined path in time.

'Oh, that's it. You're gonna get it!' Curtis called.

'Here we go.' Aaron prepared himself as Curtis legged it, bolting forward to catch Nathaniel who was already running and badly imitating Kiai sounds. Then, Aaron moved Robin to the side and went to join in some typical boisterous roughhousing with his buddies.

Robin stopped to allow Ashley time to catch up with her. After a few strides, Ashley linked arms with Robin.

'How are you doing, my love?' Ashley asked, gently stroking Robin's forearm.

'How are *you* doing?' Robin replied.

Ashley smiled and sighed. Then Robin smiled. Then, they laughed together. In seconds, desperation turned into genuine tittering as they looked forward and shook their heads at the boys before continuing to stroll.

It was a brisk morning with some wind, but not so much so that it could make things uncomfortable. Indeed, with a hat and scarf, as both girls cleverly had on, one could truly enjoy a leisurely morning walk through town, as they were.

The anticipation for the chill on your cheekbones to turn into a stinging warmth as soon as you entered a building was enough motivation for any of them to happily leave their houses that morning, to head towards a different kind of home. Everything, it seemed, beckoned them towards *Paranormal Booktivity*. The sun's beaming rays which said *"Up and at 'em!"* along with the cheeping cardinals and chirping chickadees, the fall foliage which covered trees and sidewalks alike and which appeared to form a path of their own, and the inviting smell of freshly-ground coffee beans.

In no time, they had arrived.

But as they turned the corner, off Russell Road and into Graeme Road, as soon as they joined the boys, something made them all stop in their tracks.

Not the sight of the spindly tree on the old hanging sign, nor the weather-worn door, but one of two spookily decorated bay windows. It had been broken. Broken by something or someone.

The morning light shone through millions of tiny shards of glass on the cobblestone path and reflected onto a line of bright yellow police tape surrounding the shop.

Something troubling had happened. But what could it be?

09:00 AM, *Paranormal Booktivity*

'Did you ladies display any collector's items in this particular window?'

Tamarind paused to think, tightly clinging to the large shawl which hung off her shoulders and was wrapped around Jefferson who she held close to her torso. Then, she shook her head.

'What about any limited-edition books? Any seasonal merchandise?' the deputy continued, scribbling notes into a small, black, leather-bound notebook as he questioned her.

'No. No, I don't recall,' she answered, gently rocking side to side in the morning chill.

Meanwhile, Willow made her way down the wooden staircase one purposeful step at a time, eyeing every inch of the shop as she did. The sheriff, who had been acting sheriff in Melvin for as long as anyone could remember, soon followed after her; taking *his* time due to the irritating remnants of discomfort from his recent bunion surgery, which he managed to mention in every other conversation.

'Really, sheriff. I seriously doubt whether anyone stepped foot inside overnight. And certainly not upstairs. I can't see anything out of place,' Willow asserted to a very dubious sheriff Bagan.

'No,' Tamarind called from the doorway in agreement, 'We would have heard something, right? I didn't hear anything.'

'Not a thing.' Willow shook her head in certainty, 'No, I very much feel this ought to be labeled a quote-unquote drive-by stoning, if anything, rather than theft.'

'Some local kids,' Tamarind added, 'the *undead* kind, even,' she whispered to her sister, nodding suspiciously with squinted eyes, 'Who knows this close to All Hallows' Eve?'

'It may even have been an accident,' Willow said more realistically as she made her way towards her sister and Jefferson, who she tried to comfort with a caress despite him looking perfectly fine, if not entertained, by the whole ordeal.

The sheriff's current deputy, Brett Jenkins, popped the bright yellow thumb-sized pencil he had been using into a cloth loop adjacent to the notebook. He closed it and pocketed it. Then, with both hands, he lifted his moss-green pant legs at the thigh, just above his knees, before crouching down to further inspect the affected area.

'What're you thinking there, Brett?' the sheriff asked, limping over to his deputy as the girls stepped backward and out of the way of his foreseen path.

'Welp...' deputy Jenkins started, 'The problem with that theory, Ms. Dodson,' he said, looking up towards Willow, 'is that there appear to be no *stones* here.'

Willow and Tamarind frowned towards each other—eager to commence their day and noticeably uncomfortable by this adverse shift in routine, neither was happy to hear that this petty crime might turn into something more complicated than expected.

'Mhm! Well, I'll be. Good eye there, Brett. I think you might just be right. No rock or pebble in sight!' sheriff Bagan remarked. Then, he opened the door and tottered outside to aid his deputy in the search for the missing rock.

Perhaps, if one had been used to break the window, which would be an ordinary person's first thought, it may have bounced back after the impact, and now be hidden amongst the many shards of glass and pieces of Halloween decorations which lay forlorn on the cobblestone ground underneath the bay window. But he couldn't see any. A fact he relayed to deputy Jenkins with a raise of his eyebrow, for suspense, followed by the pursing of his lips, a tut, and a shake of his head.

No, neither deputy Jenkins nor sheriff Bagan could see the inanimate accessory to the crime, to this increasingly strange misdemeanor. Although, ever-observant from decades of pounding the pavement, sheriff Bagan did see something in his periphery. It was a gang of young people he would have otherwise considered suspects, if not for the fact that it was merely Curtis Jones, Ashley Cruz, Robin Wilson, Aaron Jackson, and Nathaniel Berger—huddled together, wide-eyed and worry-faced, at the side of the road.

'Careful there, kids,' the sheriff warned, 'it's an ungodly mess 'round this way.'

The group stayed put, but, almost in unison, they all peered forward in a mixture of curiosity and concern.

'What happened?' Nathaniel asked.

'We're still on that, unfortunately,' said deputy Jenkins, propping his hands on his sides as he joined his superior outside. 'Something seems off here,' he said, looking up and around as he lowered his opaque shades.

'Mhm.' Sheriff Bagan nodded in agreement. 'I may have gone from flat-foot to hobble-foot, but I can smell something fishy a mile before I get there.'

'Wait,' Tamarind chimed in, 'I'm remembering something.'

'Oh?' Willow inquired.

'Yeah. This morning. When I came down. I saw everything on the floor and then, I opened the door and rushed outside—'

Willow sighed. 'You ran outside barefoot?'

'I wasn't thinking,' Tamarind continued, 'but yes, it was instinct. I ran outside and there was no one there, so I came back in and woke you up, Willow. And that's when we called the sheriff.'

'Right?' deputy Jenkins pushed, peering in at the girls through the empty space which would have been a window.

'Well, the door was open.'

'Right?' he pushed again.

'Well, I didn't leave it open! Willow, did you?' she asked.

'Certainly not.'

'So,' sheriff Bagan started, a lightbulb brightening above his head, 'you reckon, Tamarind, that someone might have come in after all? Used some newfangled trickery to open the door and then couldn't lock it behind them?'

Tamarind shrugged.

'Ladies,' deputy Jenkins started, 'do you know of anyone who has a spare key to the property? A landlord, perhaps? A family member?'

Tamarind winced and looked towards Willow, whose energy, she could sense, was shifting from light frustration to pure exasperation.

'No…' Willow started, 'No. We're the landlord. And we're our family,' she stated firmly. Her hands dropped from her loving grip around her sister and her gaze turned to the floor; looking out for potential rogue pieces of glass as she made her way behind the pastry display to fetch the corn broom which was propped up against the counter. 'Now,' she continued, 'with all due respect, deputy, you can file your report as is at this point. We've already told you that nothing was taken, sheriff. And honestly, we'd unlikely press charges against some misguided youths even if that were the case.'

Deputy Jenkins nearly stepped forward, as if to retort. But sheriff Bagan, preemptively apprehending the well-intended supplication, placed his hand on his deputy's shoulder and gave him a look which conveyed a simple but sure, *"No"*.

'Kids,' Willow called assertively from the hole in the wall, 'you can come on through, now, although watch your step. Have a seat in your booth, all of you, and we'll start on breakfast,' she said, sweeping up the glass, dust, and debris into a corner she would collect and dispose of later. 'And Tay,' she said, turning towards her sister, 'go put Jefferson upstairs for now, lest he cut his little paw-pads. And you go on and get some shoes on, too. Go on now.'

There was nothing more to be said—which would be the case, always, whenever Willow claimed control of whatever she deemed an unruly situation, whenever she had had enough of the abhorrent chaos, of anything that forced her to deviate from her pristine schedule.

'Welp… let us know if anything changes,' deputy Jenkins advised, holding the tip of his hat, nodding farewell to both sisters, one by one. 'Ms. Dodson, Ms. Dodson.'

'Be safe, ladies,' sheriff Bagan cautioned, tipping his hat, too, in the direction of both sisters before making his way back with his deputy to the squad car parked on the junction.

Tamarind simpered apologetically as the lawmen left. Then, as the gang carefully made their way through the door, she directed them to their seats with her outstretched hand before heading upstairs to heed the wise words of her sister.

In the time it took for the Dodson sisters to make and serve breakfast, which took longer than usual in and amongst all the chatter after the morning's distractions; Tony Woods from across the road had been and gone and come back again to help the girls with their *urgent safety hazard*, as Willow called it more than once.

He had seen the mess at the front of the shop and, after enquiring about the situation, he had kindly offered to remedy what he could.

Mr. Woods had been conveniently taught by the town handy-man, Joe Spencer, who was now retired, how to carefully deal with glass panes properly to re-frame windows.

This happened five Christmases ago, he explained earlier that morning; when he accidentally fell into his own shop's bay window and called Joe to replace it immediately to protect his stock, as well as himself and his daughter, Fiona, from the harsh cold that winter.

He had not been hurt at the time, thankfully. He was holding a rather large cardboard box filled with trinkets and ornaments he had cleared from both windows before replacing them with a newer display and tripped over himself when he saw a rare, frosted crystal bauble on the floor he did not want to step on. The box fell forward, as did he, and broke the window.

And that was that.

Now, he remembered what Joe had shown him all those years ago, and after hurriedly nipping to *Hardy's Hardware* a couple of blocks up Russell Road, he had returned with everything he needed and was currently on a step-ladder near the recess next to the front door.

Tamarind cleared plates and cups and saucers which clinked and clanked as she handled them. Grateful that he was safe, Willow generously tapped a pot of colored fish food over Prankers' bowl with her index finger and watched her little friend enjoy their breakfast despite the happenings of the past couple of hours. Then she caressed a napping Jefferson on the shelf next to the bowl, now he was allowed downstairs again, now that the floor was clean, the window was almost replaced, and the space was being guarded by Mr. Woods.

Robin and Ashley dutifully put books away in their rightful places—eyeing the reference tabs and the surrounding books on the lookout for surnames and book titles and evident gaps to guide them.

Curtis, Aaron, and Nathaniel remained at the booth; sat close together, staring at a piece of paper in silence. It comprised of a list the group had narrowed down together from the many, many suggestions Willow and Tamarind had given them of interesting places to explore and interesting things to do during their week in Melvin.

Robin and Ashley had already drawn tiny stars and love hearts next to their preferred choices. Now it was up to the boys to decide which they would rather do today.

'Hmm… What about—' Curtis started.

'Yes?' asked Aaron, eagerly sitting up.

'No…' Curtis sighed in thought.

Aaron slumped back down, again, and continued to stare at the list.

'Oh, I know!' said Nathaniel.

'Yes?' Aaron said desperately.

Nathaniel's brows furrowed as he chewed on the top of an engraved pen Willow gave him that morning in the box of birthday presents from both sisters.

'Hmm… No…' he said.

Aaron sat back into the booth and yawned. 'Okay,' he started, 'well I'm cool with whatever. So, just pick one.'

He shuffled to the edge of the booth, stood up, and stretched. Then he made his way to the kitchen. He looked at Prankers swimming contently in his little underwater world, complete with a small statue of a mermaid, an even smaller treasure chest, what looked like an artificial plant, and a myriad of colorful pebbles underneath them.

Willow patted his shoulder as she made her way to check on her friend Tony's progress. And, being done with the dishes, Tamarind shifted closer to Aaron, after drying her hands, to give him a big hug.

'Ooft! Your aura is so murky today, Aaron. Are you alright? You seem so tense.'

Aaron chuckled under his breath and hugged Tamarind back. How lovely of her, to always mean so well, he thought.

'I think everyone is a little tense this morning, T,' he said. And he wasn't wrong. But the loving, somewhat maternal, embrace made him feel a little better. And that was nice.

Then, as they separated and as Aaron smiled down at Tamarind, he noticed something in the corner of a bottom shelf underneath the till. It was a very small and very old CRT television.

'What's that, T?' he asked.

'Oh, that's just for our video surveillance.'

At that moment, silence flooded the shop as Curtis, Nathaniel, Robin, and Ashley stopped and looked up at Tamarind and Aaron, at Willow, and then back towards the counter.

'Video surveillance? Oh wow, so, we could see what happened last night?' said Curtis optimistically.

'Should we call the sheriff again?' asked Ashley, squeezing back into the booth next to Curtis.

'No,' said Willow from the doorway, 'that won't do any good.'

Robin stood next to the booth with her left hand propped on her hip and her right hand placed on top of the leather seat inches behind Nathaniel's head. 'Why not?' she asked.

'Because it doesn't work,' Tamarind answered.

A collective feeling of disappointment swept the group.

'No, it's not worked for a long time now,' Willow continued.

'I don't remember a time it did,' said Tamarind.

'Why didn't you get it repaired?' Aaron asked.

'Or replaced,' Nathaniel said, peering over the counter, 'That thing looks ancient.'

'I could have easily fixed that for you,' said Aaron.

'Well, to be fair, you probably never thought you'd need it,' Mr. Woods supposed, 'I'd hardly class Melvin as the crime capital of Massachusetts.'

'No,' Willow agreed.

'What do you think happened, Willow?' he asked her, stepping down from the ladder he had borrowed to gather his things.

'You know, Tony, I'm not sure.' Willow paused to think. 'But I honestly don't see how it matters either way. Especially with what a quick and beautiful job you've done with our window!'

Tamarind joined the two, placing her left hand on her sister's shoulder and her right on Tony's, patting him on the back for a job well done.

'Indeed. Excellent job!' she said.

'Well, that's me done, my lovelies. That should be good for years yet. You both stay safe and let me know if you need anything else doing,' said Mr. Woods.

He picked up his toolbox and the black heavy-duty bag full of sharp rubbish he would throw away on his way out. The Dodson sisters thanked him, and everyone said goodbye and waved as he headed out the door to open his shop, late, and continue with his day.

'Ah, that's better,' said Robin, looking towards the new, clean, and clear glass.

'Yeah,' said Ashley, 'now all you have to do is decorate it again. Maybe that's what we should do today! Help you guys out. We could even go shopping and see if there's anything we could add to the display!'

Robin's face lit up at the suggestion. But Curtis and Nathaniel scowled as if they had just been offered to eat an ungodly, grounded up mixture of liver and beetroot.

'Thank you, girls,' said Willow, 'but we can take it from here. You guys should be out having fun.'

'Exactly!' Tamarind agreed, 'The possibilities are endless!'

Robin smiled and shrugged, Ashley rolled her eyes, and the boys went back to staring at their list.

Just then, they all heard something bang and drop, like metal against the floor, and they all looked up in the direction of the noise.

'What're you doing there, son?' said Willow, walking to the counter and crouching down to see Aaron sat on the floor in front of the bare insides of their small television set.

Aaron grunted. 'I'm just—I'm just trying to fix it.'

'Where in the world did, he get a screwdriver?' Tamarind whispered to her sister, peering over her shoulder.

Willow shrugged. 'Don't waste your time with that old thing, Aaron.'

'But,' he started, 'it's not the camera that stopped working, right? It's still hooked up to the feed. It's just this really old screen.'

'Aaron?' called Curtis.

'Yep?'

'If that's true, wouldn't we be able to watch the stored video on a newer device?'

'Maybe. That's if I can't manage to fix *this one*.'

'You can do it, buddy,' Nathaniel exclaimed.

'Yeah, ha-ha,' Robin giggled, 'We believe in you.'

'Aaron! Aaron! Aaron!' Ashley jokingly chanted. Then, everyone joined in.

‘Ha-ha, guys. Thanks.’

Everyone waited in joint anticipation as Aaron clanked away.

‘How’s it going over there?’ Willow asked.

‘Dusty. But—’

‘But?’ said Tamarind.

‘Yeah, *but*?’ Nathaniel pushed.

‘But.’ Aaron grunted and lifted the CRT TV onto the counter, adjusting the cable at the back, and positioned it forward so that everyone could see. ‘But I think I’ve got it,’ he said, holding crossed fingers up in front of his friends before turning it on with his other hand.

‘Wahey!’ Nathaniel called, ‘You did it!’

‘That’s amazing,’ said Willow.

‘Mhm!’ Tamarind nodded enthusiastically.

‘Well done, Aaron,’ said Ashley.

‘Never doubted you, bud,’ said Curtis.

Robin took a few steps and popped both hands on Aaron’s forearm. ‘My hero,’ she said cornily.

Aaron laughed and jokingly bowed.

Robin smiled back approvingly. She knew if anyone could manage the impossible, it’d be Aaron.

Then, he started to fiddle with dials and buttons and the dusty remote he had found next to the box, hoping the camera managed to film the mysterious happenings from the night before.

Fortunately, or perhaps unfortunately as would soon be determined, it did.

It was dark and the camera recorded in black and white, but the angle was right. If you squinted just so, you could see the outline of a figure turning the corner and hovering just outside the front door of the shop.

'Who's that?' Nathaniel asked.

'It looks like a man,' Curtis pointed out, 'but he's wearing… it looks like he's wearing something on his face.'

'Is that a ski mask? Jesus, it's not that cold,' said Nathaniel.

'What's he doing there?' asked Ashley.

It seemed the sheriff was right because the strange man appeared to be hunched over for nigh on two minutes picking the lock to the door.

Almost immediately after they stood upright, it swung wide open. Then, they slowly took their first cautious steps inside. After a few seconds, the footage showed the strange person walking through the shop before passing the camera's line of sight.

Tamarind gasped and clasped a hand over her mouth.

'Oh no! You don't suppose he came upstairs?' said an increasingly worried Willow.

'But we didn't hear anything! Not a thing!' said a visibly anxious Tamarind.

'Maybe he went outside and into the courtyard?' Curtis guessed.

'Look,' said Aaron, 'in the corner of the screen. There he is again.'

'And he's got something with him,' said Curtis.

'Oh gosh. What is that? What is that?! Right there!' Nathaniel asked, frantically pointing.

'It looks like a book,' said Robin.

'Then why is it glowing?' said Ashley.

Willow and Tamarind moved their faces closer to the screen and stared intently. They simultaneously gasped, looked at each other, and ran past the gang and through the backdoor which led to the communal courtyard, home to the oldest tree in Melvin.

'Willow?' Robin called. She heard no answer, but instead an odd knocking and banging sound. She decided to follow the girls and was promptly followed by the rest of the gang.

Robin, Nathaniel, Ashley, Curtis, and Aaron, rushed to the stone courtyard to see Willow and Tamarind on their knees, sat in front of a crooked hole in the ground, alongside a small wooden plank and a large stone which they correctly assumed originally covered it.

Nathaniel gasped. 'A hidey-hole! So, something was stolen!'

'Oh no, Willow,' said Tamarind.

'Willow?' Robin pushed, making her way around her friends to investigate the hole, but something else caught her attention. It was the look on Willow's face. The eerily still, pensive, and panic-stricken look which gave Robin goosebumps. 'Willow?' she pressed, 'What kind of book *does* glow like that?'

Tamarind continued to stare at the hole and said nothing while the gang looked at each other and waited. Then, after what seemed like an eternity for everyone; Willow simply answered Robin's not-so-simple question.

'A spell book.'

12:15 AM, *Paranormal Booktivity*

It was already the afternoon of an already eventful day.

Breakfast was wolfed down, the table had been cleaned, the floor swept, and the window replaced, but the tension in the air remained.

True to form, a resilient Willow was up on the stepladder re-decorating the bay window in anticipation for the lunch-time rush of regulars she refused to disappoint.

Aaron was behind the counter, still, vigorously rewinding and pausing the tape of last night's mysterious theft, resolute to find answers or at least a clue which could lead him to them.

And Tamarind sat on a stool, with Jefferson on her lap, in front of the booth where Curtis sat with Ashley, Nathaniel, and Robin, who were all still reeling from the fantastical tale Tamarind had told them.

As it turns out, the Dodson sisters had come across a seemingly innocent book of spells when they first acquired the property years before. The book gave them no reason to be suspicious—with pages stitched like any other and an unassuming cover—initially at least. They barely flicked through it before putting it up for sale amongst other books of spells they stocked by various authors.

But the girls found over time, as Tamarind explained, that they would start to see it in different places each time. In between different books on the same shelf and then on different shelves completely. Innocently left as if moved by someone unaware of how they had categorized it. As time moved on, however, they found it would appear, as if it had a will of its own, all around the shop and worse, upstairs where they lived.

Enough was enough. They knew now that neither of them was the culprit, and that something spooky was going on.

'I honestly thought it was a ghost or something,' Tamarind had told the guys, laughing it off as soon as she had said it, '*So, we held a séance to get some answers.* But… *that didn't go well.*'

Tamarind did not elaborate further, on that aspect anyway. But she did tell them that when she and Willow finally decided to take a closer look at the book—when they read within the lines of magical words, although they would not dare to utter them out loud—they discovered that these spells were more somber than anything else they sold. Spells concerning change; beginnings and endings, life and death.

'At that point, it just started to glow,' she told them.

They wanted nothing to do with it, quite rightly, and tried to dispose of it. Time and time again they would throw it away, but it always made its way back.

Finally, they decided to bury it outside. And that seemed to work. They hadn't seen it pop up again, and they thought the ordeal was over. This was years ago, and nothing untoward had happened since.

The Dodson sisters did not know anything else about the book. But whoever that man was knew something. And, for some reason, he seemed to know exactly where it was hidden as well. Who knows what evil purposes he wanted to use it for?

‘I just don’t understand why he would smash the window once he was outside. Once he was leaving,’ said Aaron, rewinding the tape once more.

Nathaniel walked towards and then hunched over the counter with his best friend and watched as he rewinded the tape again.

‘Look. It’s like—he stops, right, just there,’ he said, pointing, ‘but then he turns back and smashes the window, and leaves. He doesn’t even run. The smug jerk. He just hobbles away.’

‘Yeah. It’s very odd,’ said Aaron.

‘Maybe he wanted us to think it was a group of meddling kids playing a Halloween prank, in case we noticed anything awry,’ Tamarind guessed.

‘Yeah. And that was your first thought, wasn’t it Willow?’ Curtis asked.

Willow said nothing and continued to hang glittery bats in front of the window, humming tensely as if she could hum the drama away.

‘Actually, my first thought was ghost kids, but whatever,’ said Tamarind.

‘Your first thought is always ghost kids,’ Nathaniel teased.

‘I just can’t believe all of this. Do you think the book is real?’ Ashley asked.

‘What do you mean?’ said Robin.

‘You know. The spells. Do you think whatever’s in that book is real… magic?’

‘Who knows.’ Tamarind shrugged.

‘Should we call a priest?’ Ashley pressed.

'No. Nope,' said Nathaniel, 'I think we'll be fine without having holy water splashed in our faces, thank you.'

'That's such a stereotype, Berger,' said Curtis.

'Yeah, well, I'm Jewish and I don't want to risk it.'

Curtis snorted and Aaron chuckled, and the tape continued to run as they were distracted.

When Aaron and Nathaniel looked down again, they saw something in the corner of the screen. A simple movement, but where they had been analyzing the footage for what felt like hours, perhaps accurately or inaccurately so, they were beginning to attribute meaning to things. From their eyes, it looked as if the thief had snagged something, his sleeve or a part of his coat, on one of the book-shelves on his right-hand side as he made his way from the courtyard, through the shop and on his way out.

The two boys looked at each other and it was as if all those years of being best friends led up to this singular moment of awesome telepathy. Aaron didn't even want to insult the moment by rewinding the tape. They had understood each other completely.

After almost managing to have an entire telepathic conversation with each other in nanoseconds; they stood up in unison and hastily made their way around the counter and towards the tall wooden bookshelves to investigate.

Robin gasped at the speed of it all. 'What the—'

'What are you guys doing?' Ashley called.

'Yeah, what are you looking for?' Curtis offered.

'Calm down, Lionel Ritchie!' Nathaniel called, 'My boy found it! Legend!'

'Found what?' Willow called with an extremely eager inflection in her tone, rushing from the step ladder.

Everyone gathered around as Aaron and Nathaniel walked towards the booth.

Aaron held in his hand a price tag, which must have been hanging from the thief's jacket. It was still intact, brand-new looking as if he had bought the puffy parka and ski mask just for this occasion.

On one side it stated the price. On the other, it had the logo of the shop he must have bought it from. Black and white embossed etching of a pair of scissors with a ribbon wrapped around its blades. That could only mean one thing.

'A clue!' Aaron exclaimed, holding it up to show his friends.

16:45 PM, ***Gloria's Garments***

Nothing on the list the gang had drawn up that morning could compare to attempting to solve their very own mystery, despite it not involving ghosts and despite the Dodson sisters' protests.

When Aaron showed his friends the price tag the thief snagged on the bookshelf in *PB*, everyone knew which shop his jacket must have come from. And although Willow and Tamarind did not want the group coming to any harm, they could not stop them from planning a stakeout later that day at *Gloria's Garments*.

Gloria Day was a seamstress all her life; originally in her mother's dry-cleaning shop when she was alive and now, after having inherited and revamped it. Now that she was in charge, she took in clothes from charity shops, or sometimes people would donate items directly to her, and she would work her magic before selling them at a higher price and donating even more to charity. She had cleverly named her shop using a play on words of *glorious garments*—which it was also called by some residents as it was considered the perfect place to find unique and fabulous garments for every occasion.

It closed at 17:00 PM, as most shops did in Melvin, and it was near the town hall, closer to the town center than *PB*. The gang had agreed the best time to scout the place would be just before closing; hoping it would be empty, or near enough, so that they would have the freedom to inspect every nook and cranny, and maybe, if it came to it, interrogate Gloria herself.

However, when they got there, they quickly found the shop was shockingly full of customers still window-shopping and queuing to pay.

There was hardly any space for the group, but they managed to slip in before closing before they could be forced on their way.

As they walked around, they saw most railings were covered with vintage Halloween costumes which, they guessed, were probably Gloria's creations.

Neither had ever recalled going to this shop for any kind of costume when they lived there. They always used Tony Woods' store, *Merry Masks*, opposite

PB. It was so close, and they knew him well. Also, they were always so colorful and fun, unlike what they were seeing at Gloria's shop. So, they weren't sure if this was new or if she made an annual effort to sell them.

It did seem odd, initially. But as they started to look through the various collections, it started to add up.

Robin recognized some puritan-style outfits she had seen her father, Christopher, and his colleagues wear at the museum he worked in. Ashley saw a small section with Día de Los Muertos inspired gowns and swore that her mother had worn something similar years ago. And the boys vividly remembered seeing Melvin townspeople in similar garb at the annual Halloween celebration which would take place in the community center opposite the town hall and surrounding square—the same celebration the group would not usually attend, as they would undoubtedly have more exciting and exhilarating plans, but which they would attend *this* year.

As they continued to look around, Ashley noticed Gloria emerge from a back room and take over the till; harping on about *"cashing up"* as she dismissed the young girl who had been serving customers from her duties. Ashley nudged Curtis and cleared her throat to get everyone else's attention. The shop was closing soon, and they could not find what they had been searching for. They would have to talk to Gloria.

They all joined the end of the queue and waited to speak to her after everyone else had gone, with Ashley at the front of the group of course. She was not one to shy away from getting exactly what she wanted from people, and she already knew what questions to ask and how innocently she'd have to approach them. She also figured it would be best not to leave it to any of the boys, who might be less tactful and end up leaving them with no answers at all.

A middle-aged couple in front of them paid, took their bags, thanked Gloria, and left. It was their turn.

Ashley stepped forward and smiled across the counter at Gloria Day; ready to pretend to be curious about *"warmer clothes, suitable for the upcoming season, like parkas and ski masks"* and *"when they would be in stock or were they already"*. But as she began her ruse, Ashley heard shuffling behind her and distracting whispers from the gang. Then, she felt a tug on her forearm and turned around to see Curtis desperately trying to signal her to leave with them. The reason, she did not know, but it appeared he had managed to whisper it to the rest of the gang who were already nervously smiling and backing away towards the door.

Ashley dismissed him with a stern hand gesture and continued her conversation.

She managed to find out the shop had stocked some items fitting Ashley's description until very recently. Until Gloria had decided to pop everything in a cheap "for sale" box near the till to make space for her annual Halloween collections, that is.

Ashley questioned after which customers may have taken items from said box, but her inquiry was met with a blockade in the form of a lecture on customer privacy.

Ashley left in a huff of frustration, having come no closer to uncovering the mystery, storming out of the shop, and stomping onto the pavement—only to come across one smiling boyfriend and three smiling friends.

It seemed Curtis had found his clue as they were queuing, but it was no price tag.

His heart pounded in his chest as he tried to describe to Ashley what he had just told his friends; what had caught his eye, the corner of his eye, as they all stood waiting to speak to Gloria.

It was an item which was propped up almost as if it were sentient and waiting for him to find it on one of the impulse-buy shelves underneath the counter filled with little sweets and treats and miniature sewing kits in line together. Something which may have well been calling his name. Something he could have sworn he saw glowing, even for an instant, like the spell book on the tape.

It was one lone page, old and delicate, with a tattered edge as if someone had ripped it out of the book and carefully placed it there for him to find.

As Curtis took it out of his inner jacket pocket, everyone huddled together to look at what was on the page: a spell.

However, they could not do anything about it, now anyway. They were all late for supper at their respective homes. Especially Nathaniel, who had still not been home all day despite promising his parents he would have seen them this afternoon.

They would have to go home. Each of them. But this was not the end. No, this journey had just begun. Because the spell the group internally read instantly produced a collective lightbulb above their heads which told them exactly where they would have to go to find a second clue: a cemetery.

23:00 PM, St. Peregrine's Church Graveyard

Beautiful in its quaint simplicity during the day, this is the first time Ashley had seen the church at night.

It was where she grew up attending Sunday morning mass with her parents, and then with her mother after her father's passing as a young girl. Its graveyard is where her father was buried still.

She would visit it after the service with her mother to bring fresh flowers and pray. As she got older, she would visit her father on her own every Tuesday after school. Sometimes Robin would come with her if she needed the support; like on the anniversary of his death or his birthday. And as her relationship with Curtis grew stronger, he would join her on the odd occasion to provide a comforting shoulder to cry on when the loss of him was too much to bear.

It would be shocking to find out and nigh on impossible to guess if you barely knew Ashley, an extremely private person; but at her lowest points, Ashley felt as though she were cursed to live with death all her life.

The Cruz household seemed as though it were in constant mourning. She remembered so many funerals from her childhood. Such a small family which seemed to shrink further every year and was nearly non-existent now that it was just her and her mother. Even with Curtis and her friends being in her life, she never felt as though it got any bigger.

At one point, she hoped, in her naivety, that her mother might remarry, and she could look forward to an extended family. But that never happened.

Having what she felt like a sister in Robin was amazing, but it was not the same. Her mother never remarried.

Indeed, it had been nearly nine years since her father's death, but he remained the love of her life, as she affirmed every day.

There were photos of him everywhere in the house, they would pray for his soul every night, and not a day went by where he was not missed.

Now that Ashley was older, and more spiritually aligned than she could have hoped to be in her youth; she understood that things happened for a reason and she would not want to seem ungrateful for the blessings in her life by wishing for another.

This, however, can be a trying and draining pursuit for anyone, even someone as strong-minded as Ashley. And this was particularly difficult for her to follow through with during a specific period of her life, almost exactly a year ago, when she was forced to suffer through another loss she was not expecting; when she and Curtis lost the baby they did not know they were expecting.

There are hardly any words to express the pain a parent, a mother, goes through when the potential of life is snuffed out like a flame before its time. So, Ashley was resigned to never speak about it. And she made sure Curtis never dared to bring it up, either.

Talking to Robin about the incident this week had been the first time in a long time, and it was strenuous enough despite the conversation being with her best friend.

For Robin, it all made perfect sense, now, looking back on it all: why, for Ashley, these little games over the years, these adventures, were quests to find proof of an afterlife, why to even attempt to delve into the mystery of life and death was so important to her. And why, of course, this week she could tolerate no more after what happened the day before.

Ashley had lost so much, she explained on Sunday morning, she vowed she would not lose Curtis or anyone she loved ever again.

Not that she had any control over the matter, Robin had thought, although the fervor in her voice might have indicated otherwise. Still, she was tense in her trembling conviction.

Robin feared that a late-night trip to the graveyard would not bode well with Ashley for many reasons which were obvious to them both but which the boys might very well be oblivious to.

At the same time, though, the girls knew that it had to be done. Whether the stolen book was magical or not, no one could just break into *PB* or threaten Willow and Tamarind's safety without consequences. And there was no way the Dodson sisters would ramble on about spooky disappearing books to law enforcement without risking being locked away themselves.

No, it was on them. It had to be done.

The spell on the page Curtis found was very clear in directing them to this location.

After sneaking out of their homes to investigate; Curtis, Ashley, Aaron, and Nathaniel were there, and Robin would be there holding Ashley's hand all the way.

The squeak of the back gate behind the church's garden alerted no one as no one was there. Only Nathaniel, Aaron, Curtis, Ashley, and Robin.

Robin and Ashley marched fearlessly into the night, arm in arm and armed with flashlights, directly towards Ashley's father's grave where they would sit and wait for the boys to be done.

Predictably, Aaron filmed everything, just in case something spookier than "spook-adjacent" occurred.

But, in all fairness, nothing appeared to be even slightly as scary as everyone expected.

Everything was oddly calm and still, peaceful even. There was no wind to rustle the trees, no nocturnal creatures to stir the ground, and barely any imposing gravestones to cast a shadow as the trail of light from their torches flickered across the graveyard.

The only slightly intimidating entity was a statue of St. Peregrine in the center of a ring of gated flowers, holding his staff and looking out onto the grave markers he protected with a serene expression on his stone face which, the longer you looked at it, appeared more and more human.

'Hand me the candle,' Curtis said to Nathaniel, who promptly took out a long and thin white pillar candle from his backpack along with a cheap lighter they bought from the packie just before closing time.

Curtis lit the candle. Then, the boys looked around and waited for something to happen.

But nothing did.

After a few seconds, he handed it to Nathaniel along with the page from the spell book.

'What am I supposed to do with this?' Nathaniel whispered, eyeing the tall statue which he felt was watching them.

'Read it,' said Curtis.

'Yeah,' said Aaron, 'you'll be fine. Go on.'

'I'll be fine?'

'Aaron's right, Berger. You'll be fine.'

'Then why would he say that? Surely, if I was going to be fine, you wouldn't have to say it. Also, I'd *be* fine, right? Like, now? And I don't feel fine you guys.'

'We're right here for you, bud,' Curtis reassured, 'What could go wrong?'

Nathaniel scoffed and Aaron couldn't help but guffaw.

'Why don't you do it then?' Nathaniel protested.

'Because,' Curtis started, before looking over at the girls sat a satisfying distance away from earshot,

'Ashley would kill me if she found out I read the spell. I'm just supposed to protect you if demons show up.'

'Demons?!'

'No demons will show up. But yeah. I can't. She would physically kill me.'

'True,' said Aaron.

'Well, then we just won't tell her then.'

'Berger,' Aaron reprimanded.

'What? She's way the heck over there,' Nathaniel exclaimed and gestured before realizing he ought to keep his voice down. 'She's literally so far away and she's not even looking,' he whispered, crouching down behind Aaron.

'Dude,' Aaron started, 'don't be a wuss.'

'You do it then.'

'I'm filming!'

'Ugh, give it here then. But I swear, if I get dragged away by a demon, I'm going to use my charms to convince it to come back for you two.'

'Yeah, okay, Berger.' Curtis chuckled as Aaron smirked behind his camera. Then Curtis took hold of the candle and held it by the page so that Nathaniel could read the spell, which he somehow managed to muster the courage to do.

Nathaniel read the spell, word for word. But nothing happened.

Aaron was not shocked, of course, but Nathaniel's face showed he was, if not also somewhat relieved. Curtis just looked confused, and for a few minutes, they stood together under the statue in silence and thought.

'Maybe I have to do a little dance while I read it. Or I can try to sing it? Or rap it? Or maybe—'

'Don't make me hit you,' Curtis interrupted, 'It's not easy trying to respect the dead while trying to enact a godforsaken spell, but especially not with you around.'

'He's right, Berger,' Aaron agreed, 'I don't believe much in this stuff either, but you don't see me taking the mick. You didn't read it properly.'

'Well, how am I supposed to read it?'

'I don't know… with feeling.'

'What am I supposed to feel? Scared? Hungry? Because right now, I'm both.'

Curtis huffed and puffed. 'Oh, dear lord.'

Nathaniel shrugged and handed Curtis the page.

'Maybe we should get one of the girls to read it. They're in tune with this stuff,' Nathaniel suggested.

'Absolutely not,' Curtis declared.

'Curtis, why don't you try it?' Aaron suggested.

Since Sunday, both Robin and Ashley had told the boys they were not interested in their original plans for the week.

Since Sunday, Ashley had also privately spoken to Curtis, although not in too much detail, as he would expect, but said enough to make it clear that she expected him to stay out of trouble this week as well.

He knew she would not be impressed if he read the spell and anything happened.

But really, what could happen?

Curtis stopped and looked at his friends. He looked at Aaron enthusiastically bent forwards, holding the camera as if he were on Ghost Adventures itself, and at Nathaniel's distracted and uneasy face. Then, he looked behind them to make sure the girls were not headed their way or looking towards their direction.

Then, he held the candle up a tad higher and brought the page closer to his face before he read the words aloud:

"Spell to make one's life endure;
burden break, encounter cure.
As my words you start to see,
radiant health blessed be.

Head to where those living are dead;
leave pasts behind and look ahead.
Summon courage and strength above,
know woeful spirits bind thee in love.

As candle burns, let sickness turn;
Avert ye tomb, ye crypt, ye urn.
Get sinful scythe behind ye first,
let Sainted staff bring blessed birth."

Sat on the cold ground with her head resting on Robin's shoulder, Ashley sighed and shivered as they waited patiently.

'Oh, Robin. I miss him so much,' she said.

'I know, my love,' said Robin, holding Ashley's hand. 'I wish I remembered to bring gloves,' she continued.

'I wish I remembered to bring flowers.'

'Flowers?'

'Yeah. Something. Anything. For my father's grave.'

'Oh.'

'My father's grave!' Ashley shouted. She stood up instantly and pointed towards it. 'Look, Robin! Look!'

In an instant, Robin stood up, too, grabbed Ashley and pulled her back to instinctively protect her from whatever it was that was agitating her so much. But she hadn't seen anything, initially.

Then, both girls gasped as they saw something on Hernando Cruz's gravestone. It looked like an orb, a ball of air, although thicker. And as seconds passed it became even more opaque. A small ball of mist which began to manifest into shape, into an object, which then began to glow.

It was another page from the same book of spells.

'CURTIS!' Ashley called.

But the boys were not far away. They were already running towards them.

Robin and Ashley turned around to see Aaron and Nathaniel already practically in front of them, along with Curtis, gripping something in his hand. A small glowing vial of mysterious liquid the girls, correctly, guessed they must have conjured, along with this second page.

WILLOW

Tuesday 27th October

11:00 AM, Melvin Town Orphanage

It did not take much convincing on Nathaniel's part for the rest of the gang to give up their afternoons in pursuit of their new quest, which Nathaniel grew more and more hopeful about. He was convinced, he ranted, that not only would they manage to find the thief and put a stop to whatever evil plan he had concocted, but that they could successfully return the supernatural book to Willow and Tamarind's protective prison, and that if they just went through the steps quickly enough, they would still be able to enjoy what was left of their vacation.

This, for Nathaniel, now meant having a good time at the Halloween party in town on Friday night or, more accurately, attempting to have a deeper conversation with Fiona Woods now that he was twenty-one and technically *"a man equipped for such things"*, as he put it.

For Ashley, only one word in Nathaniel's entire rant over the group chat that morning resonated with her: *quick*.

She didn't want to feel responsible for dampening anyone's plans on her account, something she was fearful might be remembered and brought up in the future. Also, as much as they would all leave at the end of the week, Willow and Tamarind, as well as the rest of Melvin, would be here and otherwise stuck with a dangerous thief roaming about. Ashley would not allow this to happen.

Nathaniel was right.

Ashley decided to repress the pot of emotions that began to brew in the woods, and which bubbled in all its intensity at the graveyard last night.

She kept her fingers crossed and hoped the next page reading would be as quick as last night's, that they would be onto the next one, if there was one, soon.

When Robin awoke to find Ashley's affirmative, albeit brief and neutral, response that morning; she let herself become excited about the day's upcoming events. Anything, she thought, would be better than dwelling on her situation.

Sat at home in obstinate silence with her fathers as she refreshed her various social media apps, she felt the silence was just pressure for her to decide what to do about a stranger she did not want to acknowledge.

She was game for anything today, especially if it meant helping Willow and Tamarind, as well as the town she loved so much and which, in a few short months, would be her home again.

Aaron struggled.

He struggled to believe what was happening to them, he struggled to explain last night's events and he struggled more than ever to stick to his guns in defending logic, his scientific understanding of the world or even his thoughts on chaos theory—or at the very least a firm belief in mere coincidence.

He did not see Ashley's page appear on her father's grave and certainly not as the girls had described it. He reckoned but did not dare to say, that an accumulation of the past five days had something to do with what they *thought* they saw and that the most logical explanation simply meant someone, probably the mysterious thief, was following them and, for some reason currently unknown to them, leaving pages from the book along with the vial Curtis found on the ground.

Of at least one thing he was sure; something he knew he had to do, something he could control at least. Aaron was more determined than ever to continue filming their exploits, whenever he could, and planned to scan through the footage on his own to see if he could find any stills of the strange man, anything which might enlighten them to his identity and suspicious motives.

Nathaniel would return to his own house at the end of their shenanigans. So, anything that would keep Aaron from having words with his brother and inevitably upsetting their poor mother appealed to him. Once he saw that the girls were down with Nathaniel's plan, he was the next to say yes.

Curtis, however, required more convincing.

He would support Ashley, of course. But he knew that as much as she may not want to admit it, these events affected her more than she would want to let on.

How could Ashley be involved in the search and manage to enjoy the rest of the week as well? Especially considering where the second spell book page would lead them.

They had all discussed it together. Robin's well-received point about the fifth line in the spell convinced them it would be best to venture to the orphanage in Melvin rather than Nathaniel's original suggestion of the pediatric ward at Adam's Hospital, which now made little sense.

So, off they went.

After barely any hours of sleep, after attempting to fill their bellies with food to mask their nerves, and after meeting up outside Curtis' house; they all jumped into Curtis' father's car and made their way to the orphanage.

Once en route, their energy picked up.

The gang pondered potential plans and came up with a final course of action. Robin and Aaron agreed to be the diversion—pretending to be a young couple interested in the adopting process. All the while, Curtis would help Ashley find a quiet spot for her to read the page whilst Nathaniel was the look-out, ready to use his safety word *"Sabotage"* in case any staff members appeared.

The plan was genius. What could go wrong?

'Married? And so young…' the doubtful receptionist said in response to Robin and Aaron's far-fetched ruse.

Luckily, as Aaron panicked, Robin's quick-thinking saved the day.

'Oh, yes,' she started, 'I was so surprised when he popped the question!' Robin showed the lady what she hoped would pass for an engagement ring; cubic zirconia set in plain silver she usually wore on her left middle finger, but which she swiftly switched to her ring finger under the counter seconds before. 'I just knew I wanted to start a big family, right away!'

Shocked but impressed, Aaron smiled and nodded timidly at the receptionist who hesitantly agreed to talk them through the most relevant booklets in the stack of reading materials on the front desk.

Robin touched the tip of her right thumb and index finger by her side; signaling *"okay"* to her three friends sat in the waiting area just behind them.

So, as the young newlyweds continued to distract the receptionist, Curtis, Ashley, and Nathaniel stood up and strutted through the foyer before ducking behind a corner and darting through the hall in search of a secluded area to perform the spell.

'Ugh, this place looked smaller from the outside!' an increasingly exasperated Ashley complained as they passed what seemed like endless corridors lined with countless doors.

'Wait! How about here?' Curtis suggested, stopping in front of what would be a dead-end if not for a fire-exit door.

'I mean, it's a whole safety hazard to block the door,' Nathaniel chimed in.

Curtis and Ashley shot him an infuriated stare.

'Okay, fine. But hurry up!' Nathaniel backed away and stopped in an adjacent corridor in front of a wall lined with framed photographs he pretended to curiously examine while he kept an eye on his periphery.

Curtis took the page from his back pocket and placed it in Ashley's hands, which he held for a moment before releasing them. 'Okay, hon. I'm here for you. You can do this,' he reassured her.

Ashley eyed the words one last time, feeling familiar with the flow of it all. 'I can do this. I can do this,' she whispered to herself. Then, she took a deep breath, summoning the strength to read the spell and quickly.

She held up the page and started to read, quietly but decisively. As she did, she began to feel something. She wondered whether Curtis had experienced this the night before. An odd but not uncomfortable tingling she sensed spreading outwards. *"It's working,"* she thought.

But as she continued, the tingling sensation left her body and became tension instead. Hot, uncomfortable pressure like hands on her stomach weighing her down, pulling her down. They were not hers, of course. They felt alien and foreign and inhuman; long and spindly and strong. Pushing and reaching down, reaching in, pulling, and tugging at her insides. She could feel them move inside her and it hurt more than any average cramp, more than anything most people have ever felt, a specific type of pain Ashley knew all too well. And though this was the third time she had felt this way in her life, this was already the second time this week.

'Enough!' Ashley shouted.

Ashley would not let herself cry. Not there anyway. And she would not finish the spell. Nothing was worth this.

She let the page drop from her hands and bolted past Curtis and Nathaniel before it hit the floor.

Aaron gazed at a booklet Robin held open between them whilst the receptionist went about her tasks. His legs bounced. He did not blink. He fidgeted with the edges of the strings of his sweater and then rubbed his palms along his jeans.

'I wonder how they're doing,' he whispered.

Robin looked up from the booklet like a meerkat, but there was no sign of their friends.

The receptionist had disappeared from behind her desk and emerged in the hallway on her way to a nearby door.

All the while, the weighty hands of the large clock above the main door clicked the time away.

Aaron immediately slumped back into the chair and Robin dropped the pamphlets onto the already covered coffee table in front of them. But more time passed, and they were still alone.

Robin stopped fiddling with her rings to place a hand on Aaron's knee, which she could feel begin to twitch next to her. *"It'll be fine,"* she mouthed. *"Hopefully,"* she thought. Then she yawned and settled further into her seat. She let her head fall back as she looked up and let her eyes relax as they trailed over the many bumps on the ceiling.

She was surprised at how well she was handling being where she was, considering. Truth be told, she was too tired to feel either way about anything right now.

Robin felt as though she would soon succumb to the flooding wave of exhaustion she had been battling all morning, all year even. An accumulation of tension she could not wait to release when she could finally move back home.

It would be an end to endless months of solitude, of mountains of books and scattered notes, and an ironic eternity of time management seminars amidst badly organized shifts and erratic sleeping patterns.

Robin's eyelids lowered to the rhythmic ticking of the clock. How cool would it be, she thought, to be able to control time? Perhaps by obtaining some obscure device with such a power. Like the stopwatches you would see advertised in comic books as a child. Stop-watches you could buy if you wanted a small, fragile, plastic non-time-controlling watch to arrive at your door six to eight weeks after sending a few quarters with a page clipping in the mail. One of those cartoon ones featured in an episode of a family show where the protagonist gets their hands on one and proceeds to get into all sorts of hijinks. If she had one, she thought, she would use it to speed up time. To a year from now when she would be completely settled and able to look forward to a normal Halloween filled with spooky trilogies and freshly baked cookies covered in brightly colored icing, rather than spell book pages and mysterious strangers.

Seeing the surveillance tape yesterday—watching a strange man walk in and out of *PB* like he owned the place—just reminded Robin of the stranger looming in her own life. She felt violated and wanted more than anything for things to just be as they were. For everyone. Especially Ashley, who had been through enough.

Almost instantly, as if Robin's thoughts manifested into reality—further proof that we are all living in one giant simulation, Nathaniel would argue—Ashley's fierce stomps interrupted Robin's reverie.

Robin and Aaron sat up instantly.

But Ashley did not look at them. She pushed through the main door and left, unsuccessfully attempting to hold back a river of frantic tears.

Curtis soon followed, lumbering closely behind.

'Ashley,' he called. Then, he was gone too.

Robin stood up and stood still, unsure of what to do, or how to help.

Aaron joined her. Simultaneously unsure and uncomfortable, he half pat and half rubbed the center of her shoulder blades. 'I guess that didn't go well.'

Robin shrugged. 'I guess not.'

'Where's Berger?'

Robin shrugged again.

Eventually, Nathaniel came through the corridor and walked towards them with the spell book page in hand.

'Did she do it?' Aaron asked.

'She started to,' Nathaniel replied.

'What happened?'

'I don't know.'

'What do you mean?'

Nathaniel shrugged.

'Did she spaz out?'

'Hmm, I wouldn't say that.'

'Why not?' Aaron demanded.

'Because I don't think you can say that nowadays.'

'What are you talking about?'

'You know, *spaz*. Like, *retard* and stuff. It's offensive.'

'Berger…'

'What? It's the future, Aaron, move forward with us.'

'Berger, I swear to God.'

Robin noticed a curious lady make her way towards a door, stop and stare towards the group.

'Guys,' she whispered, gesturing at the air between them as if it would cut their petty debate in half, 'go and take the page to *PB*,' she told them.

'Aren't you coming with us?' Aaron asked.

'I'll meet you there. Just let me put an end to our little ruse.'

Nathaniel gave the page to Aaron who carefully folded and pocketed it in one fluid motion. Then, they both made their way out the door to *PB*, where they would ask the Dodson sisters for some direction.

Robin walked towards the woman—making sure to step into her line of sight and distract her from her bickering friends as they left.

'I'm sorry for the noise,' Robin started, 'Adoption, huh? Such a controversial topic for everyone, isn't it?'

The false and exaggerated smile on Robin's face died out as the woman's intensely furrowed brow persisted for an inordinate amount of time.

'Right. Well, apologies again,' Robin said in a definite tone.

'Wait,' said the woman as Robin turned to leave, 'Don't I know you?' she asked.

Robin searched her memory but could not place her. However, the more she stood in her presence, the more Robin felt there was a vague sense of familiarity about her. Something in the sternness of her eyes as she looked down at her.

'I don't think so.'

'What's your surname?' the woman demanded.

'Wilson,' Robin answered like a puppy barking on cue. She was shocked at how direct and audacious this stranger was being. She was even more surprised at how her attitude brought Robin into immediate submission.

'Ah, you're Christopher's daughter,' the woman concluded, correctly.

'Oh,' Robin breathed. The tension in her neck and the top of her spine dissipated. She no longer felt as though she were in trouble. 'Yes, yes I am,' she answered.

'You're quite a young woman now, aren't you?' said the woman through what Robin assumed was meant to be a smile.

Robin smiled in response, trying to think of how she could end this awkward encounter and join her friends without seeming rude to someone who might be a friend of her father's.

The woman signaled with her outstretched finger. 'Come.' She walked past the door she had been keen to enter and made her way through the corridor, turning right into another and then left into another.

Like a trained puppy, Robin trailed the woman who had not introduced herself or made any effort to explain just why she was summoning Robin through a maze of narrow halls and framed monochrome moments of the past.

'Did my Dad organize an event at the museum for the kids here?' she wondered out loud, 'Did you need me to pass on a message to him?' she asked.

The woman simply shook her head dismissively.

When they eventually stopped, the woman pointed towards a photograph on the wall.

Robin glanced at it, nodded, and smiled back at her.

Seconds passed in silence.

'You've worked here for quite a while I take it?' Robin said, noticing the same woman in the photograph, sat in the middle of a group of children. She looked young and less careworn. It must have been taken nearly twenty years ago, Robin thought. Then, she realized her question might be considered rude; an indirect and seemingly passive-aggressive statement on the woman's appearance and apparent aging, on the evident passing of time on her face.

She panicked.

But before she could find a hurried compliment, the woman pointed again.

'No. Look,' she said, with the tip of her index finger hovering over one particular person. A small, ginger babe sat atop the woman's lap, smiling, and reaching their hand out towards the camera. 'You were so young, Robin. I didn't think you would remember your time here.'

Robin's stomach fluttered. Her arms and shoulders prickled with goosebumps. She looked closer. It was her. Of course, it was her.

'You were a delight. Really. Always happy. Always talkative,' the woman elaborated, 'You didn't know your words yet, but you sure as heck found a way to babble about whatever was going on around you. Everyone loved holding you. Such a sweet child.'

Robin lifted the frame from the nail on the wall and held it. She gripped its edges as if it might disappear, as if it might cease to exist; this surreal reality, this captured tale.

As she stared at her young self, reaching out towards her, she felt as though through some bizarre time-loop she was trying to convey something powerful to herself, now, as if to reveal some comforting secret from a time before this life, before these problems, these worries.

On the bottom of the photograph near the edge of the frame was a faded label that read: *"Miss. Bennett, group 3B, summer 1995"*. Robin read it over in her mind. She would have been two years old. Then, something clicked; like a key turning a lock deep inside her.

'Emma,' she said.

The woman beamed back. 'That's right. You tried your best to say it. I'm sure of it. You would just purse your beautiful little lips and say *"muh"*. Sometimes it would come out as *"muh-muh"*.' Ms. Bennett laughed as she looked up in thought. Then she continued, 'We would try to teach you, all of you, a variety of easy words here and there. Some of the girls thought you were trying to say *"Mamma"*, but I knew better. I knew what you meant.'

Robin continued to look down at the photo. She saw a droplet of water appear on the glass. And then another. Then, she saw barely anything as her eyes continued to well up.

Ms. Bennet took the frame, put it in its place on the wall, and then put her arm around Robin. 'Come, dear,' she said.

She led her back to where they had stood at the beginning of the conversation and opened a door to a mid-sized office, continuing to lead Robin until she was sat down in one of two armchairs facing a large desk. Then, she sat in a chair on the opposite side of the desk and reached over to hand Robin a Kleenex box, which Robin promptly took.

As Robin dried her tears with the soft tissues and tried to compose herself, Ms. Bennett struggled in the chair opposite her—bending over first to her left and then to her right. After opening and closing two drawers, she finally found what she was searching for. A brown folder she flicked through and nodded at before placing on the desk in front of Robin.

Robin tried not to become overcome with emotion, but this déjà vu was not helping.

'Now,' Ms. Bennett started, 'I've spoken to both your fathers recently. Quite a few times. And they've confided in me, naturally. I know you're not keen on the situation, Robin, but I think it's important that you think carefully before you decide, either way. And I'm always here for you, dear, if you ever need to talk.'

Robin did not know what to say. She merely clung to the box of tissues and stared down at the folder on the desk.

Luckily, she was saved by the bell, or door as it were, as after three light knocks another lady opened the door and poked her head through the gap.

'Oop, sorry, I didn't realize—'

'I'm busy,' Ms. Bennett stated.

'Yes, I'm so sorry, but you're needed—'

'Not now.'

'But Mrs. Watts said the Jones family are on the phone about, y' know, and I'm not sure I can—'

Ms. Bennett scoffed, stood up, and marched towards the door.

'Won't be a moment, Robin,' she said.

Robin nodded. And waited. And stared, at first into nothingness, then finally at the vexatious folder on the desk.

Perhaps, she thought, if she stared hard enough, it might burst into flames and out of her life.

Extraordinarily, and once again, Robin's arbitrary thought was given life by some unseen force.

At first, she thought her sight was still being affected by the resilient onset of tears, but she quickly realized what she was seeing in front of her was real, baffling though it was.

A soft, hovering flame took form above the folder. Stable, it steadily morphed and transformed into a larger shape, a rectangular shape, and maintained its new form for seconds before changing color. Red and orange to bright gold and then solid, blinding white. Then, as it stopped burning, it lowered onto the folder from where it hovered centimeters above it.

It was another page from the spell book.

Robin stood up quickly. Then, she patted it with cautious fingertips and found it was not hot. Then, she grabbed it and tossed it inside the folder, which she held close to her torso.

Robin crept up to the door of the office, opened it, slowly and only just, and peeked across the hallway. Once she confirmed Ms. Bennett and her colleague were nowhere to be seen, Robin took the opportunity and made herself scarce.

12:30 PM, ***Paranormal Booktivity***

Although, not as busy as the morning rush where patrons filled their thermoses with freshly brewed coffee before heading to their respective workplaces; lunchtime was still a busy period at *PB*.

There were few tables and booths, but most were filled with locals taking a break to eat warmed panini and a delicious slice of Tamarind's cake or pie of the day.

As Willow and Tamarind rushed around to clear the remaining line of patiently waiting customers, Aaron and Nathaniel sat in their group's booth with two sandwiches, a *PB* latte for Aaron and hot cocoa for Nathaniel.

Nathaniel drank out of his DC mug, of course, and enjoyed his meal whilst Aaron, who had barely touched his food, panicked next to him—scrolling through his phone; refreshing pages on different messaging apps to see whether Curtis had responded to any of his messages or whether there was an update from Robin.

There was nothing from either of them.

Tamarind took the last order and payment and left the rest with her sister, eager for the boys to regale her with the morning's happenings. She scooped up Jefferson from where he perched on the counter and squeezed into the booth next to Nathaniel, cheekily taking a potato chip from his plate as she sat down.

Willow carefully handed the last patrons their mugs of hot beverages and looked over her shop, at everyone sat comfortably, chatting away in their respective groups, or reading alone, enjoying their lunch.

She nodded, pleased with herself, and wiped her hands on a tartan tea towel which she folded and put away before adjusting her apron. Then, she made her way to join her sister and the boys.

'So?' she said, sliding in next to Aaron.

'Nothing yet,' he said.

'Poor Ashley,' said Tamarind, 'I do hope she's okay.'

'I'm sure she is,' Nathaniel guessed.

'She looked really upset,' said Aaron, keeping an eye on his phone. 'What happened back there?'

'Well,' Nathaniel started, 'we found a spot. A hidden spot. Like, a hidey-hole but, y' know, out in the open. And then Ashley started to read the spell. But she stopped. She stopped, dropped the page, and then left. And obviously, Curtis ran after her.'

'Oh, dear. I wonder what happened,' said Willow.

Tamarind held Jefferson close to her chin, stroking it on his forehead before giving him a series of smooches. 'Poor Ashley,' she said again in a sing-song voice as if talking through Jefferson, 'I don't think her sensitive soul is adept at these things. Dark arts and such.'

'Are any of us?' said Willow.

The four paused in thought.

Aaron sighed. 'I didn't think this week would take such a toll on us.'

'I think it's been fun. Mostly,' said Nathaniel.

Willow smiled at Nathaniel's perpetual joie de vivre, which she always admired. She brought Aaron's head into her shoulder and gave it another pat; hoping her soothing touch would preemptively shield him from any irritation brought on by Nathaniel's general way of being, which she knew he was too tense to appreciate now.

'Everything except for that creepy graveyard. And that even creepier vial,' Nathaniel continued.

'Vial?' Willow inquired.

'Curtis found a vial of liquid in the cemetery last night after he read from his page and just before the girls found the second page on Ashley's father's grave,' Aaron explained.

'Found?' Willow pressed.

'Indeed,' said Tamarind, 'how curious.'

'Actually,' Nathaniel started, 'that creepy vial kind of appeared at his feet. Just like the girls said the page did.'

'Is that right?' said Willow, shooting her sister an intrigued look.

'Yeah, but we didn't see anything like that,' Aaron insisted.

'Well, actually, you were too busy looking through your camera lens,' Nathaniel clarified.

'Curiouser and curiouser!' Tamarind cried, rather theatrically.

'I do love a good book quote,' Willow interjected.

Tamarind grinned. 'I know right!'

'Anyway, it was a strange night,' Aaron started, 'I don't blame Ashley for still being on edge.'

'Creepy is what it was,' Nathaniel persisted, 'Did you get to check your footage today at all?'

Aaron shook his head. 'Not yet. But I brought my camera with me. We can have a look now if you want. See if I caught anything.'

'As long as it's not a ghost.'

Aaron scoffed dismissively. 'More like a shot of that man in the background. He's probably been following us. That sick jerk. He probably left the vial and the page for us to find.'

'You're sounding almost as paranoid as me. I like it.'

'Right,' said Willow, sliding out of the booth, 'You guys look through the footage from last night and let us know if you find anything.'

'And keep an eye out for messages from the rest of the gang,' Tamarind reminded them.

The customers had spent the last of their lunch breaks in the familiar comfort of *PB* and cleared out as quickly as they had arrived. The only people who remained, apart from the owners, of course, were Nathaniel, Aaron, and Robin.

Robin had arrived just before 13:00 PM, soaked from head to toe. It had started to rain rather heavily on her walk back from the orphanage, she explained.

Predictably, Willow rushed her upstairs to borrow her hairdryer; lest she catch a cold, she warned. Then, Robin left her denim jacket on a heater to dry while she warmed herself with a nice blanket and a cup of hot cocoa Tamarind whipped up before returning downstairs to keep a watchful eye on the boys as they continued to weed through the videos and photos Aaron took the night before.

While they were busy investigating, Robin became toasty and at ease. But when Willow naturally inquired after the folder, Robin explained that she had protected it as best she could, clutching it on the inside of her jacket on her way there. She had since left it on the edge of Willow's bed, and it was mostly intact if not for a couple of damp, tattered edges.

Willow was still curious, though, as to the contents, and she could not be lied to.

Before this week, Willow was the only woman Robin knew cared for her at any point during her life. And even after today, she was still the most important woman in Robin's life. Her only mother.

So, she told her everything. All about her fathers' confession. About every emotion weighing her down the past few days. She told Willow about the random person only now seeking a place in her life. She described her encounter with Ms. Bennett at the orphanage and how vulnerable she felt. And how she, still, after all this, did not know what to do.

She told her everything.

'You know,' Willow started after a few thoughtful moments, 'Tamarind and I don't share the same parents. And for the longest time, from quite early on, we learned that we could only really count on each other. And that was okay.

'Tamarind and I don't need to share the same blood to be sisters. I don't need to look like her or sound like her for her to love me for who I am. She showed me that, first thing.

'Lord knows she doesn't need to close the toothpaste cap or wash the floors for me to love her.'

Robin sniggered under her breath as Willow smiled and wrapped her arms around her.

'At the end of the day,' Willow continued, 'We know what counts. We're so grateful to have a support system no matter what form it's in. We're lucky. Not everybody has that, you know?'

Robin cried into Willow's loving embrace and soaked up her kind, supportive words.

She had made no suggestions, but merely reminded Robin of what she already knew; that no matter what, she was well and truly loved. And although she was no closer to making her decision, Robin felt a million times better.

Willow had dried Robin's tears. They walked hand in hand down the wooden steps of *PB* to happily find Curtis and Ashley as well as Tamarind, Aaron, and Nathaniel.

'Ashley!' Robin called. She ran over to her best friend, crouched over her in the booth, and held her tight. 'Are you okay?'

Ashley nodded. 'Better,' she said simply.

'What happened to you?' Nathaniel asked Robin.

'I found something,' said Robin.

'At the orphanage?' Aaron asked

Robin nodded. 'Mhm,' she confirmed, before pulling the page out of her jacket pocket. She placed it on the table for everyone to pass around and squeezed into the booth next to Ashley.

'Another page from the book,' said Nathaniel.

'It certainly looks like it,' said Robin.

'Ooh! How exciting!' said Tamarind, dragging a stool close to the table and sitting on it to observe as the group passed the page around.

'How is that possible?' Curtis asked, 'Ashley didn't finish reading *her* page.'

'Yeah,' Ashley started, 'This is too confusing.'

'Hmm. I don't think it is from the spell book, though,' Aaron weighed in.

'How do you figure?' Nathaniel asked.

'Well, it's blank.'

'Yeah,' Curtis started, 'but it looks all old and scary like the other two.'

'How can a page be scary?' Aaron judged.

'Oh,' Nathaniel started, turning his torso towards Aaron, staring him down, '*it can*,' he whispered.

Ashley sniggered and tutted. Then she took Robin's page once more and inspected it fully. She looked at its corners, she held it up to the light to see if there was anything visible, any small writing or symbols or figures. But she could see nothing. 'I don't know about this one.'

'I know it's from the book,' said Robin.

'How can you be sure?' asked Aaron.

'Because it's old and creepy, right?' Curtis insisted.

Robin hesitated to describe how the page appeared to her. The boys would vote to have her institutionalized. Ashley might believe her—especially after what they witnessed last night at her father's grave—but how useful would that be, considering her state of mind?

Willow—who had heard Robin's story and believed every word—placed a hand on her shoulder as she smiled down at her. 'Go on, Robin. Tell the gang what you told me,' she prompted.

Robin looked at her friends and found the courage to speak her truth, no matter how crazy she might sound.

'Well,' she started, 'I was in a room with… I was in a room waiting and I just… I started thinking about fire, I guess.'

'Fire? Why?' Nathaniel interrupted.

'Go on, Robin,' said Curtis.

'Yeah, what happened?' Aaron asked.

'Well, I saw a flame. It just appeared in the room and changed shape right in front of me.'

'Like that ball of mist?' Ashley asked.

'Exactly. Just like that. But it was on fire. And it just changed shape, into the page. But then the page stopped being on fire if that makes sense. I touched it and it wasn't hot. So, I just took it and got out of there.'

Aaron exhaled. 'Wow.'

'Gosh. I wish I could have been there to see that,' said Nathaniel, 'Was it spooky?'

'I guess so. It was weird. Very weird.'

The group thought for a few moments.

'So, if it's a page from the book,' Curtis reasoned, 'why is it blank?'

Ashley shrugged, handing the page to Curtis who inspected it one last time before placing it in the center of the table.

'I've been thinking about this since I left that place,' said Robin, 'I think it's to do with the trail.'

'Trail?' Willow asked.

'This trail of breadcrumbs we're on. I think I found the third page because we were in the right place. We all guessed the right place to enact the second spell. So, that's where I found mine. Just like Ashley found hers after Curtis read his. Only, Ashley didn't read hers. She didn't finish the spell.'

'Ooh,' Nathaniel howled as Robin's epiphany hit.

'That's why it's blank. It's yours, and you're next, but it won't let you read it until Ashley's reads hers,' Curtis deduced.

'It won't *let* her?' Aaron pressed.

Robin nodded and then shrugged, semi-sure in her train of thought but utterly unconfident in the situation.

Ashley clapped her hands together and huffed.

'Santa Maria,' she exclaimed, exasperated.

'Ashley can't be expected to go through that ordeal again, surely,' Tamarind asserted.

The rest of the gang awaited her response by looking down in awkward anticipation.

'And, just so we're all clear, what ordeal was that again?' Nathaniel asked innocently enough.

'Berger…' Aaron warned, shaking his head and cringing after seeing a glimpse of Curtis' protective red face and clenched jaw.

'What? We still don't know what happened. And you heard Robin. It's our next step. We can all sneak in tonight after closing. We'll be together then; we can help Ashley get through it if she's scared.'

Ashley was touched by Nathaniel's kind words, his endearing thought process. She felt Robin's hand rub the inside of her left arm, and Curtis' left hand rub her right knee. She looked over at Tamarind's worried face, at Willow's patient smile, and, lastly, at Aaron's anxious expression.

'I'm not scared,' she said. And she meant it. How could she be when she was surrounded by such love?

Ashley took Robin's brave example and decided to be honest with her friends, her family. She would tell them about what had happened to her—to both her and Curtis—hoping they would understand, knowing they would support her through every choked word.

And, of course, they did.

Robin and Curtis pushed locks of hair to either side as they stroked Ashley's arms and back. Aaron and Nathaniel took one hand each and caressed Ashley's palms, her knuckles, her fingertips. Willow and Tamarind held each other and let tears fall freely as they heard Ashley speak words from a broken heart about the baby she had lost not that long ago. She could even feel the warmth of Jefferson's fur on her ankles and mustered a weak smile at the thought of him trying to be there for her, too.

Now, everyone was on the same page. And no one would force Ashley to do anything she was not comfortable with. That gave Ashley all the strength in the world.

It would be more than enough to do what she told her friends she was determined to do; to read every word from the enchanted page and enact the spell in the orphanage that same night.

20:00 PM, Melvin Town Orphanage

Ashley had made her decision. Usually, this involved everyone else following suit like dutiful children. This time, however, the group moved as one force towards their fate with an air of optimistic fortitude.

It seemed, perhaps rather unsurprisingly, that their afternoon at *PB* did them all some good.

After an evening of comfort food and diverting time with their families, they joined and made their way through the dark streets of Melvin to its center, towards the orphanage.

And someone, or something, must have been looking out for them; because although it had rained all afternoon and all evening, it had stopped minutes before they were scheduled to meet.

Moreover, when they got to the premises, as they looked around for any back entrances or unsecured gates, Nathaniel quickly noticed that one door seemed to be purposefully left wide open for them. It was almost as if someone knew they were coming and wanted to help.

They took the opportunity and snuck in as quietly as they could.

Upon entering, Nathaniel realized and mentioned, in hushed tones, that the same door which had been left open was the fire-exit door Ashley had tried to read the spell in front of that very morning.

Even in the darkness, Ashley recognized that corner of the building. It was the same spot she had hid from staff members, alongside Curtis and Nathaniel, only this time there was no rush. She could take as long as she needed. This time, she had her friends for support, should she need it.

'Okay,' she whispered, nodding to Curtis.

He nodded back, handed her the page, and gave her cheek a soft, comforting peck.

Ashley held the page close to her face as Nathaniel shone a light from his phone in her general direction and as Aaron filmed, just in case.

Then, she looked up and saw Robin. "*You can do this,*" she mouthed.

Ashley nodded again.

Of course, she could.

She thought of every single part of her. The long line of suffering in her past that made her who she was. The pure resilience of her strong Spanish blood. The example her mother gave her every day. The memory of her dear father. Her friends. Willow and Tamarind. She thought of Curtis, her absolute heart, her other half, without which she knew she would not be able to handle this or anything else.

As she thought about Curtis, her heart filled with love until there was no place for fear or longing or loss.

Ashley stood up straight began to read:

"Spell to rid life's fixed torment;
bring new day, end night's lament.
As my words you start to see,
second chance blessed be.

Head to where young babes be reared;
watch worried pasts disappear.
Summon courage and strength above,
know hopeful spirits bind thee in love.

As flora grows, all mothers glow;
forget ye grief, ye guilt, ye woes.
Get glooming thoughts behind ye first,
let true love's kiss bring blessed birth."

She had done it. But barely any moments passed before Ashley could let it sink in because all she could see was Robin's hand waving frantically a few feet in front of her.

It seemed that as soon as Ashley had said the last word, *"birth"*, words instantly began to appear on Robin's page.

An immense sense of relief washed over Ashley as Nathaniel pointed the light from his phone's torch in Robin's direction instead.

It was over, Ashley thought. Her part anyway. And she was thankful for that.

'We better get out of here,' Curtis whispered, eager to get Ashley home now that she had kept her promise.

They could all discuss Robin's page once they were away, once they were no longer illegally trespassing.

In unison, they turned around and faced the door.

But as Ashley stepped forward to join them, she grabbed Curtis on her right and Aaron on her left.

'Are you okay?' Aaron called instinctually, louder than he ought to have done.

'Did you trip?' Curtis whispered, holding her steady.

'I think I tripped over something,' Ashley said, bending over to feel her ankle.

Her fingertips ran over a sliver of fresh, stinging blood. Something scratched her. But what could have caused it?

Nathaniel lowered his phone, shining its light onto the ground, and everyone gathered round to find a small toy near Ashley's feet.

Nathaniel picked it up. 'Maybe one of the kids left this here?' he guessed.

'This is the office area, isn't it?' Curtis whispered, 'They wouldn't have toys here.'

'No. They wouldn't. I summoned it,' Ashley said, taking it from Nathaniel.

She held the toy in the palm of her hand. It was a jack-in-the-box. Quite small and brightly colored on all sides albeit slightly faded.

Ashley remembered her father giving it to her as a young girl. She would turn the crank on the side and after a few seconds of playful music, a small fabric clown would pop out and smile at her.

She remembered her mother throwing it out when she was a child after it stopped working. She wondered whether it would work now and was terrified at the thought of what might pop out instead.

But she had made it this far.

Ashley could feel her heartbeat hard inside her chest. She turned the crank for what seemed like forever until the entire group heard a loud bang. But no clown popped up. And it was nothing scary, seemingly.

It was a rectangular card decorated in light pastels.

It read; *"You are cordially invited to Ashley Cruz's and Curtis Jones' baby shower."*

23:40 PM, 8 Almond Avenue

Lying in bed with only the soft light from his camera shining onto his face—Aaron went through the last of the footage from Monday night.

As he sped through what he and Nathaniel had already analyzed earlier that day, a memory popped up into his mind. He remembered a time when he was much younger and struggled to sleep, too. He had asked his dad to read him an extra bedtime story one evening, and his dad suggested Aaron try counting sheep instead, saying; 'It helps some folks.' When Aaron asked whether it ever worked for him, his dad merely answered; 'Nope.'

After a giggle, a hug, and a kiss; an infant Aaron fell asleep that night with no sheep.

That's how Aaron Jackson was raised.

His parents never sugar-coated anything for him or his brother. They grew up questioning, learning, and debating.

No one was surprised when Aaron announced his college major choice in high school. He had always been keen to explore the challenging complexities of the world around him.

Aaron's interest in math and science piqued early. He won countless medals and awards over the years. Then, his curiosity for mystery novels and horror movies came later, followed by the joy of filming and the chilling thrills of performing amateur paranormal investigations with his friends as he got older.

As he surpassed predictable pre-pubescent angsts, Aaron's firm and rapidly formed sense of self seemed to radiate outwards and return with all manner of solutions, explanations, and theories he could put his faith in.

Now, though, he was less sure.

Alas, it is all too easy to be confident in one's youth. That is until something unfortunate should happen to rock that certainty.

Beyond thoughts of his ailing father, hostile brother, distressed mother, and apprehensive friends; something Aaron managed to catch on camera would surely put an end to any hope of him sleeping that night—something he noticed flicker in the bottom right-hand corner of the screen before disappearing almost instantly.

Aaron paused it immediately and took great care to rewind the video just enough so as not to miss it.

Then, he sat up, turned on the desk lamp on his bedside table, and magnified the paused image on the screen.

It was as clear as day.

It showed Nathaniel standing on the left, Curtis on the right, and an unknown little girl standing in between them, with her glowing eyes fixed forward, staring towards the lens.

NATHANIEL

Wednesday 28th October

11:00 AM, ***Paranormal Booktivity***

Robin and Nathaniel sat in the group's booth and took turns scrutinizing the latest spell book page as they ate their breakfast.

'I'm stumped,' Nathaniel mumbled.

'It's certainly the strangest we've seen,' said Robin, stroking Jefferson on the seat next to her.

'I bombed with the last one, but this isn't clear at all. I can't figure it out.'

'It's just a series of instructions, like the others.'

'Yeah,' he conceded, 'but what about this line?' he said, pointing at the center of the page.

Robin and Nathaniel scooched closer and zeroed in on the spell, hoping for a lightning bolt. Instead, the trill of the shop's bell signaled the arrival of another friend.

It was Aaron.

Nathaniel finished his last bite and wiped his mouth. 'Hey bud,' he said.

'Good morning, Aaron,' said Robin, sitting up.

Aaron took his damp windbreaker off and hung it on the coatrack by the door. It had been drizzling all morning after raining all night. 'I'm sorry I'm late, guys.'

'Have a seat, buddy,' Nathaniel directed, patting the space next to him.

'Any coffee?' Willow hollered as she swept the floor.

'Or a nice pastry?' Tamarind called from behind the counter.

Aaron shook his head and slid into the booth next to Nathaniel.

'Did you have something at home?' Tamarind pressed.

Aaron shook his head again.

'You don't look too good,' said Robin.

'I didn't get much sleep last night.'

'Well,' Tamarind stepped in, 'it was a full moon last night! I know because I put out several mason jars full of water to charge them with moonlight.'

'What would you need moon-charged-water for?' Robin asked.

'Spells,' Tamarind said simply.

'Ugh,' Aaron grunted, 'not more spells.'

'Hey bud,' Nathaniel started, 'speaking of spells, help us figure out this next spell, won't you?'

Aaron's face dropped.

'Maybe that'll wake you up,' Nathaniel suggested, 'It's a humdinger!'

'Wait,' Robin started, 'tell us what's wrong.'

Aaron looked at Robin, but no words came out. He was too tired, and it was all too much. If he could, he'd relay everything telepathically to save the energy. But he couldn't, and merely shrugged instead.

'We can just chill today,' she suggested, 'I heard from Ashley and Curtis this morning. They'll spend the day together. We should take a break, too. Get some snacks, watch some movies...'

Nathaniel groaned. 'Aww. What about the spell? We have a thief to thwart, a mystery to solve, a quest afoot!'

'And a ghost, apparently,' Aaron declared after a deep sigh.

Nathaniel scoffed. 'Yeah, right.'

'No. Seriously,' Aaron stated.

'Wait, what?' said Robin

'WHAT?!' Nathaniel shouted.

Aaron didn't bring his camera. Not today.

He'd had enough of filming, for now. Still, he did use his phone to take a photo of the eerie, once in a lifetime image he managed to obtain and brought it up to show his friends.

They huddled around in silence as Aaron zoomed into the translucent likeness of a doleful girl standing in between Nathaniel and Curtis in the cemetery.

Tamarind and Willow looked at each other and nodded. 'Margaret Bishop,' they asserted in unison.

'Li'l Maggie,' Robin whispered.

Nathaniel shivered dramatically. 'No. Way.'

'Who have you shown this to?' Robin asked.

'Just you guys.'

'Good. Don't you dare show Ashley. Or Curtis. Yet.'

'Yet?' Nathaniel asked, 'Try *ever*. They'll freak. Heck, I'm freaking. What the heck are we supposed to do with this information?'

Aaron shrugged.

Robin grabbed Aaron's phone. 'Would you look at that? It's just so clear. It couldn't be anything else.'

Willow took the phone from Robin. 'Well, what do you expect to see in a graveyard?'

'True,' said Tamarind. Then she took the phone and zoomed in. 'Aww, I hope she's all right. The poor dear, she's been through so much.'

Robin looked up at Tamarind and raised an eyebrow, and Nathaniel made a series of disapproving noises. Even Jefferson took his leave, and Aaron said nothing.

'I don't know if I even want to do mine now,' Robin confessed, slumping back into her seat.

'You know what I think about all this meshugas,' Willow started.

'Yiddish. Nice,' said Nathaniel.

'Well, I've said it before and I'll say it again,' she continued, 'you guys don't have to involve yourselves in any of this.'

'Yeah,' Tamarind agreed, 'you should all be enjoying your vacation. You've worked so hard.'

'T, we're well past that now,' Aaron said somberly.

'Come on,' Nathaniel started, 'you gloomy gusses! We can do this. Come on, Robin. You'll be fine. We just need to figure out where to go for this one. That line right there,' he persisted, tapping at the page in Robin's hand.

'May I?' Aaron offered, holding out his hand.

Robin hesitated slightly before handing it over. Then, she watched as his eyes scanned the words thoughtfully. His expression altered from exhaustion to exasperation.

'Okay, Willow? Maybe I will have a coffee,' he said.

Nathaniel chortled and patted Aaron's back. 'Ha-ha, that's the spirit! Another round, Willow,' he said, waving his index finger in a circular motion.

After a few laughs and a couple of refills, they were back at it, determinedly, to figure out their next steps.

'It's asking you to hold your breath, Robin,' Aaron said, relatively sure of himself, after another look.

'The question is, for how long?' Nathaniel urged.

Robin nodded. 'Until it starts to hurt, I guess.' She exhaled as if she could feel the discomfort already.

'Oh, no, I don't like that one bit,' said Willow.

'How about you go over it, again, from the beginning?' Tamarind advised.

'Robin?' Willow prompted.

Robin proceeded to read the words out loud, slowly, as everyone gathered around to ponder their meaning.

"Lock both eyes, look with thy heart,
to find the key, the missing part.
Sojourn to your coming home,
lest you become cursed to roam.

Heed these words and do not stop,
until both lungs begin to pop.
Sit in peace and hold your breath,
suffer pangs & avert ye death.

Open yourself to what ye evade,
take in only that which has stayed.
When it's done, you'll surely find,
what you need to leave behind."

Robin waited for a second. Then, another. Then, a few more passed. But nothing happened, again.

No, she was right; reading the words alone would do nothing. They all agreed, she'd have to hold her breath and do so with her eyes closed. That much was clear, but where?

'Have you tried doing it at home?' Tamarind asked.

'I tried reading it a couple of times this morning. But I didn't *do* anything,' Robin answered.

'Maybe you should *really* try,' Nathaniel insisted.

'That might not work either,' Aaron deduced.

'What do you mean?' Robin asked.

'Well, you live in Boston too, right? So, how do we know which house is the "*home*" it's talking about?'

'Or… your "*coming home*" might refer to a location in the future,' Tamarind thought aloud.

'What do you mean, T?' Aaron asked.

'A coming home, like, a home Robin will have in the future,' she elaborated.

'True,' said Willow, nodding.

'How the heck is she supposed to know where that is?' a frustrated Nathaniel demanded.

'Well…' Robin started, 'I kind of *do* know where that will be.'

Nathaniel gasped. '*What*?! News? Gossip? How have I not been informed? Why am I always the last to know?'

'In all fairness, I think I've only told Willow.'

'Willow knows and I don't know?' said Tamarind.

'She only told me yesterday,' Willow defended.

'Told you what? What's this?' Aaron asked, visibly perking up after a large cup of strong coffee.

'I'm moving back to Melvin after graduation. They offered me a position over at Adam's.'

'Adam's Hospital?' Aaron asked.

'Yeah.'

'Oh, Robin, that's wonderful! We'll get to see you every day,' Tamarind exclaimed.

'I don't know about every—'

'Every day!' Tamarind continued, 'Oh, how exciting! Why didn't you tell me?' she asked Willow, who simply shrugged and smiled.

'How long have you known this?' Aaron asked.

'Always. I guess. I mean, I've always wanted to be here. But I spoke to Dr. Warner a few months back, and she made everything… effortless.'

'Who's that?' Nathaniel asked, 'My mom must have taken me to every doctor in that place growing up, I tell you. And if I don't know her, something must be wrong. Maybe she's a ghost too!'

'Dr. Warner is the head of gynecology,' said Robin.

'Oh,' Nathaniel said sheepishly.

Then, everyone laughed. Everyone except for Aaron, evidently still processing the news.

'Why would you want to move back?' he finally said.

Robin thought long and hard. 'Why wouldn't you?' is all she could say.

The Dodsons looked at each other, cringed, and used their sororal, telepathic connection to have their private conversation without butting in.

'Well, I think that's fantastic, Robin,' said Nathaniel, slamming his arms on the table as if he could cut through the tension with his enthusiasm. 'You know what else I think?'

'What, Berger? What else do you think?' said Aaron impatiently.

'I think the next time I have a questionable boil on my back, I won't have to ask your smacked-crab face, I can just send a picture of it to Robin.'

'Or not,' Robin replied.

'But also,' Nathaniel continued, 'I think we should go to the hospital and give it a go, see what happens.'

'That might work,' Willow acknowledged, 'although, I'd prefer to picture you all safe and sound, with full stomachs, watching Scooby-Doo reruns.'

'Not gonna lie, you guys. I'm totally down for some safe Scooby snack fun,' said Nathaniel.

'Maybe later,' Robin compromised. 'So, how about it, Aaron? Are you coming with us?'

'Sure.'

12:00 PM, Adam's Hospital

'Okay. Let's try to find the baby having ward,' Nathaniel whispered.

'The maternity ward?' Robin corrected, 'Why?'

'You'll fit right in.'

'Do I look pregnant?!'

'No, but they have to do all the breathing stuff, right?'

'Lamaze,' Aaron stated.

'Yeah, they breathe in and out. I just have to hold my breath. I'll look like a frigging lunatic!'

'Okay, the psych ward then. Wait, do they still have psych wards? Like, asylums? Or did they all close down?'

'Hmm… no, I think they still have psych wards,' said Aaron.

'Right,' Nathaniel pondered, 'but I bet they call 'em "*Mental Health*" wards or something, right? All politically correct and such.'

Nathaniel tapped the forearm of a uniformed lady rushing past them in the opposite direction. 'Excuse me, ma'am,' he said as they all halted, 'where would I go if I were crazy?'

'Pardon?' said the stunned nurse.

'Sorry. Where would I go if I had *severe mental health issues*?' Nathaniel persisted.

'*Berger*,' Aaron reprimanded.

'I'm sorry,' Robin intervened, 'we don't plan to have him sectioned until *after* lunch. Excuse us.'

Robin took the lead, marching through corridors as the boys followed swiftly behind her.

'I don't think we'll find a quiet spot in a hospital, you guys,' she said, 'We have to look inconspicuous. Like visitors. There's gotta be a waiting room nearby.'

'What about the cafeteria?' said Aaron, pointing to a sign on the wall in front of them, signaling a left turn.

'Perfect!' Robin asserted, 'We'll be in and out in no time.'

'So… there's no time for Jell-O?' Nathaniel asked.

They stopped at the main entrance to the cafeteria, noticing how crowded it was.

'Here,' Aaron directed towards a small circular table with two chairs, 'sit there. I'll see if I can find a spare.'

Robin and Nathaniel sat down.

Aaron made his way through the cafeteria. He snaked through tables—narrowly avoiding people carrying trays and holding the elbows of elderly relatives—in search of an empty chair.

But he could not find one.

When he reached the archway on the other side of the dining hall, he looked towards his friends and considered whether he ought to go back through the maze empty-handed or continue to look.

Perhaps he could wait for one to become free. But Robin would probably be done during that time.

Perhaps he could find a simpler way to reach them by walking around the outside, through the hospital corridors, and back again to the main entrance.

As he stood in thought, someone bumped into his side, nearly making him buckle at the knees.

He turned around to the sound of giggling and shoes squeaking on the vinyl flooring. A mere child, playing.

Aaron stepped back from the archway and leaned forwards but saw no one. Maybe they had slipped past him and through the cafeteria.

Aaron turned around and looked for his friends, who were still sitting near the entrance. Robin had her head bowed as Nathaniel looked around nervously. They were trying to enact the spell.

"I better hurry," he thought.

But when Aaron turned around again to find a short cut, he bumped into a little girl.

'Oh, sorry, sweetie,' he said instinctually.

She looked up at him and said nothing.

Aaron looked down and tried to place her.

The faint smile on his face left.

Then, a cold chill ran along his spine as he realized where he recognized her from.

He put his hand out, slowly, reaching forwards to brush thin, blonde strands away from her face.

Her stare did not falter as he did.

The background noise disappeared behind them as everything became still, as the air around them became dense and colder.

The tip of Aaron's finger did not touch her hair or her face but seemed to go through her instead.

Suddenly, the girl ran away from him. Through the corridor and past a blind corner.

'*Aaron,*' she called as he followed.

'Wait,' he called after her.

Aaron ran through a series of empty halls in a dream-like state whilst bright, overbearing lights flickered above him. He began to sweat as he felt his pace pick up, but it felt as though time was slowing to a standstill. The clear, clean, open space turned into a prison as the lights stopped flickering, as some unknown force brought Aaron to his knees.

Helpless, there was no escape.

Rocking, he could not speak but he could hear his internal voice screaming, *"This is not real! Get up!"*

When enough was enough, he felt the entire weight of his body lift from the floor and he stood, tall and upright. Up and out of that nightmare, somewhere else. In a different room.

Blinding white gradually dulled to reveal pale wallpaper and uncomfortably cheap furniture. He had seen this place before. He looked around and took in the strong, clinical smell of bleach and something else, like off food and something foul.

Aaron looked around more, looked down, for the source, only to see a tray on a table next to a bed. On the tray were plates and bowls, abandoned, covered in remnants of moldy food, and squirming maggots.

Cringing and flinching and turning away, all Aaron could notice was the neglect and decay of every inch of that horrible room. Dust and cobwebs and bedpans, full to the brim, forlorn on the floor. The sight of it all made his gut churn as the repulsive scent filled his throat. He felt the impulse to vomit, but something stopped him.

A hand.

Fast and strong, gripping his forearm, forcing him to turn around. And as he did, he saw what it was, who it was, in the bed next to the table. A heartbreaking, skeletal version of what he knew was his father.

'How am I supposed to concentrate like this?' said Robin, flailing her page around as if to swat the noise and hustle and bustle surrounding her.

'Just drown it out,' Nathaniel mumbled, having gotten his Jell-O in the end.

'Drown it out?'

'Mhm,' he confirmed.

'I can't. It's hopeless.'

A red-faced Robin crumpled the page and threw it on the table, which bounced and landed onto the floor. Then, she slumped back into the creaky chair and huffed.

Just then, Aaron skidded through the entrance nearly crashing into the table, barely missing them.

'What the heck, dude?' said Nathaniel.

'Sorry,' a winded Aaron replied.

'What's wrong?' said Robin.

'Did you find a chair?' Nathaniel asked.

Aaron held out his arms and looked at his immediate surroundings before letting them drop to his sides.

'Okay. Message received,' Nathaniel said.

'Look, are you guys done?'

'What's the matter with you?'

'Can we just get out of here?'

'Robin still has to finish her spell.'

'I don't think I can in all this noise,' said Robin.

'Well, then, let's go,' Aaron insisted.

'Aaron, are you okay? What happened?' she asked.

'Wait,' said Nathaniel before Aaron could answer. Then, in one fluid motion, he slid down from his chair and perched underneath the table.

'Berger, what are you doing?' Aaron grumbled.

'Leave it, I'll get it,' Robin offered, standing up and walking to join Aaron.

But when Nathaniel stood up, he had more than just Robin's crumpled page in his hand. As Aaron and Robin gathered around, Nathaniel grinned as he showed his friends the small piece of paper he found stuck to the back of Aaron's sneaker. The fourth spell book page.

12:00 PM, 6 Bainbridge Drive

'Hon, come on. That's not fair. You're putting words in my mouth,' said Curtis, sat on the edge of Ashley's bed.

Ashley paced inches in front of him, walking up and down the gap in between the wall and the bed, stopping and starting, gesturing as she spoke.

'It's basically what you said. You're putting the onus on me,' she said.

'I'm not trying to.'

'You can't just tell me I need to recover or get over something as if I'm the only person who went through it.'

Curtis sighed and stood up. He looked Ashley in both eyes, held her tense shoulders and gave them a slight squeeze before moving his hands down her arms. Then he took her hands in his. '*We* need to move on,' he said.

Ashley buckled into his arms. 'I don't know how to. I don't think I ever will.'

Curtis understood now, more so than last year, the truth in Ashley's words.

When it happened—when Ashley told him she was pregnant—Curtis was terrified, initially. But it did not take long for him to imagine what their life could become. Indeed, in no time at all, he could not imagine anything better. And what could be better than having another version of Ashley in his life; albeit smaller, but just as loving and spirited? He never mentioned it, but he spent countless moments picturing their beautiful daughter. He was sure it would be a girl. A girl he knew would be just as clever as her mother. A girl he could not wait to teach how to play the piano and hoist on his shoulders at concerts. He wondered whether she would grow up to be an artist. Maybe a dancer, like Ashley, or a musician like him, or something else entirely. He thought of their little family, of the man he wanted to become, the father and husband he could be, the example his father set for him, and the love his mother would send down alongside Ashley's father, wishing they could all be together.

Curtis was not raised to be religious, particularly, but he was never against the idea—after all, he did believe in plenty of other supernatural things. Being with Ashley certainly made him more thoughtful of spiritual matters in any case—certainly more so than he would have been otherwise—especially after tragedy struck the couple the year prior.

For months, Curtis watched Ashley take solace in her faith and channel her feelings into dance.

After a while of trying and failing to talk through their loss, Curtis picked up a Bible for the first time and lost himself in its comforting verses. Gradually, he found himself feeling a powerful urge to pray. It felt alien at first, but he tried. Time and time again, doubting himself that he somehow wasn't doing it correctly. Still, the process became soothing and somewhat uplifting. And, at least, it felt better than doing nothing.

Sometimes, he would talk to his mother. He grew to understand why people like Ashley felt at ease praying to the Virgin Mary, why they would be consoled by the thought of an eternal mother listening to their sorrowful requests. And Curtis Jones only had one request. He only asked for Ashley to get better, to heal. Maybe, he hoped, two people praying for one goal had better odds.

He wasn't sure if any of it was real, or whether that mattered, but he began to appreciate the invisible support he could not obtain elsewhere. And eventually, it became a small but very real part of the person he was becoming. Soon, Curtis did not mind that he began to find meaning in things that probably had no meaning at all.

Most recently, ineffably difficult though it was for him to reach this conclusion, Curtis had come to accept the notion that everything happens for a reason—a cliché of course, but a well-intended one.

And even if there is no divine providence pulling strings behind the scenes, Curtis could at least surmise that we are intelligent and optimistic enough to find some meaning behind things, the silver lining, if we try hard enough.

A few months ago, Curtis was finally able to picture a life without a daughter, without the little girl he dreamt of every day for the most part of a year, after being told he did not have long for this world either—when he was diagnosed with terminal cancer.

He could not bring himself to tell anyone about the diagnosis, yet. But he had made up his mind. He would still propose to Ashley on Halloween night, leaving her with what little he had—if only the memories they had built together, all these years.

In desperate, one-sided reflections with his mother, with God, with whoever was listening; Curtis had come to terms with the fact that leaving behind a wife and child would have been much, much worse.

Although it seemed to be the only saving grace of the situation; it did not, and could not, make him feel better. And although Curtis would periodically advise Ashley to try to move on; he knew she could never do so, because, deep down, neither could he.

Ashley continued to whimper into Curtis' chest as he held her.

'We're so young. And so broke,' he said.

She barely managed a soft chuckle and nodded.

'Think about it,' he continued, 'you would have had to drop out of school, your career would have suffered…'

Ashley withdrew from Curtis' embrace, sniffled, and wiped her face with the sleeves of her sweater. 'What're you trying to say?'

Curtis took a moment and shrugged.

'That it's better this way?' Ashley persisted.

'No. Not like that. Not like you're saying it.'

'Then how would you say it?'

Curtis knew, without revealing his news, there was no way he could phrase his thoughts without instigating an argument. But he had to be honest.

'I just think, maybe, in time, we'll see it as a blessing in disguise.'

That was it for Ashley. What else could be said?

12:45 PM, Downtown Melvin

The streets were lined with puddles. Aaron and Robin side-stepped them as they walked, side by side, with their heads down, keeping their eye on them.

It had stopped raining. That was something, at least. That and Nathaniel being in high spirits.

'This has gotta be the most exciting thing that's ever happened to us, you guys,' he called from a few feet in front of them.

'I don't think I'd use that word, Berger,' Aaron said.

'No. Me neither,' Robin agreed.

'Well, *me* then. I mean, this stuff only happens in comic books.'

Aaron laughed. 'What comics have you read?'

'Niche ones.'

'Uh-huh.'

'Guys,' Robin started, 'this is a whole mess.'

'Uh-huh. I heard that,' Aaron agreed.

Nathaniel shook his head. 'You both really need to get your auras cleansed by that old lady that comes to see Tamarind once a month for tarot readings. Too negative.'

Aaron scoffed. 'I don't think Sant'Anna is gonna help us right now.'

'Don't you mean Ms. Greco?' Robin asked.

'I didn't think she was Greek,' said Nathaniel.

'She's not,' said Robin, 'That's her surname. But like, everyone calls her Old Lady Greco, right? I was just being respectful.'

'I thought she was Italian,' said Nathaniel.

'Yeah. But her surname… never mind.'

Aaron laughed. 'Yeah, but both T and Ashley call her Sant'Anna.'

'To her face?' Nathaniel asked.

'Probably not. But it's still respectful. It's like, she's a saint. She's saint like.'

'Maybe we should pray to Saint Anna instead,' said Robin sarcastically.

Aaron looked at Robin and smiled. 'You're starting to sound like Ashley, you know that?' he said.

She snickered back. 'Good.'

'You heard from her yet?'

Robin stopped in her tracks. She took her phone from her front jean pocket and checked for messages. Bar one failingly nonchalant message from Finn checking up on her and another from Christopher asking if she would be home for dinner, there was nothing from either Ashley or Curtis.

'Nope.'

'Let them take the day off,' Nathaniel exclaimed as he embraced them, 'It's just us, the three amigos today. The adventure's not over!'

'Knock it off, Berger,' Aaron huffed.

'Dude. What happened to you at Adam's? Spit it out.'

'Nothing. Let it go.'

Robin put her hand on Aaron's shoulder. 'You can talk to us. Is it about how you got your page?'

'I didn't even notice it 'til Berger started pawing at me. And it doesn't even say anything. It's blank, just like yours was until Ashley read hers. But you've read yours. It makes no sense. I'm tired of this game.'

Robin sighed. 'What if we spent the rest of the day—'

'Doing what? There's no way any of us can relax or have fun right now.'

'I'm having fun,' Nathaniel stated. 'You just need to shift your perspective, bro.'

'Perspective? Like you have any. Jesus, Berger. Have you ever actually dealt with anything in life? Or even had anything to deal with? You can't be positive all the time. It doesn't work that way. And I'm not your *"bro"*.'

'Woah. Where did that come from? I was just excited to get my page, too. Why do I always have to be left out?'

Aaron sniggered. 'Left out? When?'

'All the time! I'm always the last one to know stuff or have any say in anything. Last time I checked, there were five of us. Y' know?' Nathaniel held up his hand with his palm flat and his fingers spread and pointed to each of them with his right index finger. '*One, two, three, four, five*. That's an odd number. There are two couples, and then me. I'm always the odd one out. Call me Akon and make me sing *"Lonely"* every day why don't you?'

Robin stepped in between the boys and turned to look at Nathaniel. 'No one wants you to feel that way. I didn't know you ever did. Also… we're not a couple,' she outlined, pointing towards Aaron and then herself.

'Yet.'

'Hey, come on. I know everyone's tense. We've all got our own stuff going on...'

'Everyone except Berger,' Aaron interrupted.

'That's it!' Nathaniel wiped his hands in Aaron's face and began to walk in the opposite direction.

'Nathaniel, wait!' Robin called. But he merely shook his head and lifted his hands in the air as he continued to march. 'We still need to finish my spell! And find your page!' she called even louder.

But he did not reply.

'Fantastic.'

'He'll be fine,' Aaron said, 'He's always fine.'

'What? And you're jealous? Why did you have to go and talk to him like that? What *is* your problem?'

'My problem?'

'Yes.'

'My problem is that I'm even here in the first place. Here in this mess. I just wanna be back home.'

'This is our home.'

'For you, clearly.'

'What is it with you and Melvin? Is this about me moving back? What's your deal? You've been in a mood since this morning.'

Truthfully, Aaron had been in a mood since before that morning. But Robin wouldn't confront the issue now. Whatever it was. And Aaron wouldn't admit it either.

'I just don't get this pressure to come back and settle.'

'What about me coming back is settling? There's no pressure. I'm going to be a doctor. Help some people. Be around my family, my friends. I couldn't imagine being anywhere else.'

'You honestly can't imagine being anywhere else? On this massive planet? You can't imagine any other life for yourself?'

'Well, what do you want to do?'

'After college?'

'With your life.'

Aaron did not know how to answer the question.

Perhaps, quite foolishly, although understandably so for his age, he had not given the future much thought. And now he was faced with what he felt were only two options—neither of which he was keen on—moving back to Melvin to help his family or appear utterly selfish by being anywhere else.

'Why are you back here then?' Robin demanded, 'If Melvin is so… so reprehensible to you…'

'It's not *"reprehensible"*, it's just not where I belong. I guess I didn't realize it, fully, before. Before this trip.'

That's as honest as Aaron could be. For now.

'And anyway, I miss you,' he continued, 'all of you. I wanted to see you.'

Robin reached just inside her collar and tugged on the crescent moon necklace Aaron had given her as a present for time lost; a present to remind her of home and what home meant—something she thought he needed reminding of, something she hoped he would remember now.

'I've missed you too,' she said.

After a few moments of silence, a force like gravity pulled them towards each other and they hugged.

Aaron held Robin close and, for the first time in a long time, really appreciated what was happening. He understood at that moment that, at some point, he would have to say goodbye to Robin for the last time.

Whatever decision he came to with regards to his father, to his own family, he would still suffer loss in some way or another.

Loss in the form of inevitable change. Change in his beliefs, priorities, the level of sacrifice and compromise he would be prepared to give to the people around him.

Perhaps that is what he had been fighting all week. The thought of having to become someone different, with a different life, whether he wanted it or not.

Being a college student is like living in some weird limbo between a life where most things are dictated to you and a life whose paths, with all its twists and turns, either positive or negative, only you are accountable for.

If you're not prepared for the it, it is a supremely difficult transition. And nothing can prepare you for it.

Ultimately, what you grow to accept is the power in having control over how you react and how you perceive the world around you.

Maybe Nathaniel had a point after all.

Aaron couldn't control much, right now. He couldn't control how the morning went or how the rest of the day would go, but he could influence this moment, right now.

As Robin broke away to say goodbye, Aaron pulled her in closer to him and kissed her for the first time.

13:00 PM, 8 Almond Avenue

'Ma?' Aaron called as he shut the front door.

'She's not here,' Andrew replied.

Aaron turned around with a start to find his brother sat at the kitchen table, in his uniform, digging into a bag of potato chips.

'Where is she?'

'She took Pops to Adam's. Should be back soon.'

'Adam's? Seriously? I was just there.'

Aaron poured himself a glass of orange juice from the fridge and sat down, opposite his brother.

Andrew looked up briefly and shrugged.

'What're you doing?' Aaron asked.

'Eating.'

'What're you doing *here*?'

'I come home for lunch. Work is close. You'll see.'

'Not this again.'

Andrew shrugged again.

'I'm serious. I'm not having this conversation.'

'Don't, then. There's no need to talk about it. So long as you know what's good for you.'

'What does that mean?'

'It means nobody needs to hear you whine, bro. Just get it together.'

'Whine? Get it together? What does that even mean? I'm getting a degree is what I'm getting. Unlike your sorry ass.'

'That's very nice for you. And when you're done, get your priorities straight, stop being childish, you'll be here pulling your weight like the rest of us.'

'Look... Drew, I'm done arguing with you. I feel bad about what's happening with Dad but—'

'Do you? 'Cause it sure don't seem that way.'

'I don't have to give up my life to prove a point.'

'See, that's how I know you're stupid.'

'Yeah. Insult me. I'm done with this.' Aaron stood up and started to walk away.

'You're so ungrateful. How can you call having a job, a roof over your head, a shirt on your back, and food in your belly *"giving your life away"*? How is helping the people that raised you anything but the right thing to do? What are you even losing? Bring those books from Florida and read 'em on your break, dang.'

'I don't just read books... that's beside the point.'

'What is your point? 'Cause I'm getting tired—'

'You're tired. I'm tired. We're all tired.'

'Mhm. But at the end of the day, I can fall asleep knowing I did something. How well do you sleep, bro? How you gonna make your peace with Jesus?'

'Jesus? Jesus. You're such an obnoxious jerk. Do you hear yourself?'

'I'm obnoxious? Mister *"I'm gonna be somebody so don't nobody hold me back!"* is calling me obnoxious.'

'You're right. I am going to be somebody. It's not my fault you're such a failure.'

'Failure?'

'You never finished school. All you ever gave Mom were headaches. You're in your thirties, Drew. Seriously? You never committed to one girl or one apartment or one job. The only reason you've got one now is because it's Dad's company. And you're trying to act all high and mighty like you had anything to do with it before. You're using this to feel like a big man. Fine. If it's useful to Mom and Dad, fine. But you're not fooling me. I don't need a story to tell girls in some sleazy bar to make me sound like a hero or get a pity party out of my lowlife friends.'

'You arrogant, ungrateful little prick…'

Andrew was right, it would not have been long until Mrs. Jackson returned. Indeed—once again—she opened the door of her home to the sight of her two sons fighting. This time, they were not young boys, and it was not over some toy, video game, or other arbitrary reason. She had to break it up.

Aaron left the house resolved, with a black eye and a clear conscience.

13:30 PM, 13 Carmine Crescent

'Hey, Bubba,' Finn called from the kitchen, 'is that you?'

'Yeah,' Robin called back.

Robin let her keys fall into the bowl on the wooden table beside the door, hung her cardigan, exhaled, and then inhaled home-smell and something else.

'What is that?' she inquired.

'Cupcakes. You want one?'

'Uh… yes please!'

Robin went to join her dad in the kitchen.

'Red velvet,' he said, spooning buttercream icing atop the last of them.

'What's all this for?' she asked, fingering through packs of pink napkins, paper plates, and balloons.

'It's Tiff's birthday, over at *Stardust*.'

'Aww, that's so sweet. Are you sure I'm okay to have one?' she checked.

'Oh, yeah, honey. You know I made extra.'

'Of course.'

'Of course, of course! You know me.'

'Ha-ha, yes.'

Finn finished and handed Robin a cupcake. 'There.'

Robin took it and fiddled with the glittered wrapper as she leaned on the doorway in thought.

'You heard from your father today?' Finn asked.

'He asked if I was coming home to dinner.'

'And are you?'

'That depends. Are we having more cake?'

Finn laughed and hugged his daughter. 'You wish.'

'Ha-ha. No, don't worry. I'll be here.'

'That has got to be the first time I've seen you smile since you got here Friday night. Saturday morning even.'

'Yeah, it's been a tough few days. For everybody.'

'Your friends okay, baby?' Finn asked as he wiped down counters after boxing the cupcakes.

Robin shrugged. She thought of Nathaniel's outburst and Curtis and Ashley's day in seclusion, but in the end, her thoughts trailed back to Aaron.

'Ooh, okay. You just gonna smile like that and not tell me? I know it ain't because of that cupcake.'

'Ha! Bye, Dad.' Robin kissed Finn on the cheek before leaving and took the cupcake with her. 'I'll see you both later.'

'Mhm! It's that nice Jackson boy, isn't it?' he called.

'Bye, Dad!' she echoed.

Robin pinched the edge of the wrapper and pulled it away from the cupcake as she ran up the stairs towards her room.

When she was done wolfing it down, she licked the tip of her thumb and chucked the wrapper in the wicker bin in the hall. Then, she closed the door to her room before leaping onto her bed.

After a few seconds of stretching and basking in the coziness of her bed, Robin rolled over and heard—and felt—a crunch.

'What the…'

For a moment, Robin questioned whether her sleep deprivation led her to imagine bunching up and throwing the cupcake wrapper away. But the moment passed as she realized it was simply her crumpled up spell book page lodged in the corner of her pocket.

Robin sat up, took it, and crossed her legs. She stared down at it and thought about their afternoon at Adam's; wondering why Aaron's page would show up, but not be legible.

What more could she do, but try again?

She swayed slightly from side to side to find a more relaxed position. She straightened her back and closed her eyes. Then, she rested the backs of her hands on her knees.

Robin inhaled, counting, and then exhaled, counting again. There was no rush. She tried to breathe mindfully as she thought.

Then, she took in one deep breath.

She felt the weight of the necklace around her neck as well as the lightness of it. She pictured how cold it felt against her skin when she would put it on in the morning, compared to how warm it was between her thumb and index finger when she played with it.

A light pattering on the glass of her window meant it was starting to rain, again.

Robin lost her focus and had to breathe in.

But she wouldn't give up.

She tried again and thought of the rain.

She imagined it leaking through the roof, trickling onto her. In Robin's mind's eye, each droplet landed onto her skin before rolling away like pearls returning to an endless sea of warm, open water she could float atop whilst savoring powerful sun rays.

She felt her spine stretch further. Whether it was real or not, she felt her arms reach out and something tap the tips of her fingers. It was the tip of someone else's fingers. Aaron's. She felt them link hers and pull her closer into his warm embrace. Then, she felt the soft touch of his lips against hers.

Robin opened her eyes to a tingling which started in the pit of her stomach but spread to her entire body, to the overpowering, sweet smell of cocoa butter which filled her room.

She was still holding her breath, but, surprisingly, it did not feel as uncomfortable as it had done previously.

She had reached a level of peace she was sure would continue if she wanted it to, but she chose to stop and breathe in.

The smell dissipated and the rain stopped. And when Robin looked down at her bed, her page had disappeared, too.

13:30 PM, Downtown Melvin

A light pattering of rain began to fall on Nathaniel's dark curls as he marched home.

'Great,' he grumbled to himself.

He would have to take a short cut.

Nathaniel stopped to check the main road was clear of any traffic. Then, he flipped his hood up over his head and picked up his pace as he crossed.

Ahead of him, in the middle of both lanes, was a large pothole filled with murky rainwater. Nathaniel tried his best to dodge it but somehow ended up stepping into it instead.

'Ah! Great. Just great.'

It was deeper than it looked, as they tend to be.

The water had soaked through his shoe, his sock was drenched, and the water had splashed his right pant leg half-way up his shin.

He bent over to examine the damage, wiped his pants, and then wiped his hands almost instantly.

'How the… oh, no. Ugh! would you look at that?!' Nathaniel shouted to himself.

Before he could complain anymore, Nathaniel's head jerked to the sound of a car nearing the blind corner and went to cross the second half of the road.

However, when he tried to take a step forward, he found he could not lift his right leg from the puddle.

As he lifted his left leg and tried to step over it, some unseen force dragged it backward.

'What the…'

Nathaniel tried and tried, but he was trapped.

He waved his arms to signal the car coming his way, but as he looked up something else caught his eye. A little girl, standing alone, watching him from the end of the road.

Suddenly, his entire body was pulled down and he became surrounded by water.

He couldn't breathe. He couldn't escape.

He clutched at nothing and kicked for his life, only to feel as though he were being dragged down further and further into the puddle.

It seemed to last forever.

Then, as quickly as it started, it stopped.

Nathaniel found himself soaking wet and gasping for breath on the side of the road.

He tried to collect himself as he eventually caught his breath. He rolled over, put his hand out on the sidewalk, and lifted the weight of his torso as he tried to steady himself.

Getting up, on his knees, Nathaniel looked down and saw a piece of paper stuck to the palm of his hand.

He got up and studied it.

Somehow, it was perfectly dry. And blank.

But Nathaniel thought to look at its dexter side, and *that* side wasn't blank.

There was no spell—only a word that Nathaniel felt compelled to read aloud.

'Protagonist,' he read, dazed, and utterly mystified.

As the word left his lips, so too did the page from his grasp as a strong and sudden gust of wind blew it away and out of reach.

Nathaniel looked up, in the distance, in search of the ghost of Li'l Maggie he had seen and recognized moments before.

But she was gone. Just like his page.

13:30 PM, *Paranormal Booktivity*

'T?' Aaron whispered, 'Tamarind?' he pushed.

Tamarind looked up and saw Aaron by the door gesturing to catch her attention as she helped a customer decide between her newest macaroon flavors.

"Where's Willow?" he mouthed.

"Upstairs," she mouthed back.

Aaron slid by and made his way upstairs.

Both Willow's and Tamarind's bedroom doors were shut, and so was the bathroom.

Just then, a stealthy Jefferson made an appearance, arching his back and rubbing against Aaron's ankles.

'Hey, buddy,' said Aaron, bending down to administer a stroke. 'Do you know where Willow is?' he asked softly.

Jefferson chirruped in response and lifted his tail as he sauntered towards the kitchenette.

'Ah, there you are.'

'Hey,' Willow greeted, 'you guys already back from the hospital? That was quick. What happened?' she asked as she loaded the last of the dishes in the dishwasher.

Aaron took a seat near the window. 'It didn't go well, to be honest.'

'Oh, no.' Willow wiped her hands on a tea towel and sat opposite him. 'Are the guys downstairs?'

'No, it's just me.'

'What happened? How are they?'

'It was too busy, too much noise. She couldn't focus. And then Berger spazzed out and got his panties up in a bunch and split because I got my page—'

'Wait, I don't get it. If Robin couldn't concentrate and nothing happened, how did you get your page?'

'I don't know. It doesn't make sense.'

'Well, what does it say?'

'I don't know. I can't read it.'

'What do you mean?'

'It's blank. It showed up underfoot. Literally under my shoe. But there's nothing on it.'

'So, Robin *was* in the right place?'

Aaron shrugged. 'Beats me.'

Willow held out her hand. 'Let me see.'

Aaron reached into his pocket and gave the page to Willow who proceeded to inspect it.

'Look!' she hollered after a few moments, before placing it in the center of the table for Aaron to see, too.

They both sat and watched as a series of words began to appear in the middle of the paper.

'Weird,' said Aaron, 'and spooky.'

'Very.'

'I wonder what happened…'

'Who knows?! But there you go. Now, I guess we just have to figure out where you need to go and what you need to do—'

'No. I'm so done with this. With everything.'

'Hmm,' Willow grumbled, 'I did say it would be best for everyone to just stay out of this…'

Aaron shrugged. 'Yeah, well, I guess you were right.'

'Mhm.' Willow nodded.

'Well, whatever's on that page, I'm not interested.'

Willow read the spell a few times in her head. 'Can I ask you something?' she eventually asked.

'Sure.'

'Who's sick?'

Aaron stared at the back of the page in Willow's hands and pondered its contents. But he would not dare read it. He would not tempt fate.

'My dad,' he replied, looking up at Willow.

'Leave it with me,' she said simply.

That night, each friend went to sleep in their childhood beds, not having heard from each other for hours.

Each page had been and gone, but they were no closer to uncovering any answers than they were at the beginning of the week.

Soon, it would be Halloween. Then, everyone would have to return to their lives. And what of this lost week would have mattered?

TAMARIND

Thursday 29th October

11:00 AM, ***Paranormal Booktivity***

'Good morning, ladies.' Nathaniel strolled into the shop. He slid into the group's booth, sat in the center with his back propped upright, and folded his hands on the table.

'Hot cocoa?' Tamarind promptly offered.

'I think I'll have something stronger this morning.'

Tamarind squinted and looked at her sister. 'Perhaps an espresso?' she finally guessed.

'Not that strong.'

'How about a classic?' Willow suggested.

'A regular *PB* latte,' Tamarind understood.

Nathaniel nodded in agreement.

After digging around briefly, Tamarind held up his DC mug and waited good-naturedly for a second nod. But Nathaniel merely shrugged in response.

'Hmm,' Willow grumbled in the background.

'Have you ever noticed,' Tamarind started, 'that particularly out of the ordinary things always happen on a Thursday?'

'No,' Willow said simply, still eyeing Nathaniel.

'The first Independence Day was a Thursday. I think. It rings a bell from some history class,' Nathaniel added.

'Mutiny is never out of the ordinary,' said Willow.

'Mutiny?' Tamarind pressed.

'Rebellion, then. Or, whatever.'

Tamarind grumbled. 'Well, you know there's that quote from *Hitchhiker's*—'

'*The Hitchhiker's Guide to the Galaxy*?' he said.

'Mhm.'

'I loved that book. What was it?'

'I'm not sure, verbatim, but it was something like, *"I never could get the hang of Thursdays."*'

'How very anti-climactic,' said Willow.

'I simply remember noticing odd things every week, on a Thursday, ever since,' Tamarind explained.

'Indeed. Um, Nathaniel?'

'Yes, Willow?'

'Should we be expecting anyone else?'

'I doubt it.'

'Hmm.'

Tamarind's hand trembled as she served him perhaps the first coffee she had ever served. 'You seem to be handling that quite well?' she said nervously, before linking arms with her sister, as if Willow could shield her from such an oddity.

'I spoke to Aaron yesterday,' Willow announced.

'Oh?'

'Mhm. He said you, quote-unquote, *spazzed out*,' she said, gesturing.

Nathaniel grunted. 'I've told him not to say that. It's not PC!'

'Are you all right?'

'I'm just tired. It's early, still.'

'Are you sure?'

Nathaniel nodded, slowly but surely.

'Hmm.' Tamarind hesitated. 'Something has shifted,' she said, 'in your aura. Your… general being.'

'Yeah,' Willow agreed, 'I see what you mean. Or, at least, I feel what you mean. Kind of.'

'Like after a person's birthday. But more than that.'

'I've just had a birthday! You guys gave me presents!'

'Yes, but, more than that,' Tamarind repeated, 'Also, I think that might be enough caffeine for you, how 'bout it champ?'

'I like it. I feel sufficiently awake. I think I just might switch to it—permanently!' he announced after another sip.

The Dodson sisters mumbled in unison.

'In fact,' Nathaniel continued, 'I have a perfect idea! A faultless plan to fix everything. But I need your help.'

20:00 PM, *El Salero*

Robin waved through the window on the passenger's side of Aaron's father's car at Ashley and Curtis who were stood in front of Curtis' father's car in the parking lot of *El Salero*.

'There they are!' she declared.

As soon as the car was stationary, she got out and ran towards them.

'Hey, guys,' Aaron called as he locked the car.

'All right?' Curtis greeted, patting Aaron's back as he stood beside him.

Aaron buried his hands in his pockets and shrugged the evening chill off his shoulders. 'You guys got the same message from Berger?' he asked.

Curtis nodded in confirmation.

'And Willow, and Tamarind,' Ashley added.

'It all sounded very mysterious,' said Robin, crossing her arms.

'Just like Berger,' said Curtis.

Everyone nodded.

'Then, where is he?' Aaron asked.

Just then, the group heard something in the distance. The noise grew louder as they squinted, peering beyond the blinding streams of artificial light outside the entrance of the restaurant through the darkness of the night.

An energetic Nathaniel emerged from out of the darkness, bouncing towards them. He wore a large backpack full of clanking trinkets and a make-shift strap across his torso packed with small bottles of water.

'Hello, hello, hello,' he greeted, finally joining them, bowing and, in the process, making even more noise.

'Glad to see someone's happy,' Curtis said.

'Or he's finally lost it like the rest of us,' said Ashley.

'I think you'll find, ladies and gentlemen, that I have actually found it! I have acquired *it* and plan to put *it* to good use.'

'Is *it* in that bag?' Curtis joked.

'Oh, you'll see.'

Then, a confident Nathaniel adjusted the straps to his backpack and made his way into the restaurant as his friends hooted and followed him like comrades willing to face an unknown foe.

After settling into a candle-lit booth at the back near the restrooms, Nathaniel seemed shockingly unfazed as a familiar waitress took their order.

Politely but decisively, Nathaniel requested five tall tumblers of water, but no pitcher, and one long platter of nachos, but no plates.

Fiona left, came back with everything requested, and then left again.

Subsequently, Nathaniel repositioned each glass around the platter he tried to place as central as possible. He took the priorly lit tea-light and lit four others he removed from the front pocket of his backpack. Then he arranged them in between his attentive friends and set the fifth at the edge of the table, opposite Curtis who sat in the middle.

Nathaniel rubbed his hands together and licked the corner of his bottom lip. 'Okay. I think we're ready,' he affirmed.

'To eat?' asked Aaron.

'Nope.'

Curtis looked down at his watch. 'I think that's the longest I've ever seen Berger not eat food when food is around,' said Curtis.

'Or even when no food is around,' Aaron added.

'How?' Ashley asked.

Robin giggled and shrugged. 'Somehow.'

'I thought those bottles of water were for us to drink,' said Curtis.

'Oh, no,' Nathaniel started, 'those aren't for drinking. They're filled with Holy Water. They're for later.'

'Later?' Ashley asked apprehensively.

'Holy Water?' Robin inquired.

'Where did you get that, Berger?' Aaron asked.

'The Church.'

'*The* Church? Which one?' Ashley asked.

'St. Peregrine's.'

'They let you in?' Curtis asked.

'Of course, they let him in. It's a free-for-all in there,' said Ashley.

'That's offensive,' said Nathaniel.

'No, seriously,' Aaron pushed.

'I found this woman and told her about tonight and asked for some provisions. She was quite nice actually.'

'A nun?' Curtis asked.

Nathaniel shrugged in response. 'She wasn't wearing a uniform.'

'A habit,' Robin corrected.

'Yeah, that.'

'Why do we need Holy Water? What's happening tonight?' a shrill Ashley demanded.

Nathaniel reached into his bag and pulled out a book.

'A spell book?! Oh, no,' Ashely yelled, ripping it from his grasp.

'Wait… *the* spell book?' Robin said, confused.

'No, don't freak out, guys. I got this one at *PB*.'

'I thought *the* spell book was from *PB*,' Curtis said.

'It is,' Aaron stated.

'Yeah,' Nathaniel started, 'but Willow and Tamarind gave me this one. It's a nice one. Like all earthy and light and stuff. Trust me, or, trust them.'

'I don't know,' said Ashley, handing the book back.

The group paused in thought.

'I mean, realistically, where else do we go from here?' Robin reasoned.

'Exactly,' Nathaniel reaffirmed.

'It's nearly the end of the week and then we go home. I have no idea what's going on with the pages, the thief,' Robin continued, 'I mean, I tried to do mine again, but I'm not sure if it worked. And Aaron's is still blank—'

'Actually,' Aaron interrupted, 'it's not anymore.'

'What?'

'The spell just appeared. Maybe you did it right.'

'When?'

'Yesterday.'

'Great! So, where is it?'

'I gave it to Willow.'

'For safekeeping?'

'Not… exactly.'

'Then?'

'To get rid of. I guess. I'm not sure how, though.'

'What? Why? What about Nathaniel's page?'

'I already had mine,' Nathaniel announced.

Robin was speechless.

Ashley sat back in her seat, mouth agape, in shock.

'Wow, we really did miss a lot yesterday,' Curtis intervened.

'Jesus… When did you get your page?' Robin finally asked.

'Yesterday, too,' Nathaniel answered.

'See?' Aaron started, 'Whatever you did must have worked.'

'But if you gave yours to Willow, how did Nathaniel get his?'

'I have no idea.'

'Can you tell us what happened, Aaron?' a curious Ashley pressed.

'I went to talk to the girls, and T was busy, so I saw Willow,' Aaron explained, 'and while we were sat there talking, words just appeared on the page.'

'What did it say?' Robin asked.

'I didn't read it.'

'How could you not?' said Nathaniel.

'I'm so done with all of this, you guys. I don't even think I believe in any of it. And we're just supposed to be kicking back this week. I just didn't want any part of it.'

'And you just gave it to Willow?' Robin confirmed.

Aaron nodded and linked his hands on the table.

'So…' Nathaniel started, 'how did I get my page?'

'Hmm.' Curtis pondered, 'Maybe the fact that Aaron made a decision not to read it, or do anything with it, was enough.'

Aaron merely shrugged.

Ashley pursed her lips in thought. 'Nathaniel,' she started, 'how *did* you get yours?'

'Honestly? I think I saw Li'l Maggie, you guys.'

'She gave it to you?' Curtis asked, bewildered.

'No. But I saw her.'

'So, what did your page say?' Ashley insisted.

'Honestly, I don't remember.'

'Come on, Berger,' Aaron snapped.

'Seriously.'

Robin sighed, leaned in, and placed her hand on Nathaniel's. 'You can tell us, even if it is embarrassing,' she said.

'No, I'm serious. I swear on the *Beastie Boys*.'

'He's serious,' Curtis announced, slouching back into his seat.

'It's strange,' Nathaniel continued, 'I remember her face. And I remember getting it. Holding it and touching it. And I feel like I read whatever was on it? But it just flew away and then, blank. That's it. I don't even remember how I got home.'

'Hmm,' a dubious Aaron grumbled.

'I woke up this morning in my bed. Then I headed straight to *PB*.'

'Okay,' Robin started, 'So, I held my breath and mine disappeared, you gave yours away,' she said, pointing at Aaron, 'and you read yours and it… "flew away",' she said, pointing towards Nathaniel, 'then… what now?'

The group paused in thought once more.

'I'll tell you what now,' said Nathaniel, 'I have it all figured out.'

'Oh, brother,' Curtis exclaimed.

'Trust me. I spoke to the girls this morning,' he said, tapping the book in hand, 'and they agree with me. Now you guys just need to get on board.'

'With what?' Aaron demanded.

'No matter what we've tried to do this week, some out-there stuff has happened to us every step of the way. Some weird, crazy, paranormal, or supernatural things. We might as well go head-on, full force, and try to get to the bottom of it all.'

'And how do you propose we do that?' said Aaron.

'A séance,' Nathaniel suggested.

'You really have lost it,' Ashley complained.

'Listen to me, we have no other option.'

'Are you crazy?! There is no way we are doing that.'

'Wait,' said Robin, 'what did Willow say?'

'Well,' Nathaniel started, 'it was Tamarind's idea. Willow wasn't too keen, seeing as it didn't go well the last time they tried one. But in the end, we all agreed. And they said that we could go, all of us, tonight, after hours. They'll help us with it.'

'I don't know about this, Berger,' said Curtis.

'What other choice do we have? We've all had and lost a page. We have no idea who stole the book. The only thing we *do* know is that spooky stuff has been going on all around us. And I saw Li'l Maggie, you guys. I saw her. She didn't seem scary. She's kind of cute, y' know, for a ghost.'

'Jesus!' An exasperated Aaron sighed.

'For real,' Nathaniel continued, 'she looked straight at me like she would talk to me if she could. Like she was trying to help. She knows something. I just know it. We should ask her for help.'

'I don't know, Berger,' said Aaron.

'Yeah,' Curtis agreed, 'I'm not sure about this.'

'I am,' said Ashley, 'and the answer is no. Definitely not,' she ordered, 'This is not what we came here for.'

'Ashley,' Robin started, 'no one expected this week to go this way. But we're in it now. We've got to finish it.'

'That's easy for you to say. You got a page and held your breath for two seconds or whatever and then it disappeared. Nathaniel's "flew away"! And Aaron just decided to up and not read his. Who knew that was an option? Nobody told me. No one said I could choose to not have some ghost or spirit or whatever mock my loss with an invitation to a baby shower! It's sick! I won't do it.'

'What about Curtis' vial?' Nathaniel intervened.

Everyone looked at Curtis.

He reached into his coat pocket and pulled out the small flask he found in the graveyard, filled halfway with an opaque, white liquid, the consistency of milk. Then, he held it between his thumb and index finger as everyone inspected it.

'We still don't know what it does. And beyond that,' Nathaniel continued, 'we still have to help the girls, the town. When we leave on Saturday, they'll still be here. We can deal with this *now*; we just have to be quick about it.'

There was that word again.

Ashley mirrored Aaron's frown, but she struggled to ignore Nathaniel's plea.

'Listen, I'm down,' said Robin, 'If Willow's backing it up, it can't be that bad. Both her and Tamarind will be there with us, right?'

Nathaniel nodded.

'Jesus.' Aaron sat up and wiped the exhaustion from his face. 'Well, I'm not going to leave you alone to go and get yourself haunted with Berger. Someone's going to have to save both of you.'

Nathaniel grinned and nodded. 'Smooth.'

'What I don't get is why we're here,' Curtis said after a brief interval, after putting the vial back into his pocket, 'and why we're not eating, or rather, why you're not eating. Those nachos are getting cold.'

Nathaniel waved the spell book around once more. 'We're supposed to perform a bonding ritual. Willow and Tamarind said we all need to strengthen our bond, our friendship, before the séance. That's why they gave me this.'

'What are we supposed to do?' Robin asked.

Nathaniel flicked through the book. He stopped, finally finding the page with a bent ear, and held it up. 'It's simple,' he started, 'we each just say this paragraph. One at a time. And then we take a sip of our drink, and a bite out of our food. Then the next one goes. That's it.'

'What's the paragraph?' Ashley eventually asked.

'It's that one, right there,' Nathaniel replied, pointing towards the end of the page as he handed Ashley the book so she could examine it herself.

Ashley took the book and scanned the paragraph.

'Is that it?' she scoffed.

Nathaniel smiled from ear to ear. 'It's our *intent* that matters, allegedly.'

Curtis peered over Ashley's shoulder and nodded exaggeratively. 'Seems legit,' he said sarcastically.

Ashley lifted a firm hand and patted his knee twice. 'It's okay,' she said.

She stretched the book so that it would hold its place and set it down in front of Curtis. Then, she shifted in her seat and cleared her throat before reading the paragraph:

"To know you, is to always have plenty.
Boundless, I am your friend.
Henceforth, I shall never be empty.
Bonded, our journey knows no end."

Then, Ashley took a sip from her glass of water and took a nacho and ate it.

She gave Curtis' knee an encouraging squeeze and smiled at her friends.

Then, Curtis looked down at the book and did the same, followed by Aaron, Nathaniel, and Robin.

23:00 PM, ***Paranormal Booktivity***

The majority of houses were decorated for Halloween. It would be easier to count those lacking any sign of seasonal marking, if you could notice any. Bountiful as the promised harvest, each household more spirited than the last. A long-awaited sight which came once a year, bewitching in its friendly, neighborly rivalry.

Dangling bats, imitation cobwebs, and oversized creepy-crawlies covered windows. Windowsills and porch steps were lined with Jack-o'-lanterns in all sizes, carved in a series of varied leers and grimaces. And on front doors, plastic skeletons and werewolves awaited costumed trick-or-treaters to entertain with animated jigs and sinister graveyard howls.

It was the same throughout the town, even beyond shops and places of business. Lone sheets draped over branches in every other tree drifted in the evening breeze like cartoon ghosts. Strings of round bulbs hung from utility poles ready to be lit. And stapled on those poles were countless colored flyers promoting local sales and events, including the *Melvin Monster Mash*.

Now that they were adults, it seemed fitting the gang attended on Friday night, to mingle with other Melvin townsfolk before they left.

That was Nathaniel's spiel.

Besides, pleasant small-talk and cheesy music never hurt anyone, Ashley defended.

On Saturday night, it would be Halloween. While parents tucked their children into their beds after an exhilarating candy-filled night, Robin, Aaron, Curtis, Ashley, and Nathaniel would no doubt still be wide awake; binging on treats and horror box sets, soaking up the last bits of spook-adjacent fun before leaving on Sunday morning, ready for classes on Monday.

At least, that was the plan.

Nathaniel was sure they'd be able to find the thief and foil his plan with plenty of time to spare. They had to try.

But first, they would have to go through the séance this evening.

They arrived in two cars which they parked on the junction of Russell Road and Graeme Road and quietly exited before sneaking towards the back entrance.

Facing the shop, on its righthand-side, was a tight gap, like a make-shift alleyway, between it and the apartments next door. It was not lit and did not go very far. After a few steps was a small, rickety wooden door with a rusty metal latch you could squeak open. After a couple more, you would be in the courtyard behind the shop.

The gang stopped and gazed up at an endless sky with no cloud in sight. Blanketed with a million stars and a large cosmic centerpiece; the waning gibbous moon gleamed pale streaks of reflected light onto the cobblestone courtyard through each twisted, spindly branch of Melvin's oldest tree, forming eerie lifelike shadows. A mesmerizing sight hindered only by the evening chill.

Then, the click of a door unlocking made them all turn their heads. It was Tamarind, signaling for them to come in and out of the cold.

And in they went—into and through the shop, where the Dodson sisters had brought down and set up a round table and seven chairs in the middle of the room.

Three lit votive candles shone in the center next to a bowl of pastel-colored pastries atop a deep-red, velvet tablecloth patterned with Theban symbols stitched in glittering silver thread.

As Tamarind motioned for Robin, Aaron, Curtis, Ashley, and Nathaniel to sit, and directed them to their places, Willow descended the stairs with a large deck of cards in her hands. They were tarot cards.

'I thought a quick reading might warm us up,' she said, taking a seat opposite her sister.

As Willow shuffled the deck, mindfully, Tamarind raised her right index finger and cleared her throat.

'May I?' she offered.

Willow nodded, 'Of course.'

Tamarind cleared her throat again and shifted her chair closer to the edge of the table. 'Before we start, I would like to thank you, kids, for being here with us tonight. Did you do the bonding spell?'

Everyone nodded in response.

'How did it go?' Willow asked.

The group looked around at each other, bobbing their heads, and then looked towards Ashley.

'Well… it went well,' she answered.

'Good,' said Willow. Then, she placed the shuffled tarot card deck on the table.

'I think,' Tamarind started, 'it is incredibly brave of you, Ashley, to still be involved, to be here, after everything.'

'Hear, hear,' Nathaniel cried.

'It's been an extremely taxing week and you know, you all know, how grateful we are that you have tried to help us...'

'Even though you should all just be enjoying your vacation—' Willow interjected.

'Even though we don't expect you to spend your precious time this way,' Tamarind tactfully continued, 'we are grateful. And Ashley, I am so proud of you.'

'We all are,' Curtis added, patting her hand.

Aaron and Nathaniel nodded. Robin and Willow smiled.

'Thank you, Tamarind. Thank you, all.'

'I think,' said Willow, 'you should start the reading for us.'

'Hmm, I don't know about that.'

'You're stronger than you think, Ash,' Nathaniel reassured.

'Yes, but only do what you feel comfortable with,' Robin asserted.

'What would I have to do?' Ashley inquired.

'Just pick a card, no?' Nathaniel guessed.

'Cut the deck with your left hand, and then pick a card,' Willow instructed.

It seemed simple enough. Ashley would take this night one step at a time.

She reached across and cut the deck of cards with her left hand. Willow took the second half and placed it atop the first. Then, Ashley removed the first card and laid it flat on the table, face down.

The group exhaled and watched as Tamarind went to flip the card over for all to see.

'Oh, no,' Ashley exclaimed as Tamarind revealed a card depicting a hooded skeleton riding a mighty black steed over a myriad of corpses—the death card.

'No, no!' Tamarind corrected, 'Don't worry, it's not a bad one. Usually.'

'How is death not bad?' Curtis probed.

'The cards are indicative and symbolic,' Willow started, 'you have to find the meaning behind each one. If you think of death, you think of endings but also beginnings. It's more to do with change and what you can learn from it.'

The group stopped to ponder the meaning of the reading in connection to their week thus far and the evening ahead of them.

Tamarind nodded at Willow's reason, contented with the prediction, put the card back into the deck she briefly shuffled before putting away.

'So, what now?' a restless Nathaniel prompted.

'Yeah, T, how does this work?' Aaron asked.

'We will try to summon a spirit,' she replied.

'Well, it looks like everything is ready,' Robin said, gesturing at their surroundings.

Willow nodded in response. 'Of course.'

'What's this for?' Curtis asked, picking up the bowl of sweet treats, throwing a shady glance over at Nathaniel.

'It's an offering,' Tamarind replied.

'I didn't think ghosts ate much,' Aaron remarked sarcastically.

'It's out of respect,' Willow said firmly, 'we have to be respectful. No exceptions. If any should manifest or not. We are disturbing them, after all, inviting them to venture forth from the plane they now occupy.'

'Exactly,' Tamarind affirmed, 'we cannot give any reason for any disturbances back.'

Ashley shot Tamarind a concerned look. 'What do you mean by that?'

The Dodsons looked at each other as if to take a moment to find a delicate way to elaborate.

'Tamarind,' Robin said, breaking the silence, 'you said before, the other day, that you and Willow tried this once before, and it didn't go well. What happened? Willow?'

'Well,' Willow started, 'in that, we didn't get the answers we were looking for.'

'Right,' a dubious Robin said.

'There's virtually nothing to be worried about,' Tamarind reassured, 'still, it's better to be prepared, that's all. Give no indication of vulnerability or fear.'

'Hence, the bonding spell?' Curtis conjectured.

'Exactly!' Tamarind exclaimed.

‘Okay, what else can we do?’ a determined Ashley inquired, sitting up.

‘Join hands, all of you,’ Tamarind directed.

Everyone followed suit and formed a circle around the table by holding each other’s hands.

‘It is extremely important that from this second on, we do not break this circle for any reason other than to put an end to the séance,’ Tamarind explained.

‘The same goes for the candles,’ Willow added, ‘do not blow them out for any other reason.’

Robin, Aaron, Curtis, Ashley, and Nathaniel sat and nodded like dutiful children or keen students as the Dodson sisters readied them for what was to come.

‘We have the candles and the offering, we have more than three people in the circle,’ Willow listed.

‘And I will be the medium,’ Tamarind added.

‘Medium?’ Aaron inquired.

‘I will start the séance and ask the first questions; I will openly offer myself should a spirit need my energy to convey any messages.’

Ashley gulped down her nerves and straightened her back, summoning strength, sitting up straight with conviction. ‘Let’s do this.’

Some time passed in silence, mostly, bar Tamarind’s intermittent attempts to penetrate the spiritual barrier with closed questions and encouraging prompts.

She’d asked for a sign and received none, thus far.

As the group waited for a delayed climax, the atmosphere had just about lost its initial intensity when Ashley noticed something strange, or, more specifically, something strange about Curtis.

His facial expression and general demeanor were both reminiscent of their first night in Melvin.

It struck an unspoken fear into her core.

As he stared forward, and as she stared back at him, the group quickly caught on and their head jerks towards the rear of the shop, at the back door. But they saw nothing.

'Curtis,' Tamarind whispered forcefully, 'what do you see?!'

'Her,' he answered simply after a long pause.

He did not need to explain.

'Margaret Bishop,' Tamarind called loud and clear like the chime of a church bell, 'are you with us?'

The flames of the candles flickered and an audible creak on the floorboards could be heard near the back entrance of the shop.

'Please, join us,' Tamarind invited, 'you are most welcome here.'

To Aaron's astonishment, no sooner had the last word left Tamarind's lips than a sequence of footsteps could be heard approaching them.

Aaron could feel his heart race, anticipating the sight of a real-life apparition of the spectral girl who had followed them all week.

But the footsteps had stopped, and he had seen no apparition. Instead, he witnessed something else he could not explain.

If it was possible, Curtis looked more shocked than he did previously. And now, something was off about Tamarind.

She was oddly still and focused. In seconds, she became noticeably pale and rigid. Centered, her now midnight-black eyes were deep with presence. Her fixed gaze did not falter.

'T?' Aaron tested nervously.

Everyone else was speechless.

She did not respond.

'Margaret, dear?' Willow eventually whispered, knowing better.

'What would you ask of me?' a hoarse voice invited. It came from Tamarind's lips, but, of course, it was not hers.

Willow looked over the group, issuing a firm nod, prompting them to begin.

'What do you know of the spell book?' Nathaniel dared.

'The book was forged as the town, through sacrifice. The ultimate kind.'

'Who stole it?'

'The book cannot be stolen; it belongs to the town and its people. Here it will remain.'

Nathaniel shrugged towards Robin, who sought to rephrase the question. 'Who has the book now?' she asked.

'One with much to lose, but much to gain. One linked by blood.'

Now, Robin was speechless, too.

'Margaret?' Ashley prodded gently, 'we'd like to know more. You can trust us. What can you tell us about the book and the town?'

Tamarind sat with her lips slightly parted and the same hair-raising visage.

As the group waited, motionless, the entire shop darkened around them—as if a large, ominous cloud began to hover over it, encompassing the moon and the stars. Even the low flicker of each flame between them gradually faded until they disappeared completely.

Their vision had been blurred and snatched in a collective trance, briefly, before it cleared as they were transported in time nearly four-hundred-years in the past through the haunting words of Margaret Bishop.

'Great ships traveled across perilous seas for months to reach the New World. My ancestors boarded the Anne from England with hopes of finding freedom from a decadent past.

'But they would become the very thing they strived to eradicate.

'They wanted to live in their very own Eden and created an Inferno instead. Ignorant, merciless, wicked fools.

'Within a few generations, anyone could be tossed aside under suspicion of witchcraft. An impenetrable pretext.

'Power had become their new God. No one was safe. Not even me.

'Not all those tried were executed. But hundreds were punished in different ways. Shunned. They lost everything. And then… there were some who took the law into their own hands. Like the rabble that claimed me…

'So many lives destroyed… so many innocent souls…'

Tears spilled down Willow's face as she listened. Everyone's hearts broke as they heard the tale, as they witnessed flashes of harrowing scenes of agony in their mind's eye.

'I was just a girl,' she continued, *'I wasn't a witch. Neither were any of the accused.*

'The real witches were cunning, always a step ahead…'

'Real witches?' Robin blurted out.

'Yes.'

'What happened to them?'

'Many ventured south, to safety. Seven lingered, tried to fight, to protect, alongside their male colleagues. They formed their own coven, here.'

'How can you know these things?' Ashley asked.

'In death, one learns many things.'

'So, what happened to the witches who stayed? Did they write the spell book?' Nathaniel inquired.

'One such witch wielded the bark of an ancient tree to forge the book. Armed with pages flowing with defensive magick; it would ensure the safety of Melvin, its citizens, and their descendants, providing they be bound to the land.

'She sacrificed much for this. Though, as selfless as her wishes were, there was, and is, a great price to be paid by all.

'You see, even in death, I cannot escape. I cannot be freed of this land and find peace in the realm beyond. Neither can anyone whose last days are spent here. We remain as guides for the living. Connected, until the spell is broken.'

Robin, Aaron, Curtis, Ashley, and Nathaniel sat in stunned silence as they regained their sight, as the tale appeared to come to an end.

Increasingly frustrated, Curtis felt they were owed more.

'So, what now?' he demanded.

'Curtis,' Willow reprimanded in a hushed tone, 'be respectful.'

'But we still have no answers,' he pushed.

'Didn't you listen to the story…' Robin whispered.

'Yeah. But we still don't know who has the book, or why. We don't know why we each got pages, why Ashley got her horrible, horrible page, why I got this vial—'

Without thinking, Curtis unlinked Ashley's hand to reach for the vial in his pocket.

As Curtis broke the circle, Tamarind gasped and fainted, falling to the floor. In an instant, the candles snuffed out and the backdoor swung open due to an unseen gust. Then, the clock on the wall behind the counter struck twelve.

Friday 30th October

22:30 PM, Downtown Melvin

Under the Milky Way by *The Church* blasted from the speakers as twinkling lights shimmered and bounced on the walls of the community center from a number of disco and party balls.

'Milady,' Aaron teased, as he handed Robin a red plastic cup of fruit punch.

Robin curtsied and simpered in response. 'Thank you, kind sir,' she teased back.

As they waited for Ashley and Curtis to return from the refreshment table, they regarded each other with contentment as they took sips from their drinks.

'You look better,' Robin finally said.

'Better than when?' Aaron asked, grinning.

'Ha-ha, yesterday, I guess.'

'Thanks.'

'Yeah, you look good.'

'I'm just glad everything's over.'

Robin was sure that, in all likelihood, everything was far from over, unfortunately. Still, far be it from her to dampen his spirits or burst his bubble of denial, *so very typical for a Pisces to dwell in*, she thought to herself.

She downed the last mouthful of her drink and left the empty cup on a nearby table. 'Let's dance,' she said, grabbing him and luring him towards the dancefloor.

Nathaniel finally showed up—more than fashionably late, and certainly more fashionable than he usually was—dressed for the occasion. He scanned the center until he locked in on his friends, laughing and talking and bopping in a corner together.

'What are you all doing?' he hollered as he joined them.

'Good evening, Berger,' Aaron greeted, waving condescendingly as if he were trying to get through to an extremely challenged patient.

'What are you wearing?' Nathaniel interrogated.

'Clothes,' Curtis replied, grinning.

'Yeah, but where are your costumes?'

'We didn't pack any,' said Ashley.

Nathaniel gasped in horror.

'But, Berger, you're not even wearing a costume,' Aaron pointed out.

'Yes, I am,' Nathaniel confirmed.

'Who are you supposed to be?' Robin asked.

Nathaniel said nothing but merely pointed to his shirt.

'Ooh, ooh! I know. You're shirt-man,' Curtis joked.

'No, no!' Aaron joined in, 'He's shirt-boy!'

The boys laughed and slapped at each other as Nathaniel's infuriated expression only worsened.

Robin smirked. 'Oh, dear.'

'Are you supposed to be a skeleton?' Ashley guessed kind-heartedly.

'No!' an exasperated Nathaniel asserted. 'Wait,' he said, 'I'll give you a clue.'

He lifted the hood of his light gray hoodie over his head and left it unzipped so he could point, once more, at his black t-shirt with a white skeletal rib pattern, before trailing his index fingers up and down to draw attention to his jeans and classic black and white high-top converses.

'Eh? Eh?' he goaded.

Robin, Aaron, Curtis, and Ashley gawked back at him, smiling and nodding, waiting for the climax.

'I'm Donnie Darko,' he finally clarified.

Aaron and Curtis burst into a chortling fit and Ashley and Robin could not help but to chuckle along.

'Whatever,' Nathaniel dismissed, swiping his hand in the air as if he would push their mockery away, 'it's a good costume.'

'Very unique,' Robin offered, collecting herself.

As the discussion settled down, someone bumped into Robin, walking through and past the group.

'Oops, sorry,' Robin instinctively uttered as she turned around to smile at the stranger. But they did not stop. Instead, the woman continued as if nothing had happened.

Robin continued to observe her march through the crowd of partygoers towards a fire-exit at the back of the hall.

'It's a really good film,' Nathaniel started again, 'at least I made an effort, unlike you people. I mean, it's Halloween. Soon. It's almost Halloween—'

'Wait,' Robin disrupted, alarmed, 'I know her. I think I know her, you guys,' she said, waving her hands at everyone, signaling them to watch as well.

Her friends stopped and looked up towards the back of the hall but could only see the woman's back and did not recognize her.

'Excuse me,' Robin called out.

The woman stopped in her tracks just in front of the door and looked back at them for a moment before ignoring Robin's plea and leaving.

'Rude,' Nathaniel stated.

'Who is she?' Aaron asked.

'I'm not sure, but I have to speak to her,' Robin declared, 'Come on guys. We have to follow her, come on!' she ordered.

Robin left the *Melvin Monster Mash* minutes before midnight, hurrying like Cinderella fleeing the ball for her dignity. But curiosity was at the root of Robin's conviction. And instead of a morphing carriage and galloping animals, she was accompanied by her ardent friends in Curtis' father's car.

The tires screeched and skidded moments after everyone jumped in—they had barely managed to catch a glimpse of the woman escape in a car parked a few spaces behind them.

They proceeded to follow her through the town and to its outskirts, down poorly lit winding roads encircling the ravine and surrounding woods.

In a flash, the car seemed to disappear into the darkness as the woman turned off her taillights in a wily attempt to evade them.

But Curtis did not slow down.

He carried on until, before long, he was forced to slow down and come to a stop a few yards away from a large gravel pathway in front of an imposing cast-iron gate.

The gang got out of the car and saw the woman's, which was haphazardly parked on the curb.

But there was no sight of her.

As they inched closer towards the gate, stomping on countless pebbles underfoot, Nathaniel and Aaron whipped out their phones to shine two distinct rays of artificial light around them.

A large stone house covered in overgrown foliage climbing up diagonal trellises could be seen some distance beyond a patch of untended land.

No lights were on and there were no visible signs of life. The only sign they could see was an actual one, posted high above the left-hand side of the gate.

As the boys shone their torchlights in its direction, everyone tried to make out the faded writing.

'Gardner Manor,' Robin read aloud.

Saturday 31st October

00:00 AM, ***Gardner Manor***

Curtis had cupped his hands and linked his fingers to provide a boost for Ashley, followed by Robin, and then climbed over the gate himself.

All the while, Aaron tried to help Nathaniel do the same.

'Come on!' Robin hissed from the other side.

The boys grunted and huffed, slapping at each other as they struggled, before landing on a firm patch of damp grass with a veritable thud.

'Let's go!'

As they pressed on, cautiously wading through taller and more unruly plants, the group found their way to the entrance of the seemingly derelict manor.

Two hefty weather-worn doors—with a couple of intricately patterned cast-iron knockers in the center of each—had been left slightly ajar.

Upon entering, beyond a dust-covered stairwell, a myriad of forlorn antiques and sheet-covered pieces of furniture, a faint stream of light could be seen in a room across the foyer.

Venturing across creaky floorboards, to the gang's surprise, the room was fully furnished and appeared to have been used up until very recently.

They noticed that the light had come from a copper oil lamp set on a mahogany davenport near the door.

On one wall was a fireplace, aflame with burning kindling, and on the opposite wall, a horizontal, gilded mirror reflected the fireplace's flickering ambers onto the rest of them.

In an instant, Robin, Aaron, Curtis, Ashley, and Nathaniel split up and spread out. As they explored, each had hushed comments about the contents of the room; the series of documents, maps, and all manner of strange things spotted.

'No way,' Nathaniel exclaimed, 'Robin,' he called, 'look at this.'

'Oh my,' Ashley cried, as she, Curtis, and Aaron joined him, as they all stared up at the painting hung above the fireplace.

It depicted an enchanting woman with fiery locks and bewitching eyes. Gracefully sat in a forest-green dress with a fierce, soul-penetrating stare, her poised hands rested on a small, black, leather-bound book on her lap.

'She looks so sad,' Ashley remarked.

'She looks just like Robin,' Nathaniel pointed out.

Grumbling, Aaron, Ashley, and Curtis tilted their heads as they examined it further.

'Seriously,' Nathaniel insisted, 'I can't be the only one seeing this. Robin!' he called, 'Look, it's you!'

'No,' said Robin from the other side of the room, 'this is.'

Her friends rushed to join her and saw her holding a framed photograph of a small, ginger babe sat atop an elderly gentleman's lap.

Dumbstruck, Robin went to place the photograph back on the desk where she found it as if she could somehow turn back time and forget she had seen it, but as she did; a small black book magically appeared in the same spot on the corner of the desk and began to glow before their very eyes.

Aaron gasped. 'I don't believe it.'

A yelp escaped Ashley's lips. 'Oh, Dios mío…'

'It's the spell book,' said Curtis.

'Quick! Grab it!' Nathaniel shouted.

No sooner did the words leave Nathaniel's lips than a strange voice bellowed from behind them.

'There'll be no need for that,' the distinguished, orotund voice affirmed.

Everyone spun around to face the source.

Sat in a wheelchair in the doorway was a salt and pepper haired man with no end of defined creases and folds on his weary face, most noticeably underneath both doleful eyes.

Stood behind him, with her hands resting on both handles, was the woman they had chased through the town. Middle-aged, pale, with thick glasses and a full head of auburn frizz—she administered a half nod and somewhat gracious smile to the group.

'Fat chance, old man,' Nathaniel blurted out, 'that book is leaving with us!'

Ashley took a step forward and gave Nathaniel a look of reproach. 'Now, he's still our senior.'

'Yeah,' Aaron agreed, reaching for, and then grabbing the spell book, 'Still, with all due respect, Sir, my friend is right. We will be taking this,' he said firmly.

Curtis stepped forward as Aaron waved the spell book in the air, joining Ashley and Nathaniel, forming a protective semicircle around Robin.

'I'm afraid my affairs are not yet settled,' the man replied, 'it is still of use to me.'

'I could give a crap about your affairs!' Nathaniel screeched.

'Nathaniel…' Ashley rebuked.

'No! No, Ash. I'm sorry. But this selfish fuddy-duddy ruined our vacation! He broke into *PB* and stole the book from Willow and Tamarind!' said Nathaniel, standing his ground. 'You ruined Halloween, Sir!' he yelled melodramatically, shaking his index finger in the man's direction.

'Actually,' the woman started, 'that was me.'

'That was you? How?' Curtis demanded.

'Yeah,' said Aaron, 'we all saw a man leave with the book on the shop's security tape.'

Ashley thought back to the beginning of the week, to the day they first saw the grainy footage on that old television set, to the moment they stumbled upon the tag from Gloria Day's garment shop, and remembered the clothing they had tried their best to track down: the ski mask and winter parka the thief wore to conceal their identity.

'Well, with that get-up, that's what she wanted us to think,' Ashley supposed.

'The ultimate trickery,' Nathaniel exclaimed with a disapproving look. 'He can probably walk and all!

'Look,' the woman started, 'I'm sincerely sorry about the damage to the shop—'

'No, you're not!' Robin snapped, emerging from the group like a lioness protecting her pride, her tone as cold as a ferocious gust of winter frost.

The trembling pot of Robin's pent-up frustrations, delayed reactions, resentment, and exhaustion, finally bubbled to a boil, overflowed, and blew its lid.

'You could care less about the window or the shop or our vacation or anything! Don't think I don't know who you are—'

'Who is she?' Nathaniel butted in.

'I remember you from New York,' she continued, staring her down, '*Amber Grebe*?! You saved me from that mugger. Or was it all a ruse? Was he just your accomplice? Did you plan all this?'

'Of course not!' Amber defended.

'How long have you been stalking me?' a shrill Robin demanded.

Unwilling to disclose too much, Amber pursed her lips and pouted. Then, she wheeled the elderly man a few feet forwards.

'I would never let any harm come to you. Know, I would do anything for you, Robin,' he said, as he came to a stop.

'Don't say my name like you know me—'

'But I do, sweetheart.'

'No! You don't! And don't think I don't know who you are either!' she said, increasingly flustered.

'Who is he?' Nathaniel meddled again.

Robin looked down at the photograph one more time before placing the frame on the now-empty corner of the desk. She pondered its similarity to the photo she saw at the orphanage and knew in her heart that this was the person who had filed the Reversed Details Request form she had been trying to escape all week.

Her fathers knew of it, of course, and so did the members of staff at the orphanage who were involved, including Ms. Bennett, of course. But no one aside from Willow, no one important in her life anyway, had the chance to be told just yet.

Robin could not bring herself to make a revelation under such circumstances.

'My name is Gerard Gardner,' the man introduced himself to the group, 'I'm Robin's grandfather.'

Suddenly, Robin became the focal point of the room as everyone's eyes fixated on her, anticipating the intensity of her reaction. But what could be said?

Ashley faced her best friend. Taking Robin's hands in hers, she looked deep into her eyes as if to center her, to make her feel as though they were alone, to let her know she was safe. 'Robin, is this true?'

Robin dared not admit it out loud. She nodded for a split second, fearing that doing anything more might cause a flood of tears to stream down her face.

'Since when?' said Nathaniel.

Aaron lightly smacked Nathaniel's bicep with the back of his hand before facing Robin. 'Robin? Talk to us,' he prompted gently.

After a deep breath, Robin told her friends what her fathers had revealed to her at the beginning of the week. She told them about her encounter with Ms. Bennet at the orphanage before finding her page and explained that upon seeing this second photograph, she presumed, correctly, that this man must have been responsible for it all.

As Robin spoke, Curtis' face reddened, and his eyebrows pulled together until he finally exploded.

'Hold the phone,' he started, 'so all of this was just because you wanted to talk to Robin? You couldn't just show up at her house?'

'Dude,' Nathaniel said, 'he *is* in a wheelchair.'

'Well, whatever then, he couldn't have asked his evil minion to give Robin's door a little knock?' Curtis said, pointing at Amber, 'You've been stalking her for God knows how long, you sicko!'

'Mr. Gardner obviously wanted to give Robin a chance to decide for herself before barging into her life,' Amber explained.

'Well, you've both managed to barge right into all of our lives now!'

'Curtis, calm down,' Ashley advised, 'let's all take a breather.'

'No, hon, I'm sorry but Nathaniel was right. They ruined Halloween! We each got pages that made us confused and miserable all week—'

'Surely, we cannot be held responsible for that,' Amber asserted.

'But you just said you stole the book!' Curtis cried.

'I haven't been able to do much for some time now, and I asked Amber to retrieve the book for me so that I might use it,' Mr. Gardner explained, 'but we are not able to administer pages from it…'

'So how do you explain it?' Nathaniel demanded.

'Yeah, how does it work exactly?' a curious Aaron inquired.

'It must have sensed you needed help.'

'It?' Aaron pushed.

'The book,' Mr. Gardner replied simply.

'And you expect us to believe that?' said Aaron.

'Well, it's happened, hasn't it?'

The group stopped for a moment, pondering the week's events.

But Curtis only grew more enraged.

'So, which is it? That you wanted to get in contact with Robin or that you needed the book for your own selfish needs? And while we're at it, you're telling me that you're *so* selfish, you got someone to break into *PB* to unleash a sentient book just so that you could use its magic to what, I don't know, be able to walk again or whatever, and if you had left it hidden we wouldn't have been bothered at all? Ashley wouldn't have had to go through what she did—'

'Curtis,' said Ashley, trying her best to put an end to his rant.

'No! It's unacceptable!'

'Hold on, son,' Mr. Gardner beseeched, 'Believe it or not, I need the book to help you all, the town, and Robin… I would never dare *"unleash"* the book if it were capable of such evil. I cannot believe it would cause such a fuss. What happened to you, dear?' he asked Ashley.

'She got a creepy toy and a twisted baby-shower invitation!' Curtis answered for her.

Mr. Gardner and Amber looked at each other with scrunched faces, unsure how to proceed, whilst Aaron, Nathaniel, and Robin awkwardly waited, unwilling to elaborate and delve into Curtis and Ashley's private affairs.

'Well, if I may,' Mr. Gardner started, 'the only aim I can deduce, would be to inform you that—'

'I'm pregnant,' Ashley announced.

'What?' said Robin, stunned, as everyone turned to face Ashley.

'I thought about it some more after the séance and decided to take a test.'

'When?!' Robin insisted.

'Today. Well, yesterday, before the party. I went to the packie and got a pack of three. I had to convince Tara to keep quiet, she was so thrilled! But it is true. I literally did all three just to be sure. I guess Tamarind was right, or Li'l Maggie was, about helpful spirits or whatever. I guess you're right, Sir,' she said, turning towards the old man, 'I guess it just tried to help us.'

The revelation seemed to quiet Curtis, for now.

'Congratulations!' Amber offered, breaking the awkward silence as a thoroughly pleased Mr. Gardner smiled and nodded.

'Yeah, Ash, that's great,' said Aaron, hugging her.

'I'm so happy for you!' Robin's eyes welled up as she joined in.

'Just wait until Willow and Tamarind hear,' said Nathaniel, inviting himself into the group hug.

As Curtis lingered in stunned silence, Amber bent down to whisper in her employer's ear.

Then, Mr. Gardner nodded approvingly.

After the displays of affection were administered, he invited everyone to join him in another room.

'Come,' he said, 'we have much to discuss.'

In a different room, with low but sufficient lighting and wooden furnishings, Amber occupied herself in the kitchenette after wheeling Mr. Gardner to the head of the rectangular table. Robin, still evidently unnerved, sat at the edge of her seat opposite him, unintentionally making eye-contact only with her friends—where Curtis and Ashley sat on one side of the table, and Aaron and Nathaniel sat on the other.

'Dodson, was it?' Mr. Gardner asked, scribbling into the check book he retrieved from the left inner pocket of his suede jacket with the fountain pen Amber handed him moments before.

'Oh, yes.' Ashley nodded.

'You'd better make it out to Willow, Sir,' Nathaniel suggested as he wolfed down a couple more ginger cookies from one of the porcelain plates Amber placed in front of the group.

'She's the more organized of the pair, I take it?'

Ashley giggled. 'Oh, yes.'

'Definitely,' Aaron agreed.

'They must be quite the duo to have gained such fervent loyalty from you fine kids. *"One need only look at a person's friends to determine their character"* and all that. I should have liked to have met them. Please,' he said, tearing the check from the book and handing it to Ashley, 'for the damage to their beloved shop, and all the trouble I have caused. Do pass on my sincerest apologies and regards to both Miss. Willow and Miss. Tamarind when you next see them.'

'Thank you very much, Sir,' Ashley said, folding and pocketing the check, 'I'm sure they'll appreciate it.'

'You should come to *PB* with us later,' Nathaniel blurted out, 'I mean, if that's okay with everyone.'

Aaron looked at Robin, staring down at her fingers fiddling with the paper tag from the teabag dangling off the edge of the cup in front of her. 'I'm sure the Dodsons wouldn't mind,' he said, gauging whether Robin would, 'we all leave Melvin later this evening, but we'll stop over to say goodbye before we head home. You should join us, Sir.'

'Please, Gerard. And no, as lovely as that sounds, I do not think that will be possible.'

'More chamomile tea?' Amber asked the group as she poured some from a warm pot into her employer's cup.

Ashley, Aaron, and Nathaniel shook their heads politely.

'I should think you'll all sleep well enough when you leave,' she continued, 'What an eventful evening, and week, it has been for all of us.'

'It sure has, ma'am,' said Nathaniel, scoffing down more cookies.

'Might I ask…' Gerard started before taking a sip of his tea, 'what pages appeared to you all this week?'

'Well, Sir. I mean, Gerard. Mine came to me last,' said Nathaniel, 'but I don't remember it.'

'Oh?'

Nathaniel nodded vigorously. 'But at least I got to see a ghost,' he acknowledged.

'Yes… well, that does not surprise me. I suppose whatever it is you needed help with has been resolved in secret. How mysterious. What about you, young man?' he said, looking at Aaron.

'Well,' Aaron started, taking a moment to look his friends over before gulping down a nugget of nerves, 'you see, my father is sick—'

'What? Since when?!' Nathaniel interrupted.

'Well, my father is sick and, you see—'

'What's your name again?' Gerard asked.

'Aaron.'

'Aaron, I'm so sorry about your father. I suppose your page offered a way to help him?'

Aaron nodded in response.

'How very kind and unselfish a person you must be, my boy, for the book to offer you such assistance. And very mature in your young years, I can tell. I don't take it you did whatever the page required of you?' Gerard speculated.

'No, Sir,' Aaron answered, shaking his head.

'Wise. Very mature, indeed,' Gerard confirmed, nodding, 'we all get sick, don't we? But it isn't for everyone, this interfering with fate business, is it?'

Before Aaron could answer, Curtis sat up in his chair, finally snapping out of his state of shock. 'But what if we did interfere with fate?' he asked.

'In what way, son?'

Curtis ran his shaky fingers through his buzz cut and thought of a way to rephrase his question without exposing his secret.

'Curtis?' Ashley asked, concerned.

Moments passed as they all waited, as he realized he might have to do so.

In the end, Curtis reached into the zipped front pocket of his bulky puffer jacket in search of a helpful prop. His fingertips touched the edge of the black box holding Ashley's engagement ring before hitting the cold pointed edge of the vial he found on Monday night.

He took out the vial and placed it on the table in front of him.

'What is that? Milk?' Amber asked, adjusting her glasses.

'I don't know what's in it. I think it's what my page conjured,' Curtis replied.

'Hmm.' Gerard thought for a moment, 'Where did you find this?'

'In a cemetery,' said Curtis, 'In the old graveyard behind St. Peregrine's Church,' he clarified.

'Right.'

'Well,' said Nathaniel, 'What do you think it's for?'

'Yeah, what is it?' Aaron asked.

'It's a potion, isn't it?' Gerard asked rhetorically. 'I think, occasionally, Curtis, to answer your question, it isn't so much about interfering with fate as it is about going along with fate. Do you see?'

Gerard's message rang loud and clear for Curtis. Their eyes met as he spoke. And in those seconds, it was as if they had had their own private, telepathic conversation—after which Curtis finally reached his own epiphany.

Curtis smiled at Robin's grandfather, removed the vial's rubber stopper, and drank all its contents as he thought of his page, of Li'l Maggie, of Ashley and their babe to be—thanking God in his heart for this little, great miracle.

Then, he took Ashley's hand and kissed her cheek, knowing they would have more than enough to talk about on their journey home later that evening.

'Well, then! What a night,' Gerard exclaimed after a quiet interval, 'And what about you, Robin? Are you ready to talk to me yet?' he asked.

'Who is that woman in the painting?' she asked, staring him down.

'Ava Warner,' he replied.

'She looks just like Robin,' Nathaniel said, waiting for approval.

Gerard chuckled. 'Yes,' he agreed, 'I should say so. They are related, after all. And it's a strong bloodline.'

'Can you tell us more?' Ashley asked, sensing her best friend's mixed curiosity and stubbornness throb like a tingling on her arm hairs.

'Certainly,' Gerard replied before taking another sip from his tea, before regaling the group with his tale.

Gerard described Ava Warner as a woman before her time—*"Utterly kind and brave, an angel sent to earth for a most noble deed, only to be recalled again shortly thereafter."*

Unsurprisingly, the tale simultaneously simplified and complicated much. Weaving in and out of what they already knew, and what they could gather, of their hometown and its history, his story started much like Li'l Maggie's did on Thursday night.

A direct descendant of the first settlers in this great state, Ava was one of many eventually accused of the crime of witchcraft.

So many cases such as hers, he explained, ended in tragedy. Unlike the others, however, there was truth behind the claims brought against her.

Although some of her fellow witches fled, a select few would not be overcome by fear. Led by Ava, they tried with all their might to find a way to stay in the land they had claimed as their home whilst protecting the lives of those who remained, witch or not.

In giving life to the spell book they now had in their possession, Ava was prepared to sacrifice her own to ensure the eternal protection of Melvin.

However, as prepared as she was, she was not to know of the full ramifications of her actions. This is because, at the time, she was blissfully unaware that she was with child.

But the deed was done.

The book remained under the protection of Ava's coven until, over the centuries, passing from person to person, it was lost.

'It took some time and effort on my end to find its location,' Gerard continued.

'What happened to her child?' Ashley asked.

'Her long-time fiancé took the child; the little girl Ava gave birth to moments before her untimely death and raised her.'

'How do you know all of this?' Aaron asked him.

'It took some doing, I'll tell you that. And Amber has been of great help.'

'Please, tell us more,' Ashley humbly requested.

'My wife, Muriel, also died in childbirth.'

'Oh, dear… I'm so sorry,' said Ashley.

'Yes, well, these things happen. Or, so I told myself for a long time. I did not want to let my grief impact the joy of having a daughter. Healthy, alive, and well. I just wanted to be there for her.' Gerard's eyes became wet with unspeakable sadness.

Amber stood behind him and placed her hands on his shoulders after giving them a firm pat.

He took a handkerchief from the front of his jacket, wiped his tears, and blew his nose.

'What happened to your daughter?' Ashley asked.

'She died, also. Well before her natural time.'

'My mother?' said Robin, with tears in her eyes.

Gerard nodded somberly. 'Your dear mother, my darling daughter, Wren. When she passed, your father did not take it well.'

'Oh my God,' Robin exclaimed, 'I had no idea.'

'It had happened again. And the doctors were of no use, of course. They had no explanation. Because the explanation was not medical. It was not natural, but supernatural.

'I knew I had to find a way to make sense of it all.

'After looking through the town's records and tracing Muriel's genealogy, I knew something strange was behind everything.

'In my grief, I even tried to contact your mother, your grandmother… I asked for help from anyone who might guide me from beyond the grave.

'When I finally learned the truth, I knew that none of Ava's descendants could build a home here while that book still existed.

'I thought if I gave you up, my dear Robin, if I gave you up for adoption, you might have a fighting chance. A nice family would love you and take you far away from here, from this curse.

'I was told you would be taken to Boston.'

Robin nodded, wiping tears from her scrunched face. 'That's what I was told, all this time,' she said.

'I spent as much time with you here as I could, at the orphanage in Melvin before they planned to move you, but a nice couple had seen you and fallen in love, naturally.'

'Christopher and Finn,' said Robin.

'Yes. I had no say anymore. And Melvin's hold on its citizens had claimed you beyond my control.'

Everyone sat in silence, going over Gerard's words in their mind.

Robin had never been so still.

'Still,' he continued, 'they seemed so nice. And I've kept an eye on you as best as I could, over the years. And when you went off to college, I thought you might be safe. That you'd meet a nice boy and stay there or move elsewhere. But this curse… it has brought you back, my dear. And I'm going to put an end to it all, I promise you.'

'What do you mean?' Robin asked apprehensively.

'I've found a spell,' Gerard explained, 'a final spell at the end of the book which would reverse the deed once and for all. You could stay here, if you wish, or choose to leave. You would have a choice, at least. And everyone in Melvin who unknowingly is bound to this land in one way or another would have one too, finally. The town's well-intended but unnatural grip on its residents would cease to be.'

Robin's chair squeaked and screeched on the solid wood floor as she sat back, stood up, and made her way across the room.

As she reached the edge of the table, she nodded towards Amber who moved and sat in Robin's place.

Then, she took the wheelchair's handles, pulled it back slightly, and turned it around, repositioning her grandfather before kneeling in front of him. She took his cold, fragile, trembling hands in hers and rubbed his knuckles on her wet cheeks. She kissed them and cried some more.

'Grandfather,' Robin said, looking up at him, 'tell me, what would enacting the spell entail?' she asked, already knowing the answer.

'Oh, my dear girl. Do not shed tears for me.'

'But… I've only just found you. There's got to be another way.'

'Can't you see I am not long for this world? I am already gone,' he said as a tear rolled down his cheek.

All the while, everyone in the room wept at the most heartbreaking sight they had ever witnessed.

'You know what my page did?' Robin asked her grandfather.

'No, my darling granddaughter, what did it do?'

'It made me think of *home*,' she answered, 'I always thought it was a place. I thought it was *this* place. But now I know better,' she said, reaching just inside her shirt to pull out and caress the crescent moon necklace Aaron had left for her earlier that week. 'Please, don't do this.'

'Don't you know,' Gerard said, wearing the most peaceful smile he had managed in decades, 'I would do anything for you, Robin.'

17:39 PM, Downtown Melvin

The spell book's previous *"hidey-hole"* was still empty. Now, though, there was no mystery to solve.

Underneath a small wooden plank, underneath a large stone in the courtyard behind *PB,* underneath the fragmented shade of Melvin's oldest tree, remained only dirt and a memory of what was.

Gerard Gardner, Robin's grandfather, having been able to hold his granddaughter one last time, was at peace. The manor would be left to Robin, of course, which she pledged to donate to the town in due course. And Amber, who promised she would stay in touch, would mourn her longstanding friend and employer in the loving company of her family on the West Coast.

Robin, Aaron, Curtis, Ashley, and Nathaniel had said goodbye to their respective families, for now.

And, of course, they had made time to have one last round of *PB* lattes with their friends, their mentors, their chosen family, Willow and Tamarind Dodson at *Paranormal Booktivity.*

Curtis proposed to Ashley, who tearily accepted. Robin announced that she had politely declined her offer from Adam's Hospital. Aaron happily told his friends about how he had made peace with his brother, Andrew, who he vowed to help as often as possible. And Nathaniel declared that he would spend the rest of the year growing a mustache.

As the sun set on the picturesque, uncomplicated beauty that was Melvin, five best friends prepared to return to their lives—knowing that it would forever be their choice to return and that they would do so before long, to enjoy each other's company and to celebrate yet another wonderfully wholesome and memorable Halloween.

Sunday 1st November

11:00 AM, ***Paranormal Booktivity***

The shop was closed as it always was on a Sunday. But today was not like other Sundays or any other day for that matter. Midway between the autumn equinox and the winter solstice, today marked the beginning of the winter observances and the end of the harvest season.

Engrossed in their daily lives, prioritizing rest and quiet time with their families after an eventful evening, not many in Melvin would make a point of honoring this ancient holiday—save for a select few, including Willow and Tamarind Dodson.

'What a day,' Tamarind exclaimed from behind the counter, pondering the series of tributes ahead of them as she brewed some fresh coffee.

A pensive Willow merely mumbled in response.

Taking her time to flick through a sizable stack of old photographs with a wistful look across her face, Willow perched at the edge of a booth which would otherwise have been reserved for Robin, Aaron, Curtis, Ashley, and Nathaniel, had they been there.

Perhaps sensing the overwhelmingly dense air of emotion in the room, or perhaps simply desiring some attention—Jefferson leaped onto the table, sprawled across the scattered photographs, licked his paw, and shot Willow an innocent glance and affectionate blink.

'Oh, dear, Jefferson.' Willow exhaled as she petted him.

'Hey,' Tamarind called, joining her sister with two steamy mugs, 'you listen to Jefferson,' she counseled, settling into the booth.

'And what exactly is Jefferson telling me?' Willow entertained, managing a weak smile.

'That you still have us.'

Willow's smile grew. She looked at her sister, at Jefferson, she turned her head one way and glanced over at Prankers happily swimming in his bowl, then she turned her head to appreciate the cozy, organized beauty of their shop. 'Indeed,' she said simply, taking a sip of her morning coffee.

'Besides,' Tamarind continued, gesturing, 'it's not such a bad life, living amongst the many pages of these books.'

Willow chuckled softly and took Tamarind's hand. 'No. No, it isn't,' she conceded, genuinely—content in the blessed knowledge that she would forever have her sister and *Paranormal Booktivity*.

The End

Book Club

Expose yourself to new and interesting reads and encourage others to do the same! We think attending or organizing a Book Club is a wonderfully fun way to socialize and learn. So, grab your copy, some friends (and some snacks), and enjoy!

You have been cordially invited to join:

Paranormal Booktivity's Book Club

Hints: *Pick and choose random questions to keep things interesting. Some examples are provided in case you get stuck. Keep an eye out as each section has at least one task for you and your friends to complete. Have fun!*

General

1. What was your initial reaction to the book? Did you feel hooked immediately, or did it take some time to get into?
2. Did the structure and formatting of the book (e.g. using dates, locations, and timestamps to mark scenes) affect the story, or alter your reading experience? If yes, how so?
3. Think of the book's length. If you felt certain scenes were too long, what would you cut out? If you felt they were too short, what would you add?
4. Do you think the story was plot-based or character-driven?
5. What was your favorite scene and why?
6. What was your least favorite scene and why?
7. Are there any quotes that stuck out for you? If so, why?
8. What do you think of the book's cover and title? How far did it influence your interest in reading the book? Did they give you an impression of what the plot would include, and if so, how accurate or inaccurate were your impressions? What would you have named the book instead? ***Design your own book cover, complete with a different title, vote on a winner, and hand out a prize!***
9. Did the book shift your perspective about anything? Do you feel differently now than you did before you read it? If yes, how so?
10. How did you feel about the author's writing style? Did it match the tone of the book regarding the plot and genre? Would you read another book by this author? Why?

Setting

1. How well do you think the author built the various settings in the book?
2. Would you have preferred the author to have used only actual locations, or only fictional?
3. Are there any places mentioned in the book you have already visited? ***See if you can each create a checklist from memory of the locations mentioned in the book; then tick the places you have visited. The person with the most checked off gets a treat!***
4. Which place in the book would you most like to visit?
5. What made the setting unique or important, if at all? Could the story have taken place anywhere else?

Plot

1. Considering the paranormal elements of the story, how realistic did the story seem? Did this affect how you felt?
2. How original do you feel the book was? Can you find similarities with other books? What other books did it remind you of?
3. How well did events flow from one to the next? Did you find any plot holes in the story?
4. What parts of the story did you guess before they were revealed? What events surprised you? Are there things you expected to happen that did not?
5. How did you feel about the ending? What did you like, what did you not like, and what do you wish had been different? ***Jot down your own unique ending to the book, and take turns reading them out loud!***

Characters

1. Do you think there is one protagonist? If so, who would you say he or she is?
2. Would you prefer the story to have been narrated by a character? If so, who by?
3. Which character did you relate to the most and what was it about them that you connected with? Who did you feel the most sympathy for?
4. Who is your favorite main character? Who are your favorite supporting characters? ***How did you imagine the characters' appearances compared to your friends? On a sheet of blank paper, write a few bullet point descriptions next to the names of characters who were not physically described in the book!***
5. Who is your least favorite main character? Who are your least favorite supporting characters? ***As a group, decide on one character you would remove from the book! Together, think of a new character you would add!***
6. Discuss the differing levels of character development within the book. How did your opinion of each main character change by the end of the book in comparison to your initial impressions?
7. How do you feel about Curtis and Ashley's dynamic? Realistically speaking, what would you say happens to them beyond the end of the book?
8. How do you feel about Robin and Aaron's dynamic?
9. Discuss Nathaniel's place in the group. What would you like to happen to him beyond the end of the book?
10. Discuss Willow and Tamarind's potential back story. Do you think there is more to be revealed?

Themes

1. Discuss the theme of *family and parenthood* in the book. Examples: Aaron's sense of obligation towards his father, Robin's adoptive and biological family, Ashley's loss of her father and future motherhood.
2. Discuss the theme of *home* in the book. Examples: Robin's obsession with belonging, Melvin's citizens' connection to the town, the concept of creating or finding a sense of being at home within a person rather than a place.
3. Discuss the theme of *life and death* in the book. Examples: Li'l Maggie and spirits, miscarriages, Curtis' health status, Aaron's father, Robin's grandfather.
4. Discuss the theme of *sacrifice* in the book. Examples: Andrew for his father, Robin's relatives.
5. Discuss the theme of *love* in the book. Examples: friends, romance, Melvin, cross-reference with themes of family, home, and sacrifice.
6. Discuss the theme of *fear* in the book. ***Go around the room and admit your unusual phobias and greatest fears!***
7. Did you notice any other recurring themes in the book?
8. Discuss any one-off themes you may have noticed and their importance to the relevant character, event, or place.
9. What are the themes you feel were given the most importance? Do you disagree with their prominence in the book? Do you feel others should have been given more weight, and if so, which ones?

10. Which themes do you think could have been addressed differently? Which themes do you feel could have been addressed but were not? Example: homosexuality.

Fun

1. If the book were adapted into a movie, which actors would you like to see interpret which parts?
2. What songs did scenes, or the entire book, make you think of? ***Create a book group playlist together! Check out our Spotify playlists for inspiration!***
3. Some parts attempted to alleviate tension and suspense by providing comic relief. Do you think this element is appropriate considering the genre of the book? Which parts did you find funny, if at all, and what made you laugh most?
4. Which character would you most like to hang out with? ***List the five main characters and write down what you think would be the most fun activity to do with them. Vote on the best answers and give out prizes!***
5. If you got the chance to ask the author of this book one question, what would it be? ***Brave it and send your questions to the author on:***

bookclub@paranormalbooktivity.co.uk

We hope you enjoyed your stay in Melvin by reading the first book in the paranormal cozy mystery series.

Coming soon, book two in the series:

Paranormal Booktivity

The Mystery of the Enchanted Travel Journal

Follow Nathaniel to the magical city of New Orleans for another spook-filled vacation packed with breathtaking scenery, curious hijinks, charmingly eccentric locals, and an entirely new mystery to solve!

Look out for more in the Paranormal Booktivity franchise including unique, high-quality merchandise as well as a short-story series of spin-offs with all your favorite characters by visiting:

www.ParanormalBooktivity.co.uk